Sherye stared up at the ceiling, trying to find something tangible to hold on to in this strange new world she'd found.

"This is all just too bizarre," she muttered finally. After another long silence, she sighed, nodding her head slighty. "I know what this is.... I'm having some kind of a dream. They've got me on pain medication, and I'm hallucinating. I'll wake up in the morning and I'll laugh at this whole thing...." She closed her eyes, tugging the sheet up over her shoulders, trying to regain her equilibrium.

"Well," she murmured to herself some time later, as though she were alone, "this is quite a dream you're having. A husband, two children and a modeling career. If that doesn't win prizes for creativity, it should."

As she drifted off to sleep, she muttered, "Boy, I've got great taste in dream men, that's for sure...."

Dear Reader,

Welcome to Silhouette **Special Edition** . . . welcome to romance. We've got lots of excitement in store for you this April—and, no fooling, it's all about love!

Annette Broadrick, the author of over thirty-five novels for Silhouette Books, is making her debut in the Special Edition line with a book in our THAT SPECIAL WOMAN! promotion. *Mystery Wife* is a tantalizing, compelling tale about a woman who wakes up with a new lease on life—and a handsome, charismatic husband she doesn't remember marrying. . . .

And that's not all! *Shadows and Light,* the first book in the MEN OF COURAGE series by Lindsay McKenna, is due out this month. It takes a special breed of men to defy death and fight for right! Salute their bravery while sharing their lives and loves!

Loving and Giving by Gina Ferris, the new addition to Gina's enormously popular FAMILY FOUND series, is due out this month, as well as work by other favorite authors Nikki Benjamin, Natalie Bishop and Ruth Wind. April is a month not to be missed!

Sincerely,

Tara Gavin
Senior Editor

ANNETTE BROADRICK

MYSTERY WIFE

Published by Silhouette Books
America's Publisher of Contemporary Romance

This book is dedicated to Tara Hughes Gavin, my editor for eight of the ten years I've been published, for allowing and encouraging me to tell the kind of stories I want to tell in the way I want to tell them. I wouldn't have made it this far without your support.

Thank you, Tara.

SILHOUETTE BOOKS

ISBN 0-373-09877-4

MYSTERY WIFE

This edition published by arrangement with Harlequin Enterprises B. V.

Printed in U.S.A.

Books by Annette Broadrick

Silhouette Special Edition

Mystery Wife #877

Silhouette Romance

Circumstantial Evidence #329
Provocative Peril #359
Sound of Summer #412
Unheavenly Angel #442
Strange Enchantment #501
Mystery Lover #533
That's What Friends Are For #544
Come Be My Love #609
A Love Remembered #676
Married?! #742
The Gemini Man #796
Daddy's Angel #976

Silhouette Books

Silhouette Christmas Stories 1988
"Christmas Magic"
Spring Fancy 1993
"Surprise, Surprise!"

Silhouette Desire

Hunter's Prey #185
Bachelor Father #219
Hawk's Flight #242
Deceptions #272
Choices #283
Heat of the Night #314
Made in Heaven #336
Return to Yesterday #360
Adam's Story #367
Momentary Marriage #414
With All My Heart #433
A Touch of Spring #464
Irresistible #499
A Loving Spirit #552
Candlelight for Two #577
Lone Wolf #666
Where There Is Love #714
**Love Texas Style!* #734
**Courtship Texas Style!* #739
**Marriage Texas Style!* #745
Zeke #793

*Sons of Texas

ANNETTE BROADRICK

believes in romance and the magic of life. Since 1984, when her first book was published, Annette has shared her view of life and love with readers all over the world. In addition to being nominated by *Romantic Times* as one of the Best New Authors of that year, she has also won the *Romantic Times* Reviewers' Choice Award for Best in its Series for *Heat of the Night, Mystery Lover* and *Irresistible;* the *Romantic Times* WISH award for her heroes in *Strange Enchantment* and *Marriage Texas Style!;* and the *Romantic Times* Lifetime Achievement Awards for Series Romance and Series Romantic Fantasy.

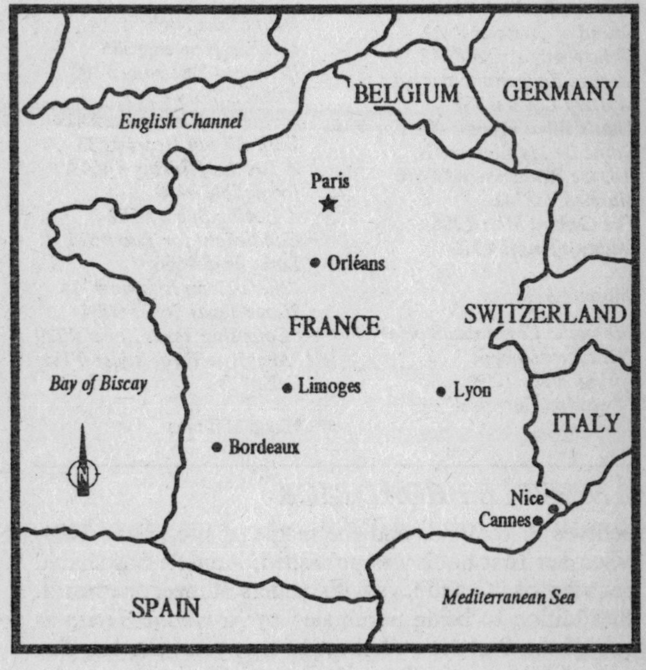

BELGIUM
GERMANY
English Channel
Paris
Orléans
FRANCE
SWITZERLAND
Bay of Biscay
Limoges
Lyon
ITALY
N
Bordeaux
Nice
Cannes
SPAIN
Mediterranean Sea

Chapter One

She fought her way to the surface, frantically struggling to escape the swirling darkness filled with demons that grabbed and pulled at her, battering her until she thought her skull would burst with the pain. Whimpering from the effort exerted, she forced herself to continue, her terror giving her the necessary strength.

Exhausted from her labors, she managed to open her eyes.

She flinched at the brightness, squinting her eyes.

Diffused sunlight poured through a tall, narrow window draped with sheer curtains, dappling the glistening sheen of highly polished flooring with an abstract pattern of shifting leaves and fingerlike branches.

The pain in her head did its best to consume her, eager to blind her to her surroundings, but she valiantly fought to ignore the invader threatening to suck her back into the nightmare.

She stirred in an attempt to shift her weight, but her body ignored her signals.

Where was she?

Once again she peered around the room, her eyelids heavy and painful, searching for something familiar to give her a clue.

Nothing looked familiar. Nothing at all.

The walls glowed with a soft peach tint. A delicate watercolor hung on one of the walls. A pair of burgundy oversize leather chairs sat on either side of a finely crafted table. An elegant lamp graced the table.

With great care she turned her head, nevertheless paying the price for movement. Wincing, she closed her eyes and rested, wondering if appeasing her curiosity was worth the accompanying pain.

Eventually she opened her eyes once more in order to study the room from her new perspective. The bed where she lay looked wholly out of place with the exquisite furnishings. There was no disguising its utilitarian design. Only then did her gaze move past the end of the bed and focus on the door, its heavy wooden surface broken by a small glass window in its center.

At last she had found something identifiable, which was comfortingly close to familiar. She was in a hospital.

Pleased with her discovery, she allowed her eyes to close as a reward, welcoming the dark relief from the glare of the sunshine. Instead of easing, however, the pounding, clanging beat in her head seemed to escalate.

She forced herself to concentrate on something other than the persistent, mind-crippling pain. *A hospital. I'm in a hospital.*

She began to identify the different areas of her body. Her legs were heavy but otherwise did not ache. She was able to breathe without hindrance. Her arms lay on either side of her body... her right hand felt weighted down. She peeked at her hand and saw the obvious signs of her stay—a drip stand with a tube running down to the back of her hand where it disappeared beneath a gauze bandage. A black machine with a video screen beeped its scrawling message in a steady, monotonous tone not far from her right shoulder.

With her left hand she touched her face and discovered a thick bandage wrapped around her forehead. She must have suffered some kind of head injury, which certainly explained the throbbing, pounding pain that seemed so real she could almost see it bouncing in front of her eyes.

What had happened to her? Where was she?

Voices impinged on her consciousness for the first time since she'd awakened, and she forced herself to listen, hoping to have some of her questions answered. The voices were hushed and feminine, speaking Parisian French. She attempted to focus on what they were saying, but her head hurt too much for her to concentrate. She caught a word here, a phrase there, but she couldn't catch enough to make sense of their conversation. They spoke the language like natives, rapid-fire and sure of their phrases.

She smiled to herself, impressed with their ability, and wondered where they had learned to speak so well. She'd like to commend their teacher for being able to eradicate their Texas drawl, something she'd never been able to accomplish with her own students.

So. She had managed to come up with a few answers. She was in a hospital with French-speaking women nearby. Now if she could only remember what had happened to her to place her in a hospital, she would feel more in control of her situation.

She forced herself to think back, to discover her last memories. The effort needed to pursue her newest line of deductive reasoning made the pounding in her head increase its throbbing beat until it seemed to fill the room, causing the walls and ceiling to waver in time to the beat.

Unable to produce the strength to fight off the waves of pain, she allowed her concerns to slip away, allowed her mind to blank out into a shimmering silver screen of nothingness....

The next time she opened her eyes she felt a new sense of serenity. Although she didn't understand why, she felt safe and protected lying there in the spacious room. She had no more answers now than the last time she'd regained consciousness. Nevertheless, she knew that no one would harm her. How could she know that she was safe? Somehow her subconscious seemed to be reassuring her.

She lay quietly and stared out the window, enjoying the view of the tree outside her window. Springtime. The new green shoots were so delicate and determined. Springtime. Always a time of hope and renewal. She would get better. She would remember. Spring offered the magic of rebirth.... She faded away into a restful, healing sleep.

Hours later a slight noise drew her into wakefulness once again. She was no longer alone when she opened her eyes this time. A nursing sister stood beside the bed, checking the drip and making adjustments. The young woman glanced down at her. When she realized she was being watched, the nurse gave a start, her eyes wide.

"Oh! Madame DuBois," she said in French. "You're awake! Merciful God, we must let your husband know!" The nurse rushed out of the room, leaving her alone once more.

A sense of surprise stirred within her. She lay there, silently repeating what she had just heard.

Madame DuBois?

Her husband?

She tested the words and phrases, repeating them carefully in her mind.

It was no use. Neither the name nor the person meant anything to her.

They must have her confused with someone else. She no longer had a husband.

Why did that thought seem so painful?

She would have to tell the nurse when she returned that there was an obvious mix-up...some kind of mistake had been made. She didn't even know a Madame DuBois. She would be polite, of course. She always tried to be polite and patient with a person's mistake. After all, human beings were not created to be perfect, she often reminded her students. They were created to learn how to experience love and joy and the abundance of life.

So she would explain that she couldn't possibly be Madame DuBois because her name was—

She paused, feeling a little silly. Well, of course she knew who she was, she was just a little confused at the moment. Obviously the pain in her head had something to do with an injury she'd sustained. The constant throbbing was distracting. Her name would come to her. She knew it would. So she was patient and she waited, but nothing came to mind.

Nothing.

After several long inexplicably blank minutes passed, a queasy sense of panic began to form within her, as though trickling through her veins. What was going on? Just because her head was pounding didn't mean her brain couldn't function, did it?

Did it?

The panicky feeling inside her grew.

All right. She reminded herself that it was not surprising she might feel confused. Obviously she had been injured in some way or she wouldn't be in a hospital. All she needed to do was to stay calm. She would allow her mind to drift back, to remember....

She couldn't remember much of anything. Brief pictures without sound—like a silent film running too fast—flashed through her mind without a hint of explanation.

Was it possible she really had a husband, that she was actually Madame DuBois, even though she couldn't remember that name or her life? She squeezed her eyes closed for a moment, the pressure calling her attention to their swollen state. She forced herself to open her eyes slowly and with a certain amount of precision, as though in some way her sight might have an effect on the door to her memories.

Perhaps the door had gotten jammed while she'd been unconscious and was now having trouble functioning upon command.

How long had she been unconscious, anyway?

The mystery was too much for her pain-filled mind. This time she actively sought oblivion, where there was no pain or confusion, slipping silently into a darkness no longer inhabited by sadistic, punishing demons.

The darkness now held only a soothing sense of peace and protection.

"Chérie?"

The sound of a deep male voice rumbling softly nearby irresistibly drew her from her place of painless safety, impelling her to seek out the source of the unusual term of endearment.

She opened her eyes.

Muted light from a small lamp nearby cast shadows over most of the tall, lean figure of the man standing beside the bed. The soft glow highlighted his long, tapered fingers resting on the railing. She couldn't seem to draw her gaze away from the sight of his large, capable-looking hands. His grip on the railing had caused his knuckles and the tips of his fingers to turn white. Drowsily puzzled by this obvious sign of tension, she allowed her gaze to wander upward, toward his shadowed head. The light glinted along the side of his face, bringing into prominence the plane of his high cheekbone and strong jawline, leaving his eyes veiled in shadow.

She licked her lips, painfully aware of how dry her throat was. "I—" She paused in her efforts to speak and swallowed painfully. Despite her efforts, she hadn't made a sound.

"Would you like some water?"

There! This time she heard the strain in his voice—his carefully modulated voice. She didn't understand why he had spoken to her in French.

She nodded and watched the graceful movement of his hands as he poured water from a crystal pitcher into a small glass with a bent straw. He brought the straw to her lips and waited while she gratefully wet them.

"How are you feeling, *chérie?*"

"My—um—my head...hurts." Her voice sounded strange to her ears, as though she hadn't heard it in a long while. She had answered him in the same language, but her tongue had felt awkward wrapping around the vowels, as though it were out of practice.

"It's not surprising, is it? You're lucky to be alive."

"What happened?"

He frowned, two vertical lines appearing above the bridge of his aquiline nose. "Don't you remember?"

She heard the surprise in his voice and was almost amused at the idea that anyone thought her capable of coherent explanations about anything. If she knew what had happened or why she was here she would most certainly share the knowledge with the handsome stranger standing so stiffly beside her bed.

As swiftly as her amusement surfaced, it disappeared, leaving her feeling confused and inadequate. She would very much like to have the answers to give to this stern, self-assured male. She felt a desire to impress him with a coherent summary of her present situation.

She frantically searched for something—anything—that might be flitting through her mind at the moment, but the images sporadically appearing were too fleeting to interpret.

"I'm sorry," she murmured after several uncomfortable moments. "I'm afraid I don't remember much of anything at the moment."

Silence stretched between them. She studied his grim expression, wondering who he was and why he was so concerned. She heard her own voice before she realized she had spoken her question aloud.

"What's your name?"

If anything, his expression grew more grim. "Raoul."

A strong sense of pleasure swept over her. "I've always liked the name Raoul," she replied with a tentative smile, then wondered about the medication she was being given. Her slurred words sounded as though she'd been drinking, and for some reason she had a tendency to blurt out whatever thought happened to cross her mind at any given moment.

"You don't know who I am?" he asked after another long silence.

Guess she was going to have to stay after school. She hadn't done her homework. He expected her to know him, she could tell. She tried to placate him with her most charming, conciliatory smile. "Please don't be offended. I mean, it isn't anything personal, you understand." She couldn't believe how difficult it was to enunciate each word. Pausing to gain some control over her tongue, she eventually confessed with a grin, "I don't even know who *I* am."

He didn't seem to appreciate her lame attempt at humor. When he didn't respond, her unruly tongue continued with "Would I lie to you?" blithely ignoring the fact that she was obviously irritating her visitor.

He stiffened, a move that surprised her, since his ramrod-straight posture had seemed too rigid to be improved upon. "On many occasions," he muttered with poorly concealed bitterness.

She blinked at the obvious explanation for his inexplicable demeanor. This man didn't like her. From what he'd just said, he might have good reason. However, she had a strong impulse to argue with him. She might not know who she was, but she knew very well that she didn't lie. She'd always had an aversion to the idea. Lies could get so complicated. Truth was much simpler.

Impulsively she reached out and touched his hand. He flinched, but didn't pull away. "I'm sorry if I've hurt you. I'm afraid I'm at a distinct disadvantage here. I don't recognize you at all. Are we related?"

She heard a slight hitch in his breathing, but otherwise he gave nothing of his thoughts away. He seemed to be searching her face for some kind of answer before he murmured, "I'm your husband."

No! She could feel the immediate denial rising in her throat and she fought not to betray her reaction. How could she possibly deny their relationship if she couldn't remember exactly who she was? He seemed to be in no doubt as to her identity.

"I see," she responded after a moment, feeling very vulnerable. "So I really *am* Madame DuBois."

"Ah. Then you at least remembered part of your name," he replied with a touch of irony.

"I'm afraid not. The nursing sister called me that. I thought she must be mistaken." Unable to contain her curiosity any longer, she asked, "What is my first name?"

"Sherye."

"Oh! I thought you were using the French endearment."

"It's spelled S-h-e-r-y-e."

She allowed the name to circle in her head, saying it to herself several times. Why didn't it sound familiar? If she'd been called by that name all her life, wouldn't she feel some sense of positive identification when she heard it?

"How old am I?"

"Twenty-six."

She pondered that piece of information. Once again pictures flitted through her mind. "Have we been married long?"

"Six years."

Another surprise. She frowned. "Why, I was just a child when we married!"

The look he gave her was filled with cynicism. "I doubt that you were ever a child, Sherye. Not in the sense you mean. You began modeling when you were eleven years old. By the time we met, you were light-years away from the innocence of childhood."

There was so much new information in that statement that she had trouble taking it all in. Once again bitterness seemed to surround the man who claimed to be her husband. What kind of marriage did they have? She hesitated to ask. When she thought about the rest of his statement, she slowly rolled her head on the pillow in a negative gesture that renewed the pounding in her head.

"I'm not certain why you're so angry with me," she finally said, "but I do know that I couldn't possibly be a model. That you should suggest such a career for me strikes me as ludicrous."

Without a word he turned and walked away. She watched him go and wondered if she'd offended him by arguing with him. However, instead of leaving, Raoul opened a side door she hadn't noticed before and disappeared into another room. He appeared almost immediately with a hand mirror. He returned to her side and flipped on the lamp beside her bed, then handed her the mirror.

Instead of looking at the mirror, she stared up at the man revealed in the light. Yes, he was very imposing... aristocratic...and no doubt arrogant, as well. His eyes were a dark gray, almost charcoal, surrounded by a heavy fringe of black lashes that in no way detracted from his masculinity.

She certainly had excellent taste in men. Too bad she seemed to have alienated him so badly.

"Aren't you going to look at yourself?" he asked, a strange note in his voice.

Reluctantly she raised the mirror and forced herself to peer at her reflection. If he was trying to convince her that she had the looks of a model, he'd certainly missed the mark. She'd always heard that love was blind, but he seemed more angry than in love. Maybe he just suffered from poor vision.

"Well?" he asked.

"Well, what?" she replied, lowering the mirror and looking back at him impatiently.

"What do you see?"

With almost a groan she forced herself to look into the mirror again. "A pasty-looking face with dark circles around the eyes. The most vivid and eye-catching feature I can see at the moment is the technicolor bruise that isn't completely covered by the head bandage." She made herself meet his gaze once again. "Why? What do *you* see?"

"A face that's been on every major fashion magazine in the Western world. With your wide-set green eyes, high cheekbones, pouting lips and—"

"Pouting," she repeated with a sense of renewed interest. She looked again. After a moment she murmured, "I wouldn't call them pouting, exactly. Maybe they're a little full." She squinted into the mirror, then widened her eyes without blinking. "At least you got the eye color right." She touched her bandaged head. "What did they do to my hair?"

"The doctor assured me he had to shave only a small portion that can easily be covered until it grows out."

She peered at the pale woman in the mirror again before she shrugged. "Well, all I can say is I must have looked considerably better at eleven than I do at twenty-six. What happened? Did I lose my looks and decide to retire at twenty and get married?"

"You didn't intend to retire right away. Unfortunately for your professional plans, your pregnancy—"

"My pregnancy!" His words set off a series of internal alarms, all clanging within her head with earsplitting dissonance. She pushed herself up on one elbow, her head spinning. She forced the next words, carefully enunciating each one. "Are you saying that we have a child?"

He nodded, watching her closely. "Yes. We have a five-year-old daughter, Yvette, as well as a fourteen-month-old son . . . Jules."

Too weak to stay propped up on her elbow, Sherye sank back onto the bed, but the move merely increased the spinning and whirling going on inside her head. She stared up at the ceiling, trying to find something tangible to hang on to in this strange new world she'd found.

"This is all just too bizarre," she muttered, finally. After another long silence she sighed, nodding her head slightly. "I know what this is. I'm having some kind of a dream. They've got me on pain medication and I'm hallucinating. I'll wake up in the morning and I'll laugh at this whole thing...." She closed her eyes, tugging the sheet up over her shoulders. She lay there for several minutes, trying to regain her equilibrium.

"Well," she murmured to herself some time later as though she were alone, "this is quite a dream you're having. A husband, two children and a modeling career. If that doesn't win prizes for creativity, it should."

She drifted off to sleep, glad to be escaping the confused feelings that had swamped her during the telling of this tall nighttime tale. As she drifted off to sleep she muttered, "Boy, I've got great taste in dream men, that's for sure."

Chapter Two

Sunlight flooded the room the next time Sherye opened her eyes. She was grateful to discover that the pain in her head was much improved, thank God. Not wanting to take a chance of reawakening the throbbing intruder, she carefully moved her head on the pillow—and saw her visitor from the night before asleep in one of the leather chairs.

She caught her breath, aware that her pulse rate had suddenly gone into overdrive. The man was real...she hadn't dreamed him, after all.

The light in the room revealed her visitor in detail, and finding him asleep gave her a much-needed moment to adjust to his presence, not only in her room but in her life, as well.

The man across from her was Raoul DuBois.

Her husband.

Or so he said.

As far as she was concerned, she had no connection with Sherye or Raoul DuBois. The names meant absolutely nothing to her. Somehow she would have to deal with her new situation. Now that the pain in her head had lessened, she was feeling more capable of coping with this strange new world she had discovered when she'd regained consciousness.

She took the opportunity to study Raoul DuBois while he slept.

His long, athletically built frame looked cramped in the chair. His head rested at an uncomfortable angle on the back of the seat while his legs stretched out in front of him, one knee bent.

He wore a cream-colored silk shirt with chocolate brown trousers. A matching suit jacket lay across the arm of the other chair. His tie had been loosened and draped drunkenly across his chest.

This man was Raoul DuBois. Her husband, she reminded herself once again.

She shivered, remembering his attitude toward her. She wished she knew more about their relationship. Why had he acted so cold, so aloof, so bitter? Feeling as he so obviously did, why had he stayed with her through the night?

She stirred, restless, wondering if she dared try to sit up. How she hated feeling so powerless! She wanted to take charge of her life instead of passively lying there waiting for the next event to take place.

She had an unquenchable desire to find out more about herself...to find out all the missing pieces of her life and her past. Raoul had mentioned their children, a thought that created so much longing within her that she felt certain if she were to see them again she would remember at least their part in her life. She had always wanted children. She knew that without a doubt, even if she didn't understand exactly how she could have such strong and fixed opinions of who she was.

Take her present situation, for example. She felt just as strongly about who she was not. She knew quite well that she was not, nor had she ever been, a model. If they could be wrong about her profession, they were no doubt wrong about who she was, as well.

Obviously there must be some mistake in identification. She would discuss the mix-up with someone in charge of her case as soon as possible. There was no reason for her to panic. She would stay calm until she could—

As though on cue, the door opened with a soft whishing sound. A slight, trim man wearing a hand-tailored suit entered, closely followed by two nursing sisters. From the corner of her eye she saw Raoul stir and straighten.

"Ahh. Good morning, Monsieur and Madame DuBois. It is good to see you awake, my dear," the man said, striding to the bed and taking her hand. "Your husband has been extremely worried about you, as have we all." He nodded to the other man before returning his sharp-eyed gaze to her. "No doubt you have many questions, which we'll try to answer for you." He stroked her fingers while unobtrusively checking her pulse. "I'm Dr. Pierre Montand. You've been unconscious for several days and under my care since your husband had you transferred to our hospital."

She glanced at Raoul, who had risen from his chair and was running his hand through his thick, dark hair, a move that did more to tousle than to tame. From the doctor's comments she decided that if Raoul had arranged for her to stay in such luxurious surroundings he must care enough about her to want her well tended.

"How are you feeling this morning?" Dr. Montand asked, continuing to monitor her pulse.

"The pain in my head is much better, but I'm very confused at the moment. My memory seems to be in something of a muddle." She smiled at him in an attempt to lessen the appearance of criticism. "I really think there's been some kind of a mistake. Although I can't remember exactly who I am at the moment, I'm positive I'm not Sherye DuBois." She kept her gaze away from the man across the room, not wanting to see his reaction to her statement.

Dr. Montand's gaze sharpened. He gave Raoul a quick glance before returning his attention to her. "You must remember that you've received a fairly severe injury to your head, my dear. It isn't unusual that you may be somewhat confused." Once again his gaze sought out Raoul's, as though checking to see if the man wished to comment. When Raoul remained silent Dr. Montand continued. "I don't think you need to concern yourself with the possibility that your identity has been confused with someone else's. I understand that the police were able to identify you at the scene of the accident from the registration of your car, as well as the papers you carried in your purse. Even if there had been some doubt in the minds of the authorities, your husband recognized you as soon as he saw you."

Sherye looked from the doctor to Raoul, trying to read something in their expressions. If she wasn't who they said she was, what would be their purpose in lying? What she had to decide was whether or not she was going to trust these people to tell her the truth.

"I don't remember the accident at all," she explained with a hint of frustration.

"Which isn't uncommon in cases such as yours. I know all of this is difficult for you. I would like to recommend that you give yourself some time. A trauma of this nature can cause a multitude of problems. A temporary memory loss isn't unusual. Fortunately the mind has marvelous healing abilities. I'll be working with you during your stay here. We have proven exercises as well as counseling techniques that we can implement to assist you in stimulating your memory." He released her hand and gently laid it across her waist. "Just be thankful that you survived with no more injuries than you received." He brushed his hand against her cheek. "You're doing quite well, all things considered."

She eyed him for a moment, wondering if this was the time to bring up the next item that was bothering her. Why not? If she was losing her mind as well as her memory, she might as well be aware of it now.

"Why is everybody speaking French?"

There was another exchange of glances between the two men, while the nursing sisters stared at her with varying degrees of astonishment and dismay.

After the brief, nonverbal exchange with Raoul, the doctor was the one who answered.

"Yes, I can see how confusing everything must seem to you. Your husband explained that you are an American, but since you've lived here in France for several years, you have a good command of the language."

She stared at the doctor in disbelief. "We're in France?" she whispered, unable to disguise her shock.

"But of course," Raoul replied. "Where do you think we are?"

"Texas!" she blurted out, then paused, rubbing her head where the ache never seemed to go away, unable to understand why she'd thought about Texas. As soon as she said the word, pictures flashed across the screen of her mind—tall buildings, multilaned highways, azaleas in bloom, the state flag...

"That's a very good sign of your returning memory," Raoul pointed out. "You're originally from Dallas. I understand you lived there for the first ten years of your life."

The doctor frowned. "Can you remember anything from that time of your life?"

She closed her eyes in an effort to recall something useful. After a moment she sighed and said, "Just brief pictures, I'm afraid. Nothing helpful."

Once again she looked to Raoul. "Can you tell me about the accident? Were you there?"

Her question seemed to catch him off guard. He hesitated, his body tensing, before he finally answered. "No. You were alone. According to the police investigation, you must have lost control of your car on a sharp curve. The car went over a steep embankment. Luckily you were thrown clear...since the car burst into flames upon impact. A passing motorist saw the flames and stopped. He saw you lying just over the edge of the embankment."

Sherye shivered at the thought of how close she had come to dying. "You're right. I'm lucky to be alive." At least she better understood why her head ached so badly. She must have hit it against something when she was thrown out of the car.

"Here," the doctor said. "Let's get these bandages off and see how your head looks. I'm sure you'll be relieved to know that we only had to shave a small portion of your hair...just the area around the wound. Luckily, because of the length of your hair, your scar will be covered." He smiled at her. "It would have been a shame to destroy that beautiful red hair of yours."

"But my hair isn't—" she began, then stopped, feeling foolish and uncertain. Nothing seemed to make any sense to her at the moment.

Only Texas seemed real to her. Nothing else. Not a husband, nor children, nor France.

The nurses efficiently unpeeled the bandages. The doctor examined the area around the wound, eliciting more than one wince from her. She bit her bottom lip to stop from groaning at one point.

"I believe we can leave the bandages off now," he said after a moment. "I'm quite pleased to see that you are healing nicely." He stepped back so that he could see her face once again. "I know you must feel overwhelmed. All you need to do at the moment is to rest and regain your strength. We'll give nature a chance to work her healing magic. You're really doing very well."

Feeling like a child who had been praised for eating all her vegetables, Sherye allowed herself to drift off to sleep once more, accepting the reassurance that everything would soon be all right.

Four days later she didn't feel quite so reassured.

Although the pain in her head had continued to lessen,

none of her puzzling memories could be explained. Nor could she accept the fact that she had absolutely no memories—not even a glimmer—of anything having to do with France, her marriage or her family.

Her body continued to heal, however, and she was now strong enough to move around without help, which gave her some sense of progress. She could at least shower without assistance, as well as take care of her personal needs. Assuming that much control over her life and body was comforting, but her continued lack of memory unnerved her more than she would admit to others.

For the past three days Raoul had come to visit her each day. She felt ill at ease with him, given their circumstances. Her lack of any memory with regard to their relationship gave him an edge that made her uncomfortable. She didn't like having to ask him to tell her about their life together. It wasn't that she thought he would lie to her, exactly, but she definitely felt that she was getting only one side of their story. There was something about his attitude where she was concerned that made her wonder why he was so antagonistic. She found what he wasn't telling her—about her attitude toward him and their children—mystifying. Surely her memories could shed some light on their relationship and perhaps explain his aloof behavior.

She'd been glad yesterday when he'd told her that he needed to leave for a day or so, in order to check in at home as well as his business. According to Raoul, home was a château that had been in his family for over a hundred years. He had explained that they lived there with his widowed mother and a sister who had never married.

His explanation immediately conjured up some kind of foreign movie in her mind, possibly starring Charles Boyer... certainly nothing she'd ever lived.

The doctor had suggested that once she was able to return to the familiar surroundings of home her memory would no doubt become more clear. Perhaps he was right, but at the moment Sherye had no desire to leave the now more familiar safety of her comfortable room and the surrounding hospital grounds.

She wasn't ready to meet more people she should remember but couldn't. Every time she thought about her two children, she panicked. What must they think of a mother who didn't remember them? She kept hoping that she would wake up one morning and every memory would be back in place, plugging the holes in her mind that made her feel so hollow and disoriented. Most especially, she wanted to be able to greet Raoul when he returned with the news that she recalled everything about their relationship.

Now she needed to shower and prepare for a session with the therapist who was working with her. She walked into the bathroom, mentally bracing herself for a routine glimpse into the mirror. She still hadn't grown accustomed to her flaming red hair that cascaded around her shoulders and neck, giving her a strange, unfamiliar look.

She knew that her natural color was a very pale blond, almost white. She'd never worn it down, preferring to keep it pulled away from her face out of her way. She had memories of sitting at her dresser each night, putting it into a loose braid to sleep. The shorter length around her face and the color were all wrong.

When she had mentioned to Raoul that she wasn't a natural redhead, he'd told her that a photographer had convinced her to change the color early in her career to enhance the contrast between her light complexion and hair.

She still had difficulty accepting the idea that she had been a famous model. Sometimes she felt as if she was truly losing her mind. Either that, or she'd been given someone else's memories in some kind of cosmic brain implant.

After showering, she dried her hair, despairing of doing anything with it other than allowing it to fall about her face, framing her pale skin with fiery color. Her eyes seemed to gleam with added color, as well. She closed her eyes, picturing the person she knew herself to be—a slender woman who easily blended in with a crowd. She wore little makeup. In short, she did nothing to call attention to herself.

The seductive-looking woman staring back at her in the mirror was still slender, but the frothy underwear Raoul had brought her seemed to accent her slender waistline and the gentle curve of her hips. The bra was engineered in such a way as to thrust her breasts up and together into a provocative cleavage. The high-cut briefs made her legs seem longer and more shapely.

Raoul had explained that these were her clothes that she had purchased herself. He'd brought them from home. She studied herself in the mirror, trying to see herself shopping for such items, but couldn't. Turning away, she returned to the bedroom and slipped into one of the dresses he'd brought. The color matched the sea green hue of her eyes, its silky texture gliding down her body in a sensuous caress.

After a few quick strokes of a brush through her hair she headed for the therapist's office, hoping that today would bring some much-needed breakthroughs.

"Ah, yes. You are very prompt, Sherye," Dr. Leclerc, the therapist working with her, said when she paused in the doorway of his office. "How are you feeling today?" He waved her to a chair across from him.

"There seems to be an inverse ratio going for me. The better I feel physically, the more frustrated I become with my lack of correct memories."

He casually clasped his hands on the desk in front of him in a relaxed manner and watched her with a slight smile. "Correct memories?" he prodded.

"You know—memories about living in France, being married, having children. Those memories."

"Instead you are having—what sort of memories, exactly?"

She sighed and leaned back in her chair. "I keep having these flashes of pictures as I drift off to sleep, or sometimes when I first wake up. I keep seeing myself standing in front of a classroom of girls, teaching, although I can't quite recall the subject. Sometimes I'm sitting on a small balcony watching a hummingbird feeding, or gazing at a skyline of tall buildings. I feel as though I live in a large city somewhere in Texas. I want to say Dallas, but I don't know if that's right. One time I was digging in a small garden, planting spring flowers, trimming around my rosebushes and azaleas."

"Is there ever anyone there with you?"

"Only when I'm in class. The rest of the time I'm alone...." She allowed her voice to trail off uncertainly. After a few minutes of silence she added, "Except the name Janine keeps surfacing."

"What does that name mean to you?"

"I see a pixie face with sparkling brown eyes and bouncy black curls as though she's seldom still. She's a friend... a very good friend. She was there for me during that terrible time when..." Once again her voice trailed off. When she met Dr. Leclerc's eyes she was frowning. "I can't remember, but something horrible happened that I couldn't face, couldn't handle at all. Janine was there for me. I wouldn't have made it through that terrible time without her."

"Do you remember the details of that event?"

After several minutes of probing into her thoughts she shook her head.

"According to your history that your husband was able to supply for us, you spent your early days in Dallas, so it isn't unlikely that you are having flashbacks to your childhood."

She frowned. "Perhaps. But I feel as though I'm an adult in these scenes. So is Janine." She shook her head in disgust. "This is so frustrating! I feel that if I could force myself to concentrate more, everything would come back to me." She shifted in her chair. "Besides, none of these fleeting glimpses have anything to do with France."

Dr. Leclerc opened the file in front of him and thumbed through some papers. He laid one of the papers aside and examined it for a moment before asking his next question.

"Has your husband discussed with you the argument the two of you had the night before your accident?"

She'd been staring blindly past him at a picture behind the doctor's desk, inwardly probing for possible memories, when he asked his unexpected question. Her gaze refocused on him in dismay.

"No," she replied slowly, "he hasn't. He seems reluctant to talk to me about anything relating to our life together. Whenever he visits we generally discuss the activities of my day." She leaned forward in her chair. "Are you saying that he told *you* about an argument we had?" She could hear the criticism in her voice, but was unable to disguise it.

"In order to help you, Sherye, it was necessary for me to consult with your husband regarding your relationship within the marriage. He was understandably reluctant to discuss such personal matters, but eventually saw the necessity for it. It is possible that the argument may have contributed to the accident, as well as to your continued memory loss."

She leaned forward in her chair. "What are you saying? That perhaps I don't want to remember anything because of an argument I had with my husband?"

The doctor peered at her over his glasses. "The severe blow to your head," he explained in a patient tone of voice, "could certainly be responsible for your initial memory loss. However, it is the continued absence of all memories regarding any part of your life in France that leads me to believe that you—on some deeply subconscious level—may be blocking any memory that you are not ready to face at the present time."

She stared at him, fighting her frustration at this line of reasoning. "What, exactly, is so painful about being married to a handsome Frenchman, having two children and living in a French château? That sounds more like a fairy tale to me... somebody's fantasy of a dream come true... than a life that anyone would have difficulty accepting."

"Your husband—with a great deal of reluctance, I must say—gave me some of the facts regarding your recent history." He picked up another page and scanned it before he said, "It seems that you had a great deal of difficulty with your second pregnancy and were slow in regaining your health after your son's birth. Although postpartum depression is not uncommon, yours seemed unusually severe, and you—for all practical purposes—rejected the baby and would have little to do with him or his sister after his birth. Instead, you began to stay away from your home for long periods of time each day."

Sherye stared at the kind-faced doctor in horror, wanting to refute the information he offered so matter-of-factly. She wasn't like that at all! How could she have abandoned a newborn baby and an innocent child? There must be some mistake, but she couldn't begin to understand where.

"Where would I go?" she asked, hoping that she'd sought professional help somewhere.

"According to your husband, you began to socialize with people you had known during your career as a model."

"Somehow I get the feeling that my husband didn't approve of my friends," she replied with a sigh.

"He said they indulged in frequent partying and he didn't find that he had much in common with any of them."

"I'm beginning to get the picture," she said out loud. To herself she added, no wonder he was so distant with her. From all indications she hadn't been any great shakes as a wife and a complete zero as a mother. "Did he say why we quarreled?"

"He wanted you to stay home that night."

"But I ignored him, and went anyway."

"Apparently."

"So I drove my car off a cliff to prove my point, that I could do whatever I wanted. That seems a little drastic, don't you think?"

The doctor removed his glasses and pinched the bridge of his nose. "What I think is that you left home angry. You did not return home that night. You did not contact your family the next day. When your accident was reported you were a considerable distance from home."

"I'm sure I saw a story similar to that not long ago on television."

"Sherye—"

"I know, I know, but this whole thing is so preposterous. If it wasn't for the fact that I have actually seen and talked with Raoul DuBois I would think you'd made the whole thing up. Everything is so dramatic. Don't you see? The former model, the aristocratic count or whatever, the scenes, the turmoil, the escape, the crash and then— Nothing. She can't remember any of it."

"Which brings us back to the crux of it all. What do you remember?"

"I've told you what I can. It's all disjointed and hazy. If I had to describe who I think I am, I'd have to say that I'm a very ordinary sort of person. I like to read, I like to work in my garden, visit with my friends, but I certainly don't do any heavy-duty partying...." She paused, then leaned forward, her hands resting on his desk. "Ever since I first woke up in this hospital, I have felt as though everyone is talking about someone else, not me. I don't feel any identification with the woman who ignored her children, partied with her friends and argued with her husband."

Unable to sit any longer, Sherye left her chair and began to pace. "Don't you understand? I can't begin to relate to a woman who behaves in the way you've described. I may have been stripped of my memory—that's certainly obvious—but I still have a strong sense of my own values. I would rejoice at the opportunity to have children and a home, to have a husband who loved me, an extended family who cared about me. Why would I deliberately behave in a way that would guarantee the loss of all that I hold most dear?"

Dr. Leclerc shifted in his chair and cleared his throat. "I believe there is a rational explanation for the facts in this case and your feelings about who you are and the behavior of which you are capable."

Sherye immediately sat in the chair she'd recently vacated. "Thank God. What is it?"

"There is no doubt that you almost died in your accident. In addition, you remained in a coma for more than a week." He paused and peered at her over his glasses, which were perched once more on the bridge of his nose.

"Yes. I understand and agree with that much, anyway."

"There is substantial evidence in the medical field, vastly reported, of what commonly has been described as near-death experiences. In many of the reported cases, the person who was near death later stated that he or she was given the opportunity to review his or her life from a less worldly perspective, in order to decide whether he or she wishes to make any changes. Whether this particular aspect of the phenomenon is true or not is immaterial. The fact remains that many people who have survived a brush with death subsequently have made radical changes in their lifestyles...have strongly departed from previously set goals and priorities. In short, in almost every way possible they have become another person."

She eyed him with more than a hint of skepticism. "Is that what you think I've done?"

"What I find pertinent in your case is the certainty you've continued to stress about what you can remember and your strong convictions about morality and acceptable behavior."

"I would like to propose a hypothesis," Dr. Leclerc continued. "What if, as a result of your full-blown career at a time when a child is trying to discover her own identity, you drifted away from your early teachings and fundamental upbringing. You may have set up a deep-seated conflict within yourself that your mind could never quite reconcile. Because of the duality in your nature there has been a continual struggle as to which side would dominate your behavioral patterns."

He held her gaze without effort. "I am suggesting the possibility that the more unlike your early training your behavior became, the more intense this conflict within you became, until you eventually could no longer function."

"Then you *do* believe the accident was intentional," she stated in a monotone.

"Perhaps not consciously, but since no one but you knows what you were feeling at the time, we can't rule out the possibility."

"How do you suggest I work on regaining my memory?"

"Once you're feeling physically well enough to deal with the emotional situations that are going to occur once you leave here, I believe that confronting your life, placing yourself in more familiar surroundings, beginning a daily dialogue with your husband and family will all help you to recover."

"You do think I'll remember eventually, don't you?"

He sat there studying her for several minutes before he said, "I don't know what you were like before the accident, of course, but I feel that I've gotten to know you quite well since we've been working together. You've been under considerable pain and emotional tension, and I believe that you have handled it as well as anyone could. You strike me as a brave, courageous woman who's had to face some very difficult choices while dealing with traumatic events in your life. In my opinion, any retreat from life, regardless of how difficult that life might seem to you at the time, would only be temporary. In answer to your question . . . yes. I believe that you will regain your memory."

Chapter Three

A week later Sherye sat near a majestic weeping willow and absorbed the panoramic scene around her. Rolling hills dotted with trees and lined with hedges and stone fences soothed her racing mind while the sound of the splashing water from the nearby fountain gave off a restful chatter.

The garden surrounding her was truly beautiful. The scented flowers added their touch to the day. She took a deep breath, absorbing the pleasing aroma, and waited for her mind to calm.

Raoul had left word with a member of the hospital staff that he would be returning today. She was to be released to his care tomorrow.

Each day of this week she and Dr. Leclerc had worked together in an effort to unlock the door of her memories. The work had been intense and draining, but it gave a sense of purpose. She'd grown accustomed to her daily routine here at the hospital. When she'd heard that she would soon be going home she'd been almost afraid of the next step in her recovery.

The truth was that she felt more comfortable with the doctors and staff of the hospital than she did with her own husband. She felt that at least she had gotten to know Doctors Leclerc and Montand on a limited basis. Raoul remained an enigma.

Just this morning Dr. Leclerc had assured her that she was more than ready to meet this next challenge. He felt certain that once she returned to her home and routine again, she would find some of the missing pieces of her memory.

What had stuck in her mind during their daily sessions was the real possibility that on some level she truly didn't want to remember.

Raoul was the key to many of the answers she needed in order to build some kind of future for herself. Now that she was going home she would be in his company on a daily basis. Since he'd assured the doctors he would cooperate fully in helping her regain her health, she should be glad to be taking this next important step.

Instead she was filled with trepidation to be giving up the sense of security she had slowly gained during her stay at the hospital. She had to prepare herself to face another group of strangers. She was being placed in a position that forced her to trust a man she didn't know, one with whom she had argued and, by all accounts, had walked out on in an anger she didn't understand. In the best of circumstances, the situation would be tense.

She found Raoul DuBois somewhat intimidating, which wasn't too surprising considering the role he played not only in her present recovery but in her life.

She could feel his dislike of her whenever he came to see her. To her his visits appeared to be made out of a sense of duty or obligation . . . possibly as a penance of sorts.

Perhaps she deserved his disdain and contempt.

Perhaps she didn't.

It was that last thought that gave her the necessary strength and motivation to keep pushing against the closed door in her mind.

She needed to learn everything she could about herself.

She needed to know how she felt about her husband.

Most of all, she had to know the true reasons that there was marital discord.

Raoul had told the doctor about her behavior since her son was born, which could be verified or disproven by others who had observed her actions at the time. If he was telling the truth—and he was intelligent enough to know she would be able to find out easily enough—she wanted to know what had happened between them to make her turn away from him and their family.

She had a hunch that this particular information, even if he told her, would be more difficult to verify.

She didn't like being in such a vulnerable position. Unfortunately there was nothing she could do about it except diligently dig into her head for answers.

Sherye rubbed her head, feeling her thoughts circling around and around inside her brain. She had come outside to enjoy the view, not to search for answers. Once again she swept her gaze across the panorama below her, consciously blocking her mind of any thought other than enjoyment of all that her senses were picking up.

Sometime later she knew she was no longer alone, although she had heard nothing to alert her to that fact. Sherye glanced around and saw Raoul standing a few feet away from her, so close to the willow that a few of the graceful limbs of the giant tree brushed his shoulder.

Feeling as awkward as a schoolgirl with her first beau, Sherye got up from the stone bench where she had been sitting and faced him. "Hello, Raoul."

He hesitated a moment before walking toward her. "You're looking much better since the last time I saw you. How are you feeling?" He paused beside her, his opaque gaze giving nothing of his feelings away.

"Fine, thank you," she murmured politely.

He glanced around the garden, then motioned for her to sit down again. When she did, he sat beside her, careful not to touch her.

"I apologize for not returning sooner. Some unexpected business detained me."

"How is everything at home?" she asked politely.

He raised his brow slightly. "You have remembered something about—"

"No." In a careful voice she went on. "I'm sorry, I didn't mean to imply that I..." She paused, searching for words.

Raoul looked away. "The doctor said it would take time."

"I was sitting here, trying to picture the children. It feels so strange to know I have children when I don't remember what they look like."

"They are doing quite well." He hesitated a moment before adding, "Would you like to see a photograph of them?"

Eagerly she turned to him. "Oh, yes, please!"

He reached into his pocket and pulled out a billfold. "I should have thought about bringing more from home," he said ruefully. "The doctor mentioned that seeing the children might trigger something, so I was concentrating on getting you home so that you could see them."

"I understand," she murmured, wishing that his aloof politeness didn't have such a strong effect on her.

He pulled two photographs out of his wallet and handed them to her. She studied the first one carefully. The professionally posed photo had been taken in a studio and revealed a young girl seated beside a toddler, her arm protectively around his shoulders. Both children had dark hair like their father. She couldn't tell from the photograph the color of their eyes.

The little girl looked very solemn, her eyes large in her face. She wore a ruffled dress that seemed too elaborate for her slight build. The boy seemed to be clapping his chubby hands together. She could faintly see a gleam of teeth in his smiling mouth.

She searched for traces of feeling within her, some hint of maternal love for these two children. Instead she felt as though she was seeing them for the first time.

"Well?" Raoul asked after a moment when she didn't say anything.

Slowly she shook her head. "I'm sorry. I don't recognize them."

He took the photo and carefully replaced it in his wallet without comment. She fought the impulse to ask to keep the images in front of her in order to memorize their likenesses. She knew any request of that nature would be futile, given the care with which he handled the treasured keepsake.

"Didn't you tell me their names are Yvette and Jules?"

"Yes. You said you'd always liked the name Yvette. Jules was named after my father."

She glanced at the second picture, her eyes widening in surprise. This one was a candid snapshot of her. She was leaning against the front fender of a bright red sports car with her legs crossed at the ankle. Her head was tilted back, showing the long line of her throat, and her hair was being tossed on the breeze. Her smile revealed sparkling teeth, while designer sunshades masked the upper part of her face. She wore a white jumpsuit that clung seductively to her body.

Sherye stared at the picture without any sense of identification with the woman.

"Is this a recent picture?"

He looked down at the photograph for a brief moment before glancing away without expression. "I took that several months ago. The car was a birthday gift."

"Was this the car I was driving when..."

"Yes."

She studied the picture of the woman who leaned so self-confidently against the car. This was a snapshot of the woman she faced in the mirror each morning. There was no doubt or chance for a mistake.

Had she really thought there was?

Sometime during the past week she reluctantly had come to accept Dr. Leclerc's suggestion that she unconsciously had blocked out years of her life rather than face the twists and turns it had taken. Regardless of what her subconscious had chosen to hide, she was determined to find out the truth about herself.

She turned to Raoul and reached for his hand. She could feel him stiffen beside her but she didn't let go. "I know this is very difficult for you. I wish I could make all of it easier somehow. I have so many questions and you're the only person who can answer them for me. As much as I know that going home is the next step, I find it a little unnerving to be faced with seeing strangers who are actually members of my family, people who know more about me than I do at the moment."

"I've discussed the matter with *Maman* and Danielle. Despite problems in the past, they have agreed to do whatever they can to assist you in adjusting."

Sherye came to her feet in agitation. She took a few steps away from him before she turned to face him. "What problems in the past?" she asked, her voice shaking. "I hate it when you imply all sorts of things, either with words or your distant manner. What is wrong between us? According to Dr. Leclerc, you told him that the two of us had argued the night before my accident. What caused the argument? Why did I leave? What was said between us?"

Raoul came to his feet, as well. "The doctor also said that you should not get upset, that it will only retard your recovery. We'll have time to discuss everything that has happened between us once you are fully recovered. Believe me, I am as eager to deal with our relationship as you appear to be, but there's no reason to go into all of that today. I came looking for you to let you know that I'll pick you up in the morning about nine o'clock. We'll be able to talk on the drive home."

"Is it far?"

"About four hours."

"You mentioned earlier that you had business to attend to. What do you do?"

"The family owns a winery and vineyards that have been part of our holdings for generations."

A winery...vineyards. She waited, hoping for some mental image to appear, but nothing happened. With a sigh she turned away from Raoul and looked over the pastoral scene that rolled into the horizon.

"Sherye?"

Reluctant to face him, she slowly turned and looked at him.

"I know that this is very difficult for you. I suppose what I want you to understand is that this situation is equally difficult for me. I'm doing the very best I can to deal with my own feelings at the moment. Just because you don't happen to remember what has transpired between us doesn't mean that none of it happened." His gaze grew bleak. "Sometimes I find myself envious of your memory loss. You see, as badly as I want to I can't forget some of the things that you have said and done. Perhaps I could forgive what you have done to me, but I'm less able to forgive the pain you've caused the children...and *Maman*...and Danielle. I can't forget. I wish to God I could."

He turned and rapidly walked away from her as though escaping her presence.

The pain Sherye felt as she watched him leave was not caused by her head injury. No, the pain was located in the region of her heart. She ached with the knowledge that she had hurt this man so badly. Only his polite good breeding had restrained his obvious contempt for and disgust of her.

How had her life become such a mess?

Whether the answer was painful or palatable she would be forced to pursue the answers. She offered a brief plea to God to give her the strength she needed to face the mistakes she must have made in her life to have brought her to her present dilemma.

Chapter Four

Raoul couldn't sleep. He'd been tossing and turning in the unfamiliar hotel bed for what seemed like hours, unable to shut out the scenes, the harsh words, the anguished feelings that continued to plague him.

Irritated with himself, he got up and went into the small bathroom off the bedroom and got a drink of water. He could try to kid himself and blame the bed, but he was too honest to accept the excuse. He knew exactly what was wrong with him.

He was dreading the next day when Sherye would be released from the hospital to go home.

He returned to bed and stretched out once again, his mind reliving the past.

From the time he'd received the call from the police reporting her accident, Raoul had been operating in a state of emotional suspension. He'd driven through the night to the hospital where she had been taken. He'd waited beside her bed for her to awaken. When the doctors had realized that she had slipped into a coma, they had warned him there was little more they could do for her.

Despite the rawness of his feelings where Sherye was concerned, he hadn't wanted her to die. Even though there was no chance that their marriage could survive, she was the mother of his children and, as such, deserved the best possible care.

He'd spent two days locating a private nursing hospital where she could receive the very best around-the-clock nursing available. For his own peace of mind he had to do everything in his power to save her.

Each decision had been based on the moment. He had not wanted to give any thought to the future.

Now he had no choice. Sherye was demanding some answers, answers that would immediately reflect the shambles of their relationship.

The irony of her having lost her memory at this time wasn't lost on him. On the contrary, had she been conscious and coherent when she'd been found, he doubted very much that she would have had him contacted. Hadn't she made it clear that she wanted no part of him—except for his money and position, of course? Given a choice, Sherye would probably have called one of the many friends she partied with, and continued with whatever plans she'd had that had precipitated their latest in a long line of quarrels.

Three months ago he'd offered her a divorce and she'd laughed at him. She'd made it clear that she liked her life exactly the way it was and that if he attempted to divorce her, she would drag his name through every scandal sheet in Europe.

Once again Raoul replayed their last scene in his mind.

He'd returned home earlier than usual one afternoon and had found her packing a bag in her room.

Her room.

Yes. Her insistence on moving out of the room they had shared since the beginning of their marriage had been the beginning of the end of their relationship, only he hadn't seen it at the time.

She had been in the last stages of her second pregnancy and very uncomfortable. She had complained that she couldn't rest, that he kept waking her up, so she had moved into the adjoining bedroom.

Once Jules was born, however, she had refused to return to his bed. Eventually they had resumed marital intimacies, but she rarely responded to him and he came to her bed less and less as time passed.

She had become involved with friends she'd known from her modeling days, people who partied more than they worked. At first she had brought them to the château on a regular basis, but gradually she'd taken to spending her time away from home. Whenever he'd attempted to discuss her behavior with her she had brushed him aside, ignoring him.

During that last afternoon he'd refused to be brushed aside. He remembered searching for her....

She was in her bedroom, packing a suitcase.

He leaned against the doorway between their rooms, his hands in his pockets.

"Going somewhere?"

She spun around and saw him. "Oh! You startled me. You're home early. Why?" she asked, tucking a wisp of satin and lace into the bag.

"You didn't answer my question."

She straightened and looked at him. "Nor you mine," she replied sweetly.

"All right," he said. "I'm home early so that I could have a word with you."

She rolled her eyes while she continued to fold resort wear and place it in the bag. "By all means, say what's on your mind."

"I just received several statements in the mail today totaling charges you've been making. I consider them rather excessive."

"Do you, now? Don't you have the money to pay them?" she asked without looking up, a small smile on her face.

"That isn't the point, Sherye. We've discussed this before."

"I know. Don't you find it a tad boring, darling?" She gave a theatrical sigh. "God knows I do."

"Now it's your turn. Where are you going?"

"Don't worry. I'll just be gone overnight."

He straightened and walked over to the bed where she was busy. "Isn't that a considerable amount of clothing for overnight?"

She slammed the lid and locked it. "Don't worry about it." She turned and faced him, crossing her arms.

"I'd prefer that you stay home tonight, Sherye. I intend for us to talk about how much money you've been spending in the past few months."

"I really don't give a damn what you intend, Raoul. It's too late for me to change my plans." She patted one of his cheeks. "But don't worry, sweetie. I'll be back before you have a chance to miss me. I promise." She giggled. "Then we can have all the talks you want. Won't that be fun?"

"What if I insist on your staying?"

Her mercurial mood shifted into anger. "Why in the hell should I sit around here all day waiting for you to show up and bless me with your presence? It's boring, can't you understand that? I'm sick to death of entertaining your stuffy friends who barely tolerate me... sick of your aristocratic mother glaring down her nose at me and disapproving of every damn thing I do. I'm sick of your mealymouthed sister cowering behind you and your mother, refusing to stand up for herself and get her own life. I'm too young to be buried alive in this blasted mausoleum. I want to enjoy every minute while I can and I intend to do just that. You aren't going to stop me."

She grabbed her bag and purse and stormed out of the room, slamming the door behind her.

He could have gone after her, but what was the point? Their marriage had disintegrated into a series of stormy scenes. Whatever love they had once felt for each other was gone.

By the time he awoke the next morning he knew what he had to do. He would call her bluff. He would see just how serious she was with regard to her threat to harm his reputation.

He went to see a lawyer about getting a divorce.

He'd had plenty of time to think while he'd sat beside her bed after the accident. The accident really hadn't changed anything between them. He'd known that once she regained consciousness all the shared animosity between them would be there waiting.

A divorce was the only sensible solution.

He'd known his choice would cost him financially, but he could put no price tag on his peace of mind.

That's all he wanted from all of this now... peace.

However, fate had decreed otherwise—and Sherye had awakened without any memory of him or their marriage.

During one of his interviews with the doctor he'd been questioned at great length about her state of mind when he'd last seen her, about the quarrel they'd had, and whether or not he thought she had deliberately attempted suicide.

No matter from what perspective he considered the matter, his answer was no. In the first place, she hadn't been all that upset when she'd left, merely determined. She'd been like one of his horses—she'd had the bit between her teeth and nothing was going to curb her from doing what she wanted to do.

In the second place, she had no reason to want to die. She had everything she could possibly want, which he could easily verify by the thick stack of charges she'd run up lately. Where other women might have wanted a husband and two healthy children, Sherye concentrated on spending lavish amounts of money on herself... which brought him to his third point. Sherye would not do anything to mar her beauty. Even if she had chosen to do away with herself, she would have found a way to have remained beautiful even in death.

No. The accident had been just that, an accident, caused by the fact that as usual she was driving too fast and lost control of the car. In addition, as usual she hadn't been wearing her seat belt. Ironically enough, that habitual lapse of hers was what apparently had saved her life.

When Raoul had visited the doctor this afternoon, Dr. Leclerc had warned him that he would find some major changes in Sherye's behavior from the woman Raoul had described to him originally.

Raoul had hoped they would be able to prove that she was faking the amnesia. Unfortunately the tests were conclusively negative. She had no recollection of anything that had happened to her since she'd lived in France. For that matter, she had no memories of modeling, living in New York or traveling. The only memories they'd been able to evoke were around her childhood in Dallas, and those were sketchy at best.

The doctor had also mentioned some possible theories for Sherye's new and rather bewildering attitude toward life. She had almost died. Now she was being given a second chance.

Raoul wasn't at all certain that he wanted a second chance with Sherye. No matter what the doctor said, she was the same person who had caused so much grief in his home and his life. He'd been honest with her today. He didn't know if he could forget what she had done. He wasn't even certain he was willing to try.

However, the doctor insisted that she be returned to her home in hopes that the familiar surroundings would more quickly trigger something in her memory. Raoul couldn't deny her the chance to completely recover from her injuries. He could only hope that allowing her to come home wouldn't create additional turmoil for everyone concerned.

With that last drowsy thought, Raoul fell into a deep, exhausted sleep.

Sherye awoke the next morning with a sense of foreboding. She glanced around her, recognizing the familiar room with a relieved sense of safety before she recalled that today was the day she would be leaving the hospital.

She'd grown accustomed to being there. For all practical purposes, her life had begun here in this room, when she'd opened her eyes for the first time after her accident.

Her room had become a refuge for her to return to whenever the intense therapy regarding her lack of memory seemed to be too much for her to face.

In a few hours she would have to leave everything that was familiar and comforting to her. Her sadness wasn't eased by the knowledge that she would be leaving here with a man who was a stranger to her—a stiff, unbending man whose cold aloofness made her feel instinctively guilty without the slightest notion why.

She'd had trouble sleeping the night before, waking time and time again from some vague nightmare feeling of being pursued by ravenous animals.

Despite her anxiety, she needed to prepare herself for her trip to a place Raoul called home, to meet people she couldn't recall, which included her children.

She felt hopelessly inadequate. She also felt as though she had knowingly and willfully let everyone down. She wished she had more confidence in herself. Surely her years of modeling should give her something from which to draw. Perhaps she hadn't been a very successful wife, but she'd been told that she was a very successful model.

She quickly showered and dressed, wearing another one of the dresses Raoul had brought for her. She must have gained some weight while she had been recuperating. The dress was a trifle snug. Studying herself in the mirror, she objectively noted the changes since she'd regained consciousness—her cheeks didn't appear so gaunt, her eyes had a healthy shine and her skin glowed with a light tan. The ivory silk shift she wore seemed to bring out the bright red of her hair and the green of her eyes.

When she returned to the bedroom she found Raoul standing by the window, looking out.

"Oh! I didn't hear you arrive. You should have let me know you were here."

Slowly he turned away from the window, his hands in his pants pockets. His gaze assessed her from head to toe without giving away a hint of what he was thinking. "I was early," he replied in a low voice. His face could have been carved from wood.

Her heart sank. For an instant Sherye felt the urge to plead with him to give her the opportunity to make amends for whatever she had done to cause him to treat her so coolly. Either that, or to allow her to go somewhere alone to continue her healing process, to a place where she would feel accepted and welcomed.

Of course, she didn't say any of what she was thinking. What good would it do? Instead she walked over to the bed and packed the last few articles that had been lying beside her bag. "I'm ready to go whenever you are." Her voice sounded as cool and calm as his, she was pleased to discover.

"You look tired," he surprised her by saying. "Did you sleep all right last night?" He reached past her and picked up the bag.

"Not really. I'm nervous about leaving here."

He raised an eyebrow. "Why?"

She didn't want him to know about her misgivings, but perhaps he would understand. "I've grown accustomed to being here. The hospital and the routine here are all that I can remember at the moment."

They were standing beside the bed, within touching distance of each other. He scanned her face as though searching for something. A slight line appeared between his brows. "The doctors warned me that I might see some pronounced changes in you since your accident. I'm beginning to see what they meant."

"I'm not certain I understand what you mean."

"In all the years I've known you, I've never seen you nervous or unsure of yourself. Even if you had been, you would never, ever have admitted it to anyone."

His voice hadn't warmed exactly, but his tone was more neutral than she had ever heard him. He sounded puzzled, as though she had presented him with a view of her he'd never seen and that didn't fit with any of his perceptions.

Impulsively she took his hand and said, "Raoul, it would help me so much if we—what I mean to say is...everything is so strange to me right now. I feel as though I woke up in somebody else's body, that I'm trying to live somebody else's life. What's worse, the more I learn of this person I'm being told I am, the less I like her." She looked down at their clasped hands, then up into his narrowed gaze. She almost lost her courage, but realized that she had to try to make him see how difficult all of this was for her. "I know that you're upset with me, but it's very difficult for me to deal with your attitude when I don't know what I have done to cause it. If I could go back and undo whatever actions of mine created the pain you mentioned yesterday that you and your family have suffered, believe me, I would. You said that you wished you could forget. Well, so do I. Unfortunately we're faced with the unfortunate circumstances where I can't remember what you can't forget, and we're going to have to accept that fact regardless of our personal feelings. I know I'm asking a great deal of you, but if we're going to get through today and the rest of the days while I'm working to recover my memory, we're both going to have to leave the past behind, at least temporarily."

She waited but he didn't say anything, although he seemed to be considering what she had said. With a slight sense of hope, she decided to say it all.

"What I want to ask of you is...would it be possible for us to start over...to pretend we just met? As far as I know

I saw you for the first time the night I opened my eyes and found you standing beside my bed. Can we just continue from there?"

She stopped talking when her voice began to shake. She hated feeling so emotional and so out of control. She hated feeling like a supplicant for royal favor. However, she also knew that she couldn't function with so much tension between them. She had to do whatever she could, say whatever was necessary, to effect a truce until her memory returned.

He continued to stare at their joined hands as though he found the sight unusual. Perhaps he did. After a tense, lengthy silence he carefully withdrew his hand from her clasp, put down her bag and moved away toward the window where she could no longer see his face. With his back to her, he said, "I will do everything I can to accept as bona fide your offer of a truce between us. I'll admit that you have seemed very different since you regained consciousness. However, there's too much between us for me to pretend none of it ever happened. What I will do is attempt not to allow the past to color the present."

Sherye felt as though a giant hand had just squeezed her chest so tightly that she could scarcely breathe. He had turned away from her but he'd been unable to mask the pain in his voice. She stared at his stiffly held back and for the first time felt as though she'd gotten a glimpse of the man behind the mask. He'd been hurt very badly, she suspected, just as she suspected she knew who had inflicted so much pain on him.

Despite his pain he'd seen that she was well cared for in those first harrowing days after her accident.

Despite his pain he was here today to take her home with him in an effort to help her heal.

Here was a man with deeply held convictions, a man who appeared to love deeply despite unknown—to her—but obvious setbacks. Whatever his feelings for her now, he was doing his best to deal with them without inflicting more of a burden upon her.

Sherye searched for something to say, but her new insight and understanding of the man could not help her to ease the tension between them.

After another prolonged, weighty silence she heard Raoul sigh before he turned to face her once more. His expression was carefully composed, his voice even when he spoke again.

"I will do my best to treat you with the respect you deserve as my wife and the mother of my children while you are in my home. I will assist in your recovery by answering whatever questions you may have in hopes that you will more quickly regain your memory. That is all that I can promise you."

He stood alone, facing her, much as she suspected he might face a firing squad—with fearless courage and undeniable dignity.

"Thank you, Raoul. I have a hunch it's more than I deserve."

They stood there in the spacious room, he by the window, she by the bed, silently acknowledging their truce. Sherye could feel the tension ease somewhat between them. As though released from hidden restraints, Raoul strode to the bed and again picked up her bag. "Come. We need to be on our way. We have a long drive ahead of us."

The sunlight that greeted them when they stepped outside gave Sherye a buoyant feeling of hope that the day would bring answers that would ease the ever-present tightness in her chest.

Raoul escorted her to a silver luxury sedan and politely opened the door for her. She sank into the soft leather seat with a sigh, automatically buckling her seat belt, while he came around the car and slid behind the steering wheel.

They pulled out of the long driveway onto a country road. Although it was only midmorning she recognized that she was already feeling weak, which frustrated her. Perhaps it was the continued tension that so exhausted her.

Remembering that he had promised to answer her questions on the drive home, Sherye asked, "What have you told the children about the accident? Did you tell them I don't remember them?"

"We told them you'd been in an accident. We didn't tell them about your memory loss. There was no need to alarm them more than was necessary."

"We?"

"*Maman* and Danielle."

His mother and sister who lived with them.

She recalled that the doctor had told her she had had little to do with her children. "Do your mother and sister look after Yvette and Jules?"

"They spend as much of their time as possible with the children, of course, but we have a full-time nanny who looks after them—Louise."

"What sort of woman is she?"

"Very competent. She came highly recommended."

Once behind the wheel Raoul had placed shade glasses over his eyes, effectively masking his expression. She turned in her seat so that she could see him in profile.

"What I meant was..." She paused, searching for the most diplomatic way to phrase what she wanted to know. "What sort of person is she? Is she warm and laughing? Does she give them hugs and plenty of affection? Does she play games with them...maybe teach them little songs?"

Raoul gave her a quick glance, frowning. "Louise takes her job quite seriously. The children are well trained—obedient with good manners."

She sighed and straightened in her seat. What could she expect? If she had allowed another woman to care for her children, she couldn't complain about the way they were taught. As far as that goes, they could still be warm, exuberant children who had enough family around them to mask the absence of their mother's attention.

She prayed that was so and vowed to make up for her long absence by spending as much time with them as possible from now on.

"Before we arrive home," she began in a firm voice, "I would appreciate your giving me some kind of idea of our relationship. According to Dr. Leclerc, we quarreled the last night I was home. I also got the impression that you didn't approve of my friends."

This time she kept her gaze straight ahead, suddenly grateful that they were seated side by side so that she didn't have to look at him.

She could hear the tightness in his voice when he said, "I'm sorry that you had to learn of our relationship through a third party. I regretted having to discuss the matter with the doctor, but I understood his need to have some information about your past in order to work with you."

"Yes, he mentioned your reluctance."

She waited, silently reminding him that she was waiting for him to answer her question.

After several miles of silence Raoul cleared his throat. "I'm finding this much more awkward than I had imagined it to be. It's very difficult to discuss what you have said and done in the past when you have no way of knowing whether or not I'm telling you the truth."

Impulsively she touched his shoulder. "When I first regained consciousness I wondered about that, myself, but I feel that I've come to know you a little better now. I find that I trust you to tell me the truth, no matter how disagreeable you find the telling. I've already guessed that my behavior hasn't been anything to brag about. The thing is, I've imagined all sorts of things. It would be a relief to know the truth."

"Yes, but whose truth, you see. I want to be fair with you. However, you've never been one to explain the motives behind your actions so I have no idea why you've done the things you've done. You've refused to discuss your feelings with me. It's as though the woman I fell in love with and married became someone else during your second pregnancy. For the past two years I've lived with a stranger whose inexplicable, erratic behavior has created many problems in our household."

"So our argument wasn't unusual?"

"No. Over the past several months you've been spending a great deal of money without bothering to account for it. You've gone on shopping sprees that were excessive, even for you. You've been moody and unpredictable. Laughing one moment, snapping at someone the next." He massaged the back of his neck before he said, "However, this was the first time you decided to go somewhere overnight."

"You mean you knew I was leaving?"

"Yes. I found you packing, but you assured me you'd be back the next evening, despite the fact you packed a rather large bag, which made no sense to me. When I questioned you, you got defensive and sarcastic, refusing to answer my questions. I asked you not to go but you ignored me. I decided to face you when you returned and deal with our situation. Instead of your return, I received a call from the police reporting your accident."

"Did I tell you where I was going?"

"No."

"Or why?"

"No."

She fell silent for several minutes before she asked, "In the weeks that I've been at the hospital I haven't heard from any of my friends. Isn't that unusual?"

"I haven't given the matter much thought. I suppose it is, although we managed to keep a low profile in the papers. Perhaps they weren't aware of what happened."

"But if I spent most of my time with them, wouldn't they have called for me at home?"

"Perhaps they have. I haven't asked."

Sherye made no effort to fill in the silence that took over between them. At least she had a better understanding of their relationship, some specifics to go with the generalities the doctor had outlined for her. Unfortunately there seemed to be no one who could tell her why she had behaved the way she did.

After nearly an hour had passed, Sherye said, "I have no explanations to give about my behavior. All I can do is repeat what I said earlier. I'm sorry for causing so much turmoil in your life. I keep thinking about something the doctor said to me—about second chances."

He glanced at her. "What do you mean?"

"Perhaps my accident was God's way of getting my attention and making me aware of my mistakes. Maybe I've been given another chance to look at my life and make some much needed changes." She gazed out at the passing landscape before adding, "Perhaps we have been given the chance to begin again, as strangers, to get to know each other."

When he spoke, his voice sounded gruff. "That would be a little difficult, wouldn't you say, considering we've had two children together."

She could feel the heat in her cheeks as she grasped the implication of his statement. "I know...at least, a rational part of me acknowledges that you and I have a history together, but at the moment it's difficult to accept the fact that I have shared a life and a bed with you, when it feels as though we met only recently."

"You needn't concern yourself about sharing my bed. You've had your own room since shortly before Jules was born."

"Oh."

"Given the present circumstances, I certainly wouldn't expect you to be a wife to me in the intimate sense. Perhaps I should have reassured you on this point much earlier. I suppose I keep forgetting that you truly don't remember anything about us." He glanced at his watch. "Perhaps you should try to get some rest. We'll be stopping for lunch in little more than an hour. The doctor warned me that you would tire easily and that I should make certain you aren't overtaxed."

In other words, she thought to herself, he was through answering her questions. Not that she blamed him. Nothing that she had learned had surprised her, but she was depressed to learn the condition of her marriage was as bad as she'd been told to expect.

The reason she was saddened by the confirmation was that she had discovered today that she liked Raoul DuBois. Given his perspective of their situation, she knew that he had handled himself well despite his personal feelings. She was sorry he had such a poor opinion of her, even while she understood why he did.

She adjusted her seat into a reclining position and closed her eyes with a sense of relief. Sleep had become her haven when she no longer wanted to face the life she had made for herself. For a little while she could escape.

Raoul awakened her sometime later. She opened her eyes and blinked, looking around in surprise. From the change in the landscape she realized she must have been asleep for some time.

They were on the outskirts of a village that looked as though it hadn't changed in a hundred years. Enthralled by the sight, she couldn't seem to look fast enough to see everything she wanted to see. Small shops, narrow streets, flowers in bloom . . . all of them caught her eye.

"Oh, this is beautiful. Where are we?"

Raoul told her the name of the town while he turned into a side street and parked. With his usual grave politeness he helped her from the car and guided her down the sidewalk to a small outdoor café.

A waiter immediately joined them, rattling off a list of the day's specials and discussing the wine list with Raoul.

Once the waiter left, Sherye leaned forward in her chair and asked, "Could you explain something to me?"

He sat across the table from her, still wearing the dark shades so that she couldn't see the expression in his eyes.

"I'll try," he replied.

"Tell me how we met. Help me to understand what drew us together in the first place. There's so much I don't know."

As though discussing two other people, he spoke in a matter-of-fact tone of voice. "You were with a crew doing a modeling shoot on the Riviera. I was there on business. We met on the beach and began talking. You had just arrived, while I was scheduled to leave the next morning."

The waiter appeared with their orders. While they ate, Raoul continued his story. "I ended up staying another week, despite the need to return to my business concerns. I went with you each day and watched you work." His expression softened and his voice lowered. "You were magnificent. You knew how to project whatever image necessary to make a man see you as the fulfillment of all of his fantasies." As though focusing on the present once more, he shrugged and in a hard voice said, "You still do."

Taken aback by his sudden bitterness, she could only ask, "What do you mean?"

"You play the bewildered amnesiac so well. You've portrayed the woman I fell in love with most convincingly since your accident. I thought she was gone. I had accepted the fact that she had never existed anywhere other than my own mind." He picked up his wineglass and silently saluted her before finishing the wine. "You have quite a gift, my dear. That's the way you ensnare us, you know."

"I've done nothing, Raoul," she protested, sorry to see the grim mask appear once again.

"I know," he agreed immediately, surprising her. "It's all second nature to you."

When he didn't say anything more, she asked, "How long did we know each other before we married?"

His cynicism hit her like a winging dart. "Long enough for you to convince me that your career meant nothing to you in comparison to your love for me. I returned home when you flew back to New York at the end of your assignment. I needed to clear my brain, to try to look at the situation logically...sanely. But I couldn't resist calling you. We talked many times over the next few weeks. I wanted you, but was realistic enough to understand that we came from different backgrounds and cultures."

Raoul leaned back in his chair and crossed his arms. "You explained to me how you'd spent your entire life yearning for a home. That you had been raised by a single mother who'd had difficulty supporting the two of you. You finally convinced me that living with me and my family at the château would be a dream come true for you." His smile held no humor. "I allowed myself to become convinced." He shrugged. "And so...we were married."

"And I set out to make your life miserable forever after, from the sound of things," she added.

He looked at her in surprise, taken aback by her unexpected response. "Not at first," he finally said. "You were very taken with the château. You said it looked like something out of a Hollywood movie. You said you felt like a princess living in a castle."

Since that was the same reaction she'd had when she'd learned of her life in France, she remained silent. What she wished she could understand was what had caused her to change her mind about her life with Raoul.

The only way she was going to find out was to return to the château in hopes of having her memory triggered by familiar surroundings.

Chapter Five

Sherye didn't know how long they had driven before Raoul slowed the car and turned between two very old stone pillars just off the main road. She straightened in her seat and looked around, hoping against hope that something... *any*thing... would look familiar to her.

After following a winding lane to the crest of a hill, the car topped the hill, revealing a panorama that caused her to catch her breath.

Nestled among a growth of well-preserved trees, the château sat like an old but well-loved dowager, content to watch the passing of time from its comfortable perch halfway along a hillside across the valley from where they were.

"Oh, Raoul, it's beautiful... absolutely, perfectly beautiful," she breathed in awe.

"Yes."

His simple answer gave nothing of his feelings away. However, his expression spoke volumes of the love he felt for his home.

How could she not remember such a place? she wondered. How could she have spent the past six years of her life here and ever want to leave it, for any reason? Without realizing her intention, she spoke her thoughts out loud with calm certainty. "I have never been here before in my life."

"You mean you don't remember," he corrected her.

"No. I mean that I could not possibly forget something so memorable and striking."

He made no comment, allowing the car to pick up speed once more. They drove for almost twenty minutes before they arrived in front of the château. Leaving the car, Raoul walked to Sherye's door and opened it, then guided her up the steps. He opened the door and allowed her to precede him inside.

The foyer soared upward two stories high to an arched dome, dwarfing the occupants below. Her gaze slowly fell from the ornately decorated ceiling to the stairway that wound downward from the upper floor. She saw a pair of wide green eyes peering down at them from around one of the balusters located in the upper hallway.

Sherye unobtrusively edged toward the stairway without taking her eyes away from the child crouched upstairs. She smiled and in a soft voice said, "Is that you, Yvette?"

The child edged away from the railing, her eyes, if anything, growing larger. Frustrated, Sherye looked over her shoulder at Raoul, who was speaking to a woman in a starched uniform. When Sherye glanced back upstairs, the child was gone.

A pang of loss hit her unexpectedly. Had she been mistaken? Or was her own child unwilling to come greet her mother?

"It is good to have you back with us, *madame,*" Sherye heard behind her, and turned. The woman standing beside Raoul had spoken. "You are in time to join the others for tea."

Ready or not, here I come, she thought to herself as Raoul took her arm and escorted her into one of the rooms off the foyer. She had a brief sense of connection with the young child she'd glimpsed on the balcony. She felt as alone as the child had looked—alone and uncertain of her welcome.

The room she and Raoul entered was a formal salon from a much earlier and more gracious era. Each piece of furniture was a work of art, each accessory chosen by a discerning eye. She felt awed by her surroundings.

Why, the place should be roped off to visitors! And yet...somehow the room managed to invoke a sense of welcome and comfort to the weary, a soothing source of permanence and peace emanating from it.

"Ah, there you are," Raoul said and for the first time Sherye realized that they were not alone in the room. Two women had been seated in a grouping of chairs and love seats. Both of them stood when Raoul spoke.

There was no denying their relationship to Raoul or to each other. They had the same strong bone structure, similarly shaped noses and eyes. The older woman was dressed in expensive black silk, and her hair—a mixture of silver and black—was swept back from her face into a tidy knot at the back of her head.

Here was a woman who faced whatever life threw at her without flinching. She held her head proudly while she gazed at Sherye without blinking.

The younger woman was similarly dressed in black, but where the color was striking and dramatic on the older woman, on the younger one the color made her skin look sallow. She wore her hair in braids wound around her head in a coronet. She could be anywhere from Sherye's age to thirty years older. Without makeup or any attempt at fashion, she appeared older than her slender build and smooth complexion might indicate. She, too, looked at Sherye without speaking.

"Leandra will have our tea here shortly," Raoul said to the waiting women, while indicating that Sherye could sit on one of the love seats. Her knees had suddenly started to shake and she was glad for the opportunity to sit down before her nervousness was made obvious to everyone.

Raoul took one of the chairs nearby, facing the two women across a low, wide table.

"How was your trip?" the older woman said as though Raoul was alone.

"Uneventful."

Sherye clasped her hands in her lap, not sure what to do or say. She glanced up and saw Danielle looking at her with curiosity, but when their eyes met, Danielle immediately looked away.

A heavy silence seemed to fill the room.

"How are the children?" Raoul asked when no one seemed inclined to speak.

Danielle showed the first signs of animation Sherye had seen in her since they had walked into the room. "They're quite well. I spent most of the morning with them. We went for a walk, and I told them that—" her gaze darted toward Sherye, then away "—their mother was coming home today."

Silence filled the room once again.

Sherye realized that she felt more alone, now that she was at home, than she had all the time she was in the hospital. She could feel the animosity toward her from the two women and didn't have the faintest notion how to deal with it. She felt cut off from the world around her, an unwanted spectator attempting to discover where she fit in to the scheme of things.

The arrival of tea managed to ease the tension that had seemed to build in the room. There was something almost cheerful about sharing food and drink with others. Raoul continued to talk to the women as though nothing was out of the ordinary about their situation, and they began to relax and respond to him. Feeling more like an invisible observer, Sherye noticed how well Raoul ignored the atmosphere. He appeared comfortably relaxed, voicing his relief to be home.

No one spoke directly to Sherye or included her in the conversation. If this was the way she was generally treated by the family, she could better understand why she'd reverted to the company of old friends.

She was actually relieved rather than more nervous when the children appeared with their nanny.

"Ah, yes, Louise," Raoul said, rising and heading toward where the trio stood just inside the doorway. "Thank you for bringing the children down." Sherye watched him walk over to the young, slim woman with reddish blond hair and attractively large blue eyes, and take the child she held into his arms. A little girl stood just behind the woman, shyly peering around her. Sherye recognized the green eyes and hesitant expression from her glimpse of the child in the hallway earlier. She felt a tug at the tightness in her chest.

"Hello, Yvette," she offered softly. Holding out her hand, she added, "Won't you come here to see me?"

With a dignity far beyond her years, Yvette walked across the wide expanse of rug toward her. Only her expressive eyes gave her away.

Raoul followed Yvette with Jules in his arms.

"Mama!" Jules announced gleefully. The exuberant word triggered unexpected tears and Sherye blinked rapidly in an attempt not to betray her reaction. When Yvette reached her side, Sherye pulled her stiff little body into the circle of her arms and hugged her daughter, feeling the rigidness of her spine beneath her fingers. Yvette suffered the hug but didn't lift her arms in response.

When she allowed her daughter to step back from her, Sherye looked up and saw Jules jabbering to his father with a great deal of waving. "May I hold him?" she asked, holding out her arms. Raoul moved closer to her and started to hand Jules to her, but instead of going to her, Jules clung to Raoul and whimpered.

Raoul's gaze met hers. "Perhaps we shouldn't force him," he said in a low voice. "He will need to get used to you."

"But he knew me! He seemed so glad to see me that I thought—"

"Oh, yes. He recognizes you. He just isn't used to being close enough to touch you."

With those simple words ringing in her ears, Sherye could feel all her hard-won courage to face the consequences of her previous behavior crumble. She couldn't control the tears that filled her eyes.

She turned her head away in an effort to hide her embarrassing reaction to her child's instinctive response to her. She swallowed in an attempt to speak around the lump in her throat. "I see."

As though taking pity on her, Raoul sat beside her so that they were shoulder to shoulder. Jules continued to cling to his father's neck.

Blinking away the tears, Sherye realized that Yvette was watching her intently. She gave her a wobbly smile. "Is your brother shy with everybody?"

Yvette shook her head.

"Are you shy?"

Yvette tilted her head in a way that immediately brought Raoul to mind. "Sometimes."

"Is this one of those times?"

Instead of answering the question, Yvette said, "You're different."

The statement seemed to bounce around the room like an echo. All the adults froze.

"I am? In what way?"

Yvette continued to look at her for a long moment. "I don't know, but you are."

Raoul reached out and tenderly brushed a strand of Yvette's hair off her forehead. "Your mama has been ill for a while, remember? She's better now, though, so she could come home."

Yvette turned her clear gaze back to Sherye. "Did you almost die?"

Sherye glanced at Raoul, unsure of what to say. He answered for her. "The important thing is that she's well enough to come back home." He looked down at Jules, who had released his death grip on his father's neck and was staring at Sherye from eyes as dark as his father's. "Are you going to say hello to your mother, Jules?"

Jules immediately hid his face in Raoul's shirt.

Danielle spoke up. "Would you like me to take them out into the garden?"

"I'll take them," Raoul said, standing. He looked down at Sherye. "Perhaps you could go upstairs and rest for a while. Danielle can show you the way."

"Doesn't she know where she sleeps?" Yvette asked, not missing a trick.

Refusing to start off with evasions, Sherye made an instant decision, instinctively wanting to be truthful with her daughter. "You see, Yvette," she said, taking the child's hand between both of hers for a moment, "I got a bad bump on my head, see?" She pushed back her hair and showed her the area that had been shaved. "Ever since then my memory plays tricks on me. I can't always remember everything that I used to."

"Do you remember me?"

Oh, help! she prayed, still not wanting to lie to the little girl. Sherye cupped her heart-shaped face gently between her hands and asked, "How could anyone possibly forget such a special person like you?"

Yvette's solemn stare seemed to look deeply into her soul. Then she grinned and threw her arms around Sherye's neck. "I'm glad you're home, Mama," she said, immediately backing away as though suddenly shy.

"Me, too," she managed to say.

She watched the tall man walk away from her, leading the little girl by one hand and carrying the boy with ease. They looked so comfortable with each other. Once again she had a flash of being alone and separate from her family.

"Very touching," her mother-in-law said once Raoul was gone. "Perhaps you should have gone into the theater. If I didn't know better, I would have believed you've really missed your children."

"Maman," Danielle murmured, her cheeks glowing.

"I know, I know, I told Raoul that I would accept her presence here," she replied as though Sherye wasn't there. "I'm afraid I'm not as gullible as these men you've managed to wrap around your finger."

Sherye blinked. "I beg your pardon?"

"And so you should, but seldom do. I'm talking about this act you're carrying on, pretending to have forgotten everything. It's most effective, to be sure."

"Maman," Danielle began, "please don't. There's no point in—"

"I know. She's here now." She turned back to Sherye. "I never faulted your intelligence, Sherye, and your ability to survive. It's beyond my comprehension how you were able to find out so quickly about Raoul's plans to divorce you. Now, of course, he must wait until you can—"

"Divorce me?" Sherye repeated in a whisper. She felt as though all the air had been knocked out of her.

"Don't try to pretend you don't know at this late date. You were certainly quick enough on your feet to fake an accident and pretend to helplessness before he could have the papers prepared, signed and filed."

Sherye managed to stand, although her knees were shaking so hard she wasn't at all certain her legs would hold her. "I knew nothing about a divorce."

"So you say."

"I'm sorry that you don't believe me. I'm not faking anything. As far as I'm concerned, this is my first time here. You and Danielle are strangers to me." She knew she had to get away from these people. She walked toward the door, praying that her knees would continue to support her.

"Sooner or later you'll give yourself away," her mother-in-law said behind her, "and you'll be out of here, out of our lives."

Sherye continued through the doorway, out into the foyer and as far as the newel post of the stairs before her knees gave way. She grabbed the post and held on, taking deep breaths. Thinking she was alone, she was startled when Danielle spoke from immediately behind her.

"I apologize for *Maman*'s outspokenness," she said, pausing beside Sherye. "She's been under a considerable strain. We all have."

Sherye straightened and started up the stairway on sheer determination and willpower. "She has every right to say whatever she wishes," Sherye replied. "This is her home, after all."

She could feel Danielle's gaze on her but she needed all her concentration to place each foot on the next riser.

"Yvette is right. You're different."

Sherye gave a tiny shrug. "I wouldn't know," she said indifferently. At the moment all she wanted to do was to lie down before she collapsed. When she finally reached the top she paused to catch her breath, gripping the rail.

"Your room is down this hallway," Danielle said.

Taking a deep breath, Sherye followed her.

Danielle opened one of the doors and stepped aside. "It's just that we love Raoul so much. It's been so painful to watch him deal with everything and not be able to do anything to help."

Sherye paused in the doorway and looked at her sister-in-law. Standing this close and in better light, she could see that the woman wasn't much older than she was. She couldn't be more than thirty. With her dark eyes and creamy complexion she could be very attractive. Sherye wondered why she dressed so severely and wore her hair in such an unflattering style.

"Thank you for showing me to my room," she said quietly.

"Dinner is at eight. We generally meet in the salon at seven-thirty."

"Thank you." Sherye closed the door and leaned against it, exhausted.

The room before her had been decorated in gold and white, with touches of royal blue. Once again she was reminded of an earlier era, where massive furniture did not shrink the size of the room. A large four-poster bed with a canopy that matched the drapes and spread stood at one end of the room, facing a fireplace. Floor-to-ceiling windows filled with leaded panes let in the light. She made her way across the wide expanse of carpet to the windows and looked down at a formal garden that stretched out toward a thick stand of trees.

She saw Raoul seated on a stone bench beside a fountain. Yvette leaned beside him, her elbow on the bench, her chin resting in her palm, listening attentively to him while Jules stood in the shelter of Raoul's knees.

She didn't bother to fight the tears that slipped down her cheeks. She had been counting on this day for so long. Dr. Leclerc had been so certain that her memory would be jogged once she returned home.

Nothing looked familiar.

She hadn't expected her mother-in-law's anger to be quite so aggressive. She hadn't expected to be accused of lying. Even more unnerving was the news that Raoul planned to divorce her.

She turned away from the window, unable to handle looking at a family that she would lose so soon after she'd found them. All her life she had yearned for a family of her own. She and Janine had often talked about—

Janine?

Her heart gave a sudden thump in her chest. There was that name again. The doctor had suggested that she was a childhood friend. Perhaps she was, but there was more to it, wasn't there? They were still friends.

Sherye closed her eyes in an effort to see Janine more clearly, to picture her surroundings, but all she got for her efforts was a pounding in her head.

Why did some memories seem to pop up without rhyme or reason, while others refused to surface, no matter how strongly she wanted them?

She hated the position she was in. If only she could remember why Raoul wanted a divorce. Of course the news shouldn't have surprised her. They had separate rooms and went their separate ways. She was obviously unhappy living here and after meeting her in-laws she had a much better understanding of why.

Yes, a divorce was probably the best solution. The problem was she didn't know where she would go or what she would do, particularly if her mind continued to play tricks on her. No doubt Raoul had decided to wait until they'd arrived home to tell her about the divorce in the hope that, once home, she'd suddenly remember everything and could discuss the matter intelligently.

He hadn't asked her if she remembered anything when they'd been having tea downstairs. As perceptive as he was, he hadn't needed to verbalize a question whose answer was obvious to him.

She didn't know how she was going to be able to face all of them again over dinner, but she had very little choice. In the meantime, she would rest.

After removing all but her underwear, Sherye slipped into bed, deliberately seeking oblivion from a cold and bewildering world.

Chapter Six

Sherye woke to shadowed light. For a moment she felt disoriented, unable to place where she was or why she was there. The wide, comfortable bed was nothing like the hospital bed she'd grown used to during the past few weeks. She lay still, allowing her gaze to wander around the large, high-ceilinged room with its opulent furnishings.

Was this how Sleeping Beauty must have felt, waking up after a hundred years? Nothing looked familiar to her, and for an agonizing moment she thought her memory had deserted her.

Then she remembered the events of her homecoming. She was at Raoul's château. She'd come upstairs to rest . . . now she remembered.

She propped herself up on her elbows to get a better glimpse of the clock. The hands pointed to a few minutes past seven. If she didn't hurry, she'd be late meeting everyone downstairs before dinner.

The rest had done her good. She felt restored, with no sign of the headache that plagued her whenever she grew tired or was under pressure to force a particular memory. At least she had time to shower and change before returning downstairs to meet her family once again.

She sat up in bed before she realized that she didn't know whether or not her room came with a bath. She hadn't taken time to explore when she'd come up earlier. There were two doors in the wall opposite. Perhaps one of them led into a private bath.

She slipped out of bed and silently crossed the floor to one of the doors. When she opened it she discovered not a bathroom as she had hoped but another bedroom. Despite the drawn drapes she could make out a figure asleep in the bed. How strange. Who else would be sleeping at this time of day?

The figure on the bed stirred and she froze, several realizations hitting her at once.

She'd been mistaken about the time of day. It was no longer evening, but morning...and the figure in bed was Raoul, sound asleep.

His movement had disarranged his covers and her startled gaze took in the fact that he slept nude. Only a small corner of the sheet covered most of his groin area, revealing a part of his bare hip and the long muscled length of his hair-covered leg.

Drawn to him as though by some magnetic force, Sherye moved on silent feet to the side of the bed. He looked much younger in his sleep without the lines that bracketed his mouth and marked his forehead. His dark hair fell across his forehead in a boyish way and her fingers tingled with the strong desire to brush it away.

She resisted the impulse. Instead she took the opportunity to study the body of the man she knew intimately, if only she could remember.

His body was tanned as though he spent considerable time in the sun without his shirt. Only the small lighter stripe across his hip gave her a clue to his natural color, which was still darker than her own. His skin tanned beautifully, all golden and sleek. She wished that—

His arm unexpectedly snaked toward her and he caught her by her shoulder, pulling her down onto the bed beside him. Caught off guard, she tumbled onto the bed in a graceless heap, embarrassed to have been caught looking at him. She had started to apologize when she noticed that his heavy-lidded eyes were scarcely open. He was still more asleep than awake.

"Mmm," he muttered in a wordless sound of satisfaction just before he wrapped his arms around her and tugged her against his bare body. Without a pause he rolled until she was beneath him on the bed, his thigh snugly tucked between hers.

"I've missed you," he murmured into the side of her neck, his lips brushing against her skin.

Sherye's heart pounded against her chest as she faced the situation that her curiosity had created. Raoul cupped her breast in his hand, lazily drawing his thumb across the lace-covered tip. His body pressed against hers, leaving her in no doubt of his early-morning arousal.

Her body seemed to come alive, vigorously reacting to the sudden onslaught of sensation. Somehow in all the movement her arms were securely wrapped around him and her fingers—as though unconnected to any thought—lightly examined the smooth expanse of back muscle, causing a ripple of sensation to run over him.

She tried to think clearly but her brain had gone dead and her sensory organs had taken over. She felt as though tiny electrical charges were going off all over her body, sending urgent signals.

Muttering something beneath his breath he shifted until his lips found hers, then he seemed to take complete possession of her in a searing, mind-numbing kiss that promised her some passionate consequences if she didn't do something to stop him.

The problem was that she had no desire to stop him. Not now. How could she have thought him cold or aloof when the bedclothes must be singed and smoking by now by her heated response to him?

He nudged her mouth open and slipped his tongue inside, lazily exploring before he began a pulsing rhythm not only with his kiss but with his thigh that pressed firmly against the apex of her thighs, until she automatically pushed against him in a rhythm of her own. She felt like a victim of spontaneous combustion. All she wanted was to draw him closer and closer to the flaming center of her need.

Suddenly he stiffened and jerked his head up, staring down at her in shock. His eyes had darkened with passion, but now they were open fully and he was seeing her as though for the first time.

Like a man suddenly confronted with a deadly snake, he jerked away from her and rolled, coming up on the far side of the bed, his back to her.

"What the *hell* do you think you're doing!" he growled between clenched teeth.

"I—uh—" The change was too abrupt for her to get her mind to function properly.

"You must think you still have some control over me to try this one, Sherye! It won't matter how many times you seduce me, nothing's changed between us. Nothing."

Horrified that he thought she'd come into his room to deliberately— She moaned, his words sufficient to douse all the flames that had been started moments before. "No. I didn't mean— You see, I—"

Grabbing the sheet and twisting it around him, he turned and faced her once more, his gaze running up and down her body with a look of contemptuous lust. "Well, I see the trip must have been a success. You've regained your memory and hope to do everything in your power to erase mine." His gaze lingered on her breasts and she immediately crossed her arms in an attempt to shelter her body from his cold stare.

She shook her head, her hair tumbling around her shoulders and down around her face. "I'm sorry. It was inexcusable of me, I know, but I—I woke up and I didn't know where to find the bathroom, so I opened the door and I saw—" She dropped her head, wishing she could disappear without a trace. Never had she felt so humiliated.

He didn't speak. Nor did he move. She couldn't look at him, nor did she have the necessary nerve to get up and walk out of the room wearing no more than her lacy underwear, which revealed more than it concealed.

When he finally spoke, his voice sounded tired. "There's no reason for you to apologize. I was dreaming and I thought you were part of that dream, that's all."

She glanced up and saw that he was once again wearing his impassive expression, revealing nothing. She kept her gaze on his eyes, not wanting to visually explore the body that had been giving her so much pleasure only a short while before.

"But you're right. I had no excuse coming in like that, invading your privacy."

He stood, looking dignified and regal despite the fact that only a sheet protected him. He nodded toward a door and said, "We share a bath—through there."

There was nothing she could do except gather her courage and her dignity and walk across the room to the door he had indicated. Just as she opened the door he said, "Have you discovered anything—or anyone—that looks familiar to you?"

She could feel her face flame at the memory of how close they had been to making love despite the fact that she didn't remember him at all. Unable to speak, she managed to shake her head before closing the door behind her.

This room must have been added at a much later date, or perhaps it was a dressing room that had been converted, because the bathroom fixtures were quite up-to-date and very luxurious. In addition to a whirlpool tub that could seat two quite comfortably, there was a large, glass-walled shower and a long marble counter with double sinks.

She might have moved out of Raoul's bed but she continued to share the intimacy of a bathroom with him.

Their encounter had shaken her, revealing a sensuous nature she hadn't realized she had. She rubbed her fingertips across her lips, feeling the slight puffiness caused by his passion. She traced her mouth with the tip of her tongue, tasting him, and shivered at the remembered sensation of him lying on top of her, his leg thrust between hers as though claiming what he knew was his.

She shook her head in an effort to shake off her memories and her embarrassment at her abandoned response before she turned on the water in the shower, adjusted the temperature and pressure, then stepped inside. Her skin was unusually sensitive while she soaped her body in a fruitless effort to forget how he had felt pressed so intimately against her. Was this how she'd reacted when she'd first met him, all weak and trembly, wondering what his lovemaking would be like?

He hadn't said, but she guessed that they had made love soon after they had met. Had their lovemaking convinced her to forget about her career in order to be with this man? If so, what could have happened to make everything go so wrong between them?

After she finished her shower, Sherye dried herself with a thick, overlarge towel before she returned to her room. By the simple process of elimination, the only door she hadn't tried must be her closet. When she opened the door she discovered a walk-in dressing room with two long rows of clothing for all occasions. The back wall was filled with shelves upon shelves of shoes of all colors and styles.

She was shocked by the amount of obviously expensive clothing and accessories. No one could possibly need so much. From the looks of things she wouldn't need to buy anything more until after the turn of the century.

Sherye searched through the clothing, looking for something simple to wear. By the time she'd looked through both sides of the long closet she faced the fact that there was no such thing.

Each piece of clothing she touched was specifically designed to call attention to the wearer. The shift she had worn yesterday was the most unobtrusive item in her wardrobe. She frowned. She certainly couldn't continue to wear the shift every day.

With a sense of the inevitable, she grabbed one of the outfits and put it on, more interested in getting something to eat rather than how she looked. Now that she was awake, her stomach was letting her know that she had missed dinner the night before.

She sat in front of the vanity to do something with her hair. She'd finally grown accustomed to the color over the past few weeks and no longer received that sharp jolt of unease whenever she happened to look into a mirror. She brushed her hair until it lay smooth, then in a practiced twist of her wrist coiled it into a neat knot at the nape of her neck. Unfortunately her hair didn't want to stay neatly coiled. Wisps of hair sprang around her face, determined to rebel.

After a light coating of lipstick she felt ready to face a new day.

Nothing like sleeping around the clock to make you feel like a new person, she thought, following the hallway to the stairway. *Or a passionate kiss from your handsome husband first thing in the morning to get all your juices flowing!*

When she reached the bottom of the stairs she looked around, wondering where she would find the kitchen in a place like this. She had a sudden picture of twenty-five or thirty men all dressed in white with tall, floppy hats racing around preparing food in a giant kitchen. Hadn't she seen that in a movie once?

Her biggest problem was believing that any of this was real—the château, Raoul, the children, the inflexible matriarch. Somewhere deep inside her lurked the inescapable belief that at any moment she was going to suddenly wake up to find herself back home in Dallas, having fallen asleep on the couch from watching a late-night movie and overslept...running the risk of being late for school. There would be—

Late for school?

Once again she saw the same picture of a classroom filled with teenage girls. She clung to the picture, trying to understand. She focused on a blackboard that was actually green, and saw handwriting—hers—conjugating French verbs.

She taught French?

She smiled to herself. That made sense in a surrealistic kind of way. If she taught the language, then she would be able to speak it fluently, and understand it, as well. No wonder she had been impressed with the Parisian French spoken by the nursing sisters.

Feeling as though she was finally making some kind of progress in her search for her own identity, even if it made absolutely no sense in her present environment, Sherye went in search of some coffee.

The first door she opened looked as if it was used as a study. She made a sound of frustration and was closing the door when a voice spoke behind her.

"Good morning, *madame*. You are up quite early this morning."

With relief Sherye faced the housekeeper and smiled. "I'm afraid I slept through dinner last night. So I was hoping to find some coffee this morning."

"But of course. Breakfast is already set up in the dining room."

"Unfortunately I'm having a little trouble *finding* the dining room, which sounds strange, I'm sure."

"Not at all, *madame*. Monsieur DuBois has already explained to us about your head injury."

Sherye wondered what, exactly, he'd said. From her tone, the housekeeper sounded as though she thought the head injury had caused her to misplace a large portion of her brain, as well. Come to think of it, she wasn't far off. Her memory bank certainly had gotten jiggled around, if not completely erased.

She followed the older woman through a doorway that led into another hallway. Maybe she should make a map of the place so she could find her way around.

The dining room was in keeping with the rest of the house in that the furniture looked as though it belonged in a museum and the room was tastefully and richly furnished.

She also discovered that she wasn't the first one in the household to be searching for coffee. Danielle stood with her back to the room, facing the sideboard. She was filling her cup with a hot, aromatic liquid whose scent lured Sherye onward.

Danielle wore a tan shirtwaist dress, another unfortunate color choice that did nothing for her skin tones. Sherye waited until Danielle had set the coffee carafe down before speaking.

"Good morning."

Danielle whirled in surprise and faced Sherye with widened eyes.

Sherye glanced over her shoulder, convinced an ax murderer must be hovering immediately behind her to get such a shocked reaction. "Is something wrong?"

Danielle flushed a brilliant scarlet. "Uh—no. That is—I've never seen you up this early before," she stammered.

Sherye smiled at the other woman and nodded toward the tempting array of food on the sideboard. "I managed to sleep through dinner last night and woke up hungry as a bear this morning." She walked over to the buffet that displayed croissants and brioches, fruit juice and coffee. "Ahh! This looks wonderful." She filled a plate, poured a cup of coffee, inhaling the aroma with undiluted pleasure, and sat down across from the other woman.

"Raoul said that you were sleeping so soundly he didn't want to disturb you," Danielle said defensively, as though hearing an implied criticism in Sherye's comment.

"He was probably right. I don't remember rousing at all during the night."

Danielle kept her eyes on her plate and ate without saying anything more.

Sherye did the same. Since she wasn't much of an early-morning person anyway, she found the silence soothing. Danielle, on the other hand, appeared uncomfortable, giving Sherye brief glances before looking away to avoid making direct eye contact. Since she couldn't think of anything to say that would make the woman more comfortable, Sherye mentally planned her day as though she were alone.

She was on her third cup of coffee when Danielle finally met her gaze, her expression puzzled. Sherye smiled at her in hopes of putting her more at ease. The smile must have encouraged Danielle because she finally spoke, her voice soft and hesitant.

"I've never seen you with your hair pulled back like that. It makes you look very different."

Sherye touched the coiled mass of hair at her nape before she remembered how she was wearing it. Now that Danielle had called her attention to the style, Sherye realized that she had tried to wear it this way in the hospital but hadn't been able to keep it pinned back. In the following weeks it had grown enough to stay in place except for the short pieces around her face.

She had put it up unconsciously this morning out of some forgotten habit while her conscious mind had been focused on reliving the embarrassingly intimate scene with Raoul.

"I found this to be a comfortable style," she admitted. "Although you're right. Hairstyles can make a big difference in how a person looks."

It was only when the other woman's face flushed once again that Sherye realized Danielle thought she was making pointed remarks about her own choice of hairstyle. She almost groaned out loud. She hadn't meant anything by the comment, but how could she explain without making matters worse?

Sherye chose to let the moment go and continued to enjoy her coffee. She was admittedly surprised when Danielle spoke up after another lengthy silence between them.

"Raoul told us over dinner last night that you've been spending hours every day in therapy trying to regain your memory." Her voice was so soft that Sherye had to strain to hear her.

"That's right," she agreed in as pleasant a voice as possible in an attempt to encourage her shy sister-in-law's efforts at conversation, even though she didn't particularly care to be the subject of the conversation.

"You can't remember anything?"

With a sudden sense of recklessness, she grinned. "Actually, I do have memories, but they really can't be rationally explained unless I could prove that I'm not Sherye DuBois."

Danielle almost choked. She set her coffee cup down, coughing, unable to take her eyes off Sherye, who continued to grin at her, encouraging her to share the humor in her comment. After a moment Danielle returned the grin, with a soft chuckle. "You're joking, right?" Her eyes filled with amusement.

Sherye was struck by the change in Danielle. She looked years younger, almost youthful. Sherye was delighted to see such an abrupt change caused by her attempt to defuse the seriousness of what had happened to her.

Danielle suddenly sobered, her expression stricken. "I'm sorry. I didn't mean to laugh at you."

"It's okay. I guess it was a silly thing to say, under the circumstances." With a lightness she didn't feel, Sherye gave an airy wave of her hand and said, "Be my guest and laugh all you want."

Danielle shook her head, obviously embarrassed once again. "I can't imagine you thinking you're not Sherye, that's all. There are obvious changes in the way you wear your hair and your lack of makeup, but you can't hide your features, the shape of your chin, that sort of thing. If you weren't an only child, perhaps you might be able to pass yourself off as your sister. Otherwise..." Her voice trailed off into another puzzled look. "If you don't think you're Sherye, who do you think you are?"

Sherye paused for a moment, trying to decide what to say. She was pleased that she had somehow broken through Danielle's reserve. She decided to tease a little, despite the accuracy of what she said. In a pseudosolemn tone of voice she intoned, "A teacher from Dallas, Texas." Her tone invited Danielle to enjoy the humor.

Sherye was delighted when Danielle erupted into a new round of giggles. She covered her mouth as though to obstruct the flow, which only seemed to make the laughter worse.

Sherye knew her statement sounded absurd under the circumstances and she began to laugh, as well. When she paused to draw breath she added, "I even know what I teach—French!" which immediately sent both of them into another round of choked laughter.

Raoul walked in as they were tapering off, his expression somewhere between shock and utter bafflement. Sherye had hoped to avoid him this morning, but in her enjoyment of getting the opportunity to visit with Danielle she'd lost track of time.

He walked over to the sideboard, shaking his head. "I can't believe what I'm hearing. As I was coming down the hallway I was convinced we must have company. The two of you sound like a couple of schoolgirls, giggling over secrets."

His remark was close enough to the truth that their gazes met in acknowledgment of the nature of their discussion...which set them off again.

Sherye was also enjoying seeing Raoul in a more relaxed atmosphere. He seemed pleased to see his sister enjoying herself, just as he seemed puzzled when he looked back at Sherye.

Whatever her relationship with Danielle in the past, she must have behaved differently toward her today.

Well, if so, that was too bad. She was growing rather weary of trying to live up to some unspecified form of behavior. For the first time since she'd awakened in the hospital she discovered that a lack of memory could be a sort of liberation from the past. She was free to behave in any way she wanted. What difference did it make, anyway? Even though he hadn't bothered to tell her, Raoul was already planning to divorce her. He'd made it clear that he didn't see any future in their relationship, so why should she attempt to work so hard not to incur his displeasure?

"If you will excuse me," she said to Danielle with a quick glance at Raoul, "I'm going to go visit the children." Before either of them could respond she left the room, feeling as though she'd set off a bomb and wanting to escape before it exploded.

Chapter Seven

Once again Sherye had to explore the château before she found the rooms where her children spent most of their time. The area was easy enough to find once she returned upstairs and listened for the sound of young voices.

She tapped and waited until Louise opened the door before she entered her children's domain. She wasn't certain who was the most surprised to see her—Louise or Yvette.

Her daughter sat at a small table eating, while Jules was in a high chair, obviously being fed by his nanny. Louise looked perfectly composed, far from the way Sherye felt. She felt like an outsider, hoping to be included in a highly selective club.

Louise was the first one to speak. "Good morning, *madame.* May I help you?"

So polite. Obviously she made a very good example for the children, but did she have to appear so cold? Perhaps she only behaved that way around her employers. Sherye sincerely hoped that the woman showed some warmth and friendliness to her two charges.

"I came to visit," was all Sherye could think of to say. She stood just inside the room and looked around.

A small frown appeared between Louise's brows. "I'm afraid the children are still at breakfast. Perhaps if you'd like to come back later—?"

Sherye displayed her most confident smile to the woman. "Oh, I don't mind helping with breakfast," she replied, walking past the woman and sitting across the small table from Yvette.

Yvette's eyes had grown wider during the conversation between her mother and her nanny. As soon as Sherye sat down, Yvette quickly stared down at her bowl of hot cereal.

"How are you this morning?"

Yvette glanced up through her thick lashes. "Fine."

"Did you sleep well?"

This time Yvette's gaze went to Louise before she nodded.

Meanwhile Jules had begun babbling again while beating his spoon on the tray of his high chair. Sherye grinned at him. "You're looking quite rested, little one. Would you like me to feed you?"

He bounced, giggled and waved the spoon. Sherye held out her hand and he gave the utensil to her. Before long she was making a game out of his food and Yvette was giggling at her silliness.

Louise had gone into the other room, leaving Sherye alone with the children, for which she was grateful. By the time Yvette and Jules had finished their meal they seemed to be more relaxed in Sherye's presence.

"Now what do you usually do?"

"We get dressed and when the weather's nice we go outside," Yvette responded.

"That sounds fun. Where are your clothes?"

Yvette hopped off her chair and headed toward the door where Louise had gone. Sherye cleaned Jules's face and hands and lifted him from his chair. "My! You're a big fella, did you know that? You're going to grow up to be a tall, strong man just like your papa, aren't you?"

Jules had gotten over his shyness with her and willingly came into her arms. He patted her cheek, touched her ear and talked to her in his very special and to her totally incomprehensible dialect.

Sherye smiled and nodded as though she understood and agreed with every word. It didn't matter. He was talking to her and beginning to accept her presence. She would spend as much time as possible with him until she could understand everything he said.

She hugged him to her, inhaling the baby smell of talcum powder, freshly laundered clothes and warm skin. Her heart seemed to swell in her chest with joy. She'd always loved children. When she was growing up she'd laughingly planned to have half a dozen or more. Unfortunately things hadn't worked out that way. She'd given up hope that she would ever—

Sherye paused, wondering where those thoughts had come from. When nothing more came, she shrugged and shook her head. She didn't have time to think about her memories and lack of them at the moment. She had an exciting day planned—to learn her children's routine and to become an integral part of their lives.

They went outside until time for Jules's nap, then Sherye offered to read to Yvette until lunchtime. Yvette gave her one of her favorite books and listened with shining eyes while Sherye read to her.

Sherye spent the morning with the children and, together with Louise, supervised their lunch. When it was time for Yvette to rest and for Jules's afternoon nap, she gave each of them a hug and a kiss, promising to come back later.

Their hours together had made a significant difference in the children's behavior toward her. She had played games with them and made up stories—enlisting Yvette's help in the creative process. She'd found gentle ways to tease them and was delighted to witness Yvette's awkward attempts to tease her in return. Yvette's giggles at Sherye's reaction touched a wellspring of contentment somewhere deep inside.

She found the children endearing and came away with a sense of well-being that had been absent in her life. For the first time in a long while Sherye felt good about herself, as though she had finally accomplished something worthwhile.

She entered the dining room smiling to herself at some of Jules's antics. What a little clown he was. Sherye was already in the room when she became aware that Danielle and her mother were already there. All right, here was another test, one she was determined to pass. *Think pleasant thoughts, set an example,* she reminded herself as she nodded to both of them and sat down, placing her napkin in her lap.

She turned to Raoul's mother. "I know how strange this request must sound to you, but under the circumstances I'm afraid it's unavoidable. What would you like me to call you?"

The woman blinked, stared at her for a moment, then nodded regally. "My name is Felicity. Of course, Raoul and Danielle—"

"Would never use your given name," Sherye finished smoothly, determined that she would not call this frosty—and unquestionably rude—woman *Maman.* "May I have your permission to call you Felicity?"

Taken aback by Sherye's forthright request, the older woman hesitated for a moment, then nodded.

"Thank you." Sherye turned next to Danielle. "I have a favor to ask of you."

An apprehensive expression crossed Danielle's face. Sherye could see her steel herself. "Of me?" she repeated timidly.

Oh, boy, I'm coming on too strong. It was because she was nervous and trying to compensate by sounding self-assured. *Take this one step at a time,* she coached herself. *You can't turn things around overnight. This is going to take time and you've got plenty of that.*

Sherye smiled at Danielle. "Yes. I'd like to go to town but I don't have any transportation at the moment. Besides, under the present circumstances I'd probably become hopelessly lost. I was wondering—that is, if you have some time in the next few days, if you would mind taking me to town."

Once again Sherye was painfully aware of being the outsider, and she watched Danielle and Felicity exchange glances. Felicity suddenly showed a great deal of interest in her salad fork, while Danielle slowly met Sherye's patient gaze.

"You want *me* to take you to town?" Danielle repeated carefully, seemingly convinced that she had misunderstood Sherye's request.

Sherye gave an inward sigh and nodded. "I just need a few things. There really isn't a rush, of course."

Danielle looked around the room and down at her plate before she finally answered. "I don't have anything planned—that is, if you'd like—this afternoon would be fine."

Sherye let go of the breath she'd been unconsciously holding. "Oh, good. I'll jot down a list so I don't forget anything." She looked at each of the women, experimenting with a neutral topic of conversation. "The château is breathtaking in its beauty and design. You must be very proud of it."

Both of the women stiffened and looked away from her.

Oh, no. What now? Sherye waited but when neither one of them looked up or made an effort to respond, she grew impatient. "What? What did I say? What's wrong?"

"You've often referred to it as a prison or mausoleum."

Here we go again. She tried a light approach. "The blow to my head has obviously improved my appreciation of classic architecture."

One of the staff brought in their lunches and the three women ate their meal in silence. Sherye felt unbearably uncomfortable but forced herself to deal with her almost ungovernable need to bolt from the room.

By the time she had finished her meal, Sherye had developed a whale of a headache. No wonder. Tension had crept into the room, filling even the corners until she wanted to scream. No one made an effort to break the silence and she was at a loss to find a topic that didn't contain hidden land mines.

It was really too bad. She'd felt so good this morning, certain of her progress toward establishing healthier relationships with her children.

Perhaps she expected too much, she reminded herself. Just because she had no memory of these people did not mean that they could forget some of the things she must have said and done.

She fought the urge to blurt out apologies for her past behavior. She wanted to reassure them, to explain that she had changed, but she knew that would be pointless. What she would have to do was show them that the changes in her were real. Hopefully they would some day accept that, for whatever inexplicable reasons, she had experienced a major shift in her personality.

As soon as they finished the interminable meal Danielle placed her napkin beside her chair and nodded toward Sherye. "Why don't we meet in the foyer in half an hour? I'll have my car brought around."

Although she had made no comment regarding the arrangements, Felicity made her attitude clear. She was suspicious of Sherye and of her motives.

Sherye could hardly blame her.

Nevertheless, there was so much that she didn't understand about the household and the routine. So many things that she wanted to ask about, but discovered an unexpected shyness.

She'd wanted to ask if Raoul ever joined them for lunch. She felt awkward that she knew so little about her husband's routine. Since no place had been set for him today, she decided to wait and ask him the next time she saw him.

She'd gained the impression that the two of them did not spend much time together. Actually, she was relieved . . . or at least, she should have been. From every indication, she and Raoul did not have a very close relationship.

Since he was practically a stranger to her, she couldn't be bothered by that knowledge. She'd been surprised at her own reaction to the news that he planned to divorce her. A relationship she didn't remember was ending before she'd had a chance to salvage it. She'd felt dismayed.

The bewildering question to her was why now did she feel so strongly that she wanted her marriage to work when her past behavior had shown a distinct disregard for her husband and his family?

Puzzling questions with no answers. She felt as if there was a swarm of bees buzzing around inside her head, making her dizzy and driving her to distraction.

Getting away for a while would help, she was certain. Anything would be better than the present oppressive atmosphere.

She went upstairs and, after painstakingly searching, found a dress that she felt was more or less her style and changed into it. After checking the time, she quickly ran a comb through her hair and hurried downstairs so that she wouldn't cause Danielle to wait for her.

As soon as Danielle saw her come down the stairs she turned away and went out the front door, leaving it ajar for Sherye to follow. Not a great beginning, but at least Danielle had agreed to go. Wasn't that a start?

She found Danielle waiting in a late-model sports car, its sleek lines and bright metallic color unexpected for someone as quiet as Danielle. The woman had hidden depths.

Sherye was encouraged to think she might—with enough patience—eventually reach those depths.

"Hi," she said in a casual voice. She opened the passenger door and crawled inside. "I hope you didn't have to wait long," she added, fastening her seat belt.

Danielle shook her head and made some noncommittal sound as they started down the long driveway.

"I like your car."

"Thank you."

"Did you choose it yourself?"

Danielle glanced out of the corner of her eye before asking, "You don't think it fits my personality, do you?"

Nothing like a hint of hostility to add richness to the occasion. Sherye caught herself counting silently to ten, gave her head a tiny shake and replied, "I don't really have an opinion of your personality, Danielle. The most I'm guilty of at the moment is attempting to make conversation, that's all."

They rode in silence for a long stretch, a silence that Sherye refused to break. Instead she admired the countryside as though this was the first time she'd seen it. At long last Danielle said, "I'm sorry." She seemed to be at a loss for words. In a sudden burst she said, "I realize I'm oversensitive. It's just that—" Abruptly she stopped speaking.

Sherye waited. When Danielle didn't say anything more, Sherye decided to push her luck with Danielle by prompting in a quiet voice, "It's just that—what?"

Danielle shook her head without looking at Sherye. Danielle's tenseness showed in every line of her body. When Sherye made no more attempt to draw her out, Danielle once again blurted out what she was thinking.

"I guess I'm having trouble adjusting to the difference in you."

Ah. Now we're getting somewhere. "In what way?" she asked casually.

"In the past you've always ignored me."

Whatever she'd been expecting, that wasn't it. "Ignored you!" she repeated slowly. "Why?"

Danielle shrugged, keeping her eyes on the road. "Oh, I understand. After all, we don't have anything in common. You're a famous model, while I—" Once again she came to a complete verbal halt as though anything she might add was self-evident.

Sherye felt sickened at being given another glimpse of herself. "How dreadful," she said in a low voice, feeling ashamed. "I've been going around bragging about being a famous model and ignoring my husband's sister? How embarrassingly rude!"

After a brief silence Danielle offered, "See? This is what I mean. It's your reactions that seem so different."

Sherye made a face at her faint reflection in the glass window. "Maybe the blow to my head knocked some sense into me," she replied with irritation at herself. "All I can say is, it's about time!"

Danielle chuckled, sounding more relaxed. "I must admit that you're much easier to talk to now."

Sherye leaned her head on the headrest and sighed. "I'm not at all certain I want to regain my memory if I'm going to discover that I've been playing the role of Queen Bitch of France."

Danielle burst out laughing and after a moment Sherye joined her, finally seeing the humor in the exchange. If nothing else, they had managed to lighten the mood of their afternoon outing, which was a relief.

Once again Sherye felt that she had managed to pass a tough—because it was so nebulous—test.

When Raoul arrived home later that afternoon he found Felicity alone in the salon, working on her embroidery.

"Ah, there you are," he said, walking over and brushing his lips against her cheek. "What are you doing sitting in here all alone?" He glanced around. "Where's Danielle?"

Felicity sniffed. "Sherye complained over lunch that she had no transportation and demanded that Danielle drive her into town for her usual round of shopping."

Raoul's jaw tightened. "I'll take her to town tomorrow to get a car. Danielle shouldn't have to play chauffeur."

"Exactly what I told her, but you know Danielle. She's always trying so hard to please everyone and ends up letting them run all over her. When I pointed out to her that she was just allowing herself to be used and she certainly wasn't responsible for the fact that Sherye had so carelessly destroyed her car, Danielle insisted there was no reason she couldn't help. She's so protective of you. She probably thought if she could entertain Sherye that you'd have an easier time of dealing with her once you got home."

Raoul rang for tea before he sat in his usual wingback chair. "I thought the two of them were getting along quite well at breakfast. I'll admit that I was surprised when I came downstairs this morning to hear them laughing together."

"Well, they certainly weren't laughing over lunch," Felicity replied with a sniff of disapproval.

When the tea tray was brought in, Raoul poured each of them a cup, then sat back with his.

"Did Sherye say how she'd spent the morning?"

Felicity looked up from her own cup, her eyes snapping. "She didn't have to. I know what she was doing. She insisted on spending the entire time with the children."

Raoul lifted his brows. "All morning?"

"Yes. She totally ignored their routine. I could hear how excited the children were becoming while they played outside. She showed no sense of decorum. Instead she seemed to encourage them in their childish behavior."

He hid his smile behind his cup. "I don't suppose there's any real harm in that."

"Of course there is. She's just using them, and it's the children who are going to suffer for it in the long run because they'll think she's being sincere in wanting to become part of their lives. Of course, I see through her. I always have. She's trying to convince you not to continue with your plans for a divorce by pretending she's forgotten the past. She's hoping you'll forget it, as well."

Raoul thought about her remarks, weighing them, before he responded in a mild tone. "I might agree that there's possibly some truth in what you say if I'd given any indication to Sherye that I was contemplating divorcing her. However, I've never discussed the subject of divorce with her since the accident."

"Why not? Why shouldn't she know that you've made up your mind—finally—to get out of this ridiculous arrangement?" After a moment she added without looking at him, "Besides, I mentioned the divorce to her yesterday and she didn't seem all that surprised."

Raoul froze, his cup halfway to his mouth, his amusement gone. "You mentioned the divorce to her?" he asked in a carefully neutral voice.

"Yes, I did," she replied, filled with self-righteousness. "She needs to know that you are no longer a fool who will continue putting up with her outrageous behavior."

Raoul fought not to show his irritation with his mother. He understood how many times Sherye's actions had hurt and embarrassed his mother, but she'd had no business discussing their personal business with Sherye, particularly under the present circumstances.

He set the cup down on the small table beside his chair. "*Maman,*" he began patiently, "there was no reason for you to discuss the matter with her. Until she regains her memory she—"

Felicity gave him a disapproving look. "Just what makes you think she has any intention of suddenly regaining her memory, when it's to her definite advantage to continue playing this helpless, pitiful role she's chosen?"

"You know, *Maman,*" he said, determined to stay calm, "she could have faked the amnesia without resorting to her abrupt attitude change."

"Of course, but it wouldn't have been nearly so convincing or effective. Sherye has always known exactly how to behave to get what she wants. She knew that her leaving when you asked her to stay would provoke you into taking steps to end the relationship. It's no wonder that she faked the wreck, faked the blow to the head, faked the amnesia..."

He shook his head and she paused in her recital of Sherye's latest transgressions. "The blow to her head was very real, let me tell you. I saw the wound and it was a nasty one. It easily could have killed her. She was very fortunate to have regained consciousness at all." He took his time refilling their cups before he continued. "I also believe her amnesia is equally real. I was there, *Maman.* I saw how she behaved. For one thing, she didn't believe she was Sherye DuBois. When we discussed who she was, she kept denying it."

Felicity stared at him in surprise. "Why in the world would she deny such a thing?"

"The doctor believes that while she was in a coma she somehow restructured certain events from a deeply subconscious desire—a yearning, actually—to escape her present life-style. He believes that those dreams became more real to her than the life she presently leads."

Felicity sniffed, shoving her needle into the material with short jabs. "Sounds ridiculous to me."

"Perhaps, but her new behavior supports the idea that she may truly wish to make substantial changes in her life. Spending her morning with the children, suggesting that she and Danielle spend time together this afternoon—all of this appears to me to point out some obvious shifts in her priorities."

"Obviously she's managed to impress you," she grumbled.

Once again his sense of humor surfaced. Raoul smiled. "Oh, I don't know, *Maman.* I don't think I'm all that easy to impress."

"We'll see."

He'd been home almost an hour when Raoul heard the front door open. Feminine laughter made it clear to him that Sherye and Danielle had returned, obviously in good spirits. There was a rustling of packages before he heard Danielle instruct one of the staff to take their purchases upstairs.

The two women appeared in the doorway. Raoul stood to greet them and Felicity gasped. "Danielle! What in the world have you done to your hair!" Her sewing slipped out of her lap unheeded and fell to the floor.

Raoul's gaze went to Sherye, who had a decidedly guilty look on her face. Then he glanced at Danielle and felt a small shock of surprise. He'd never seen his sister look quite so vibrant. Danielle's cheeks bloomed with color as she approached them. She raised her hand and lightly brushed her fingers across her cheek in a nervous gesture.

Her coronet of braids was gone. Her hair had been drastically shortened until it feathered in wisps around her forehead and ears, like a pixie. Shortened, her hair had an unexpected tendency to curl, softening her features and giving her a gamine look. Her eyes, always her best feature in Raoul's mind, seemed more noticeable, perhaps because they were shining with anticipation. She glowed. There was no other word for it.

"Do you like it?" she asked shyly.

Raoul glanced around at his mother. It was obvious she hadn't recovered from the shock of her daughter's drastic transformation. Danielle needed reassurance, and he could see that his mother was too taken aback to say anything.

He moved toward his sister, smiling, and took her hand. He raised it to his lips. "You look smashing. What a clever idea to make a change."

"Well, I got the idea this morning from something Sherye said."

"I knew it!" Felicity exclaimed. "I knew you wouldn't have done anything like this without someone forcing you to—"

"Oh, no! Sherye didn't force me in any way. Actually, I brought the subject up. I was the one who mentioned that I was thinking about experimenting with a new hairstyle. She just went along to the shop with me to give me a little extra courage. It was Pierre who suggested that I had the features to wear this style." She turned around and Raoul could see how the cut flattered the shape of her head. He could hear the hint of anxiety in her voice when she asked, "Do you really like it?"

Raoul glanced at Sherye, noticing that she was taking no part in the conversation. Instead she stood quietly by, watching the scene without comment. He returned his attention to Danielle. Still holding her hand, he gave it a gentle squeeze and said, "Yes, I do. Very much."

He stepped back and gave his sister an all-encompassing look. "Do I detect that you are wearing something new, as well?"

Color filled Danielle's cheeks. "Sherye happened to see this in a window we were passing and suggested that it looked like something I might enjoy wearing." She spread her hands along the skirt of her coral dress. "Since we weren't in any hurry, we went inside so I could try it on." She gave a nervous chuckle. "I must admit that I've never worn anything like it. The skirt is shorter than I'm used to wearing." She tugged at the pleats that fanned out around her. "It's probably too short."

Raoul smiled. "On the contrary. The men will appreciate the generous view of your shapely legs, Dani. I agree with Sherye. That particular color looks very becoming on you. You made a wise decision." He motioned to the grouping of sofas and chairs. "Why don't the two of you join us? We'll have more tea brought in."

Raoul waited until the women were seated before he said to Sherye, "You should have mentioned to me this morning that you wished to go into town. There was no reason to insist that Danielle take you."

"Oh, but she didn't, Raoul!" Danielle said. "Insist, I mean. I had nothing else planned to do this afternoon and Sherye wanted to see about—" She paused, looking uncomfortable. "Well, I suppose she can tell you...." She trailed off, her color heightened.

"Tell me what?" he asked abruptly, looking at Sherye without bothering to disguise his suspicions of her behavior.

This was not the time she would have chosen to have this discussion. Nor did she like the idea of having a marital discussion in front of Raoul's mother and sister. However, she saw no way to get around the matter. It was obvious that Raoul found nothing unusual about their lack of privacy.

Smothering a sigh of frustration, Sherye said, "While I was looking through my closet today I discovered that I have nothing casual to wear here at home. I want to be able to do some gardening. I find it very soothing and relaxing. I mentioned the idea to Yvette and she was excited about the idea and wanted to help me. I also discovered that she didn't have anything appropriate to wear, either. I decided to see what I could find for us to wear and surprise Yvette."

"Gardening?" Felicity asked faintly.

Sherye smiled. "Yes. I enjoy working with flowers and keeping a garden healthy." She paused, suddenly feeling confused. "Surely that isn't unusual, is it?" She looked around at the people watching her. "I remember gardening. I remember how much pleasure I get from it. Surely I—" She stopped, feeling as though she'd said or done the wrong thing again.

Felicity looked over at Raoul without comment. He ignored the look. "Tell me, Sherye," he asked, "how was your visit with the children today?"

Feeling as though this was a trick question, she studied him for a long moment before she quietly responded, "I enjoyed it very much."

He glanced at his watch. "It's almost time for Louise to bring them down to see us."

More tea arrived. Raoul sat back and quietly observed the interaction among the three women in his household. From his mother's expression he could see that she was still a little dazed by the changes in Danielle.

Now that the general attention had moved away from her, Danielle looked much more relaxed. She was animatedly telling Felicity about something she'd bought, and had lost her self-consciousness. Raoul took his time about studying the changes in her. He was really quite amazed. The combination of a new hairstyle, a brighter color and younger dress style seemed to take several years off her, leaving her looking vibrant and very attractive.

Whether the two younger women were willing to acknowledge it or not, he knew that Sherye's influence today had helped to create the changes in Danielle. She was the one who had first spotted the dress Danielle wore. She was the one who had convinced her to try it on, or, as Dani might say, encouraged her to try it.

He leaned back in his chair, pondering the ramifications of what he was witnessing. For years his sister had shown little to no interest in her looks or in her style of dress. If anything, she had seemed to go out of her way to be as unobtrusive as possible.

In the past Sherye had ignored her, dismissing the idea of a friendship with his sister, claiming that they had absolutely nothing in common. He hadn't tried to persuade her to change her mind because he tended to agree with her. His only request was that she show his family respect. To a great extent she had ignored them completely.

So what had brought on this new attitude of friendliness? Was his mother right, and she was trying to make sure of her standing in the family?

Now that he was thinking about it, he realized that Sherye was wearing something that looked out of character for her—a simple shirtwaist dress and low-heeled shoes. With most of her hair pulled back, leaving only escaped curls framing her face, she looked very young. Almost innocent.

While he sat watching her, Sherye glanced past him. He saw her expression change from one of social politeness into one of warm pleasure. He blinked, surprised at the change in her. He couldn't remember ever having seen her so animated since she'd regained consciousness. Raoul glanced around to see what had caused the transformation.

Louise had entered the room with the children.

Today Jules's sturdy legs carried him immediately to Sherye, his arms stretched out, while he babbled something incomprehensible. Laughing with obvious delight, Sherye scooped him up onto her lap, oblivious to the wrinkling effect on her clothes. She gave him a hug and murmured something too low for Raoul to hear from where he sat. Whatever it was made Jules giggle.

Yvette came directly to Raoul, hugged and acknowledged him with a kiss on the cheek, then immediately broke into an animated description of her morning with her mother.

A sudden sense of unreality swept over him and for a brief moment he had a flash of empathy for Sherye's dilemma when she seemed to have awakened in another world.

Had he been in the habit of fantasizing, the scene before him couldn't have been closer to what he could have wished for his family—Danielle looking young and pleased with herself, Sherye playing with their son, Yvette bubbling with plans she'd made to spend time with her mother.

Only *Maman* deliberately held herself aloof from all the changes. Perhaps she was feeling the same sense of confusion he was experiencing. How had Sherye managed to create such a difference in their family during one twenty-four-hour period in their lives?

What had caused such a radical change in her?

More to the point, how long would the change last?

Chapter Eight

Four weeks later Raoul stood at the window of his office at the winery, gazing out at the long rows of the meticulously kept vineyard, thinking about the changes that had taken place in his home since Sherye had returned.

The sound of children's laughter rang through the château.

Danielle had met a young man who seemed to spend an increasing amount of time visiting the château.

Maman had actually complimented Sherye about something over dinner the night before.

He'd never seen Sherye so happy.

Sherye's happiness was the most bewildering of all to him. Although she hadn't seemed to regain anything of her lost memories, she appeared content to spend each day enjoying her life.

Only with him did she maintain a polite distance.

After that first morning she had never ventured into his bedroom. If anything, he got the feeling that she did her best to stay out of his way.

He remembered the day he took her to buy another automobile. She had strongly resisted the idea until he had pointed out to her that other members of the family might not find it convenient to provide her transportation whenever she felt the urge to leave the château.

She had given in, but had refused to consider any of the expensive sports models she'd been drawn to in the past. Instead she had found a sedan that she felt would be more practical when she wanted to take the children with her.

Although he still saw many changes in her, Sherye's stubbornness hadn't lessened in the slightest.

He had bought the car she wanted, fully expecting her to change her mind within a week. Instead she appeared delighted with it, installing an infant's seat for Jules as well as a safety lift seat for Yvette.

Sherye continued to spend most of each day with the children, until Louise had approached him wondering if he still wanted her to oversee them. Since he hadn't been certain how long this new phase would last with Sherye, he had assured Louise that her services were still needed and appreciated. He had suggested that she learn to enjoy having more free time.

Raoul had discovered something about himself today. He didn't know how it had happened, or when, because the change had been so gradual. He probably wouldn't have become aware of it even now if the attorney he'd consulted hadn't called him earlier in the day with regard to the status of the divorce.

He heard himself tell the attorney that he would have to get back with him and quickly hung up.

The truth was, he no longer wanted a divorce. The revelation had stunned him.

What he wanted was his wife.

Her flamboyant, shallow behavior in the past had effectively and relentlessly killed any of the feelings he'd had for her. Or so he had thought. However, he'd seen no sign of that behavior since her accident. Perhaps the close brush with death had frightened her enough to cause her to grow up a little and to appreciate what she had.

Whatever the reasons for her change, Raoul had discovered a disquieting fact—once again he was becoming more and more attracted to the woman he'd married, and he didn't know what to do about it.

How did a man begin to court the woman he'd been married to for six years? How did he go about convincing her that he wanted her back in his bed? How did he admit that she had managed to convince him that the changes he'd seen in her were real and long lasting?

He had to do something soon. The tension that he felt whenever they were together couldn't be entirely his imagination. She was just as aware of him as he was of her. Of course, there had always been a strong chemistry between them. The chemistry hadn't been enough for him, though, once she began to ignore the children and spend most of her time with her own set of friends. Now he would have to rethink the relationship. He would have to build on what had drawn them together in the first place.

Turning, he walked over to his desk and picked up the phone, irritated by the prickly realization that he felt like an inexperienced boy calling for a first date.

Sherye sat back on her heels and brushed her gloved hand across her forehead where perspiration had gathered beneath her straw gardening hat. Yvette was on her knees beside her, energetically pulling weeds, while Jules was busy nearby making hills and valleys out of the rich loam for his brightly painted wooden cars.

She smiled at the sight. Her children looked like little urchins rather than the elaborately scrubbed and dressed miniature adults she'd been shown all those weeks ago when she'd first arrived home from the hospital.

She loved the change in them. Even Louise had commented on how happy they appeared, which had surprised Sherye. To get Louise to admit that anything Sherye had done was positive was a major accomplishment on Sherye's part. Nowadays the nanny didn't appear to be as threatened by Sherye's sudden participation in the children's lives as she had been those first weeks.

Now Louise enjoyed two extra half days off, knowing that Sherye took pleasure in entertaining the children until she returned in time to supervise their evening meal. Louise admitted to her that bedtime was quite pleasant now that Sherye had set up the routine of reading to them until they fell asleep each night.

When Sherye had first suggested the ritual, Louise had felt certain the children would be too on edge to sleep after another visit from their mother. Sherye had been pleased that Louise admitted she'd been mistaken in her assumption.

Sherye made certain that the children got plenty of fresh air and exercise each day, plenty of fresh milk and vegetables, and an abundance of hugs and kisses from their mother.

The summer sun had turned them both a silky tan even with the lavish sunblock Sherye put on all of them. Eventually she'd gotten herself included at bathtime, one of her favorite times of day, right up there with reading to them the hour before they went to bed.

Once she had set up a routine with the children, her life had taken on almost a dreamlike sequence. Each morning she woke up to find herself once again in her beautiful bedroom, knowing she didn't have to rush off somewhere to work, that there were servants who saw to the running of her massive home, who fed her family and looked after her children. She felt as if she was living the life of a princess in an enchanted castle, knowing that her dream was much too wonderful to last. Instead she woke up each day, looked around to make certain her dream hadn't suddenly vanished overnight, then gave a daily prayer of thanks to God.

She spent each day as though it might be the very last one she would have with each family member. She'd discovered a wealth of patience with Felicity, whom Sherye had finally understood from observing her behavior and remarks. The older woman was afraid of growing older, afraid of not being needed, afraid of dying.

Sherye decided to plan outings with Danielle where Felicity could be included. They took her shopping with them and out to lunch. Together the two younger women encouraged Felicity to find other women her age who were alone and lonely to get together and develop new hobbies.

Sherye enjoyed thinking about all the changes in her sister-in-law. All Danielle had needed was some encouragement and a stronger belief in herself. She had blossomed with new ideas and attitudes that touched Sherye deeply, because Danielle continued to give Sherye the credit for the changes.

Only her relationship with Raoul remained the same—distant and polite. There were times when she lay alone in her bed at night thinking about the wall between them. There was so much more than the physical wall dividing them.

Raoul's reaction to finding her in his bedroom her first morning home had made his feelings clear on the subject of their marriage. The only way he expected her to be in his bed was if he was dreaming . . . probably having a nightmare.

Over the past few weeks she'd had ample opportunity to study the man who'd given her so much and asked so little for himself.

He worked long hours and yet always seemed to have time for his children, his mother and his sister. Being around his wife, however, seemed to create a wariness within him. She didn't know how to get past his aloofness.

Sherye wasn't certain she even wanted to, except for the times when he seemed so lonely. He gave so much to all of them and expected so little in return.

Once when Yvette had exuberantly thrown herself into his arms and given him an unrestrained hug Sherye had seen a flicker of expression in his face that stunned her. He'd been surprised by his daughter's affection. He'd also been touched by the unexpected gesture.

Because he was such a private man, Sherye had resisted the impulse to discuss Raoul with Danielle. Instead she contented herself by unobtrusively observing his behavior.

She watched and learned.

The more she saw the more her heart ached for him.

The more she learned the more she loved him.

As her love grew, she discovered that the most loving thing she could do for him was to give him the distance he so obviously wanted from her. Consequently she poured the love and gratitude she felt for him into loving those who were closest to him—their children, his mother and his sister.

A slight noise brought her back to the present, and Sherye glanced around to see her sister-in-law walking across the wide expanse of lawn toward them.

"So there you are," Danielle said, laughing at the sight before her eyes. "All three of you look as though you've been rolling in the dirt and having a grand time of it."

Sherye smiled. The dress Danielle wore reflected the newer, shorter style and showed off her slender build to a flattering degree. Her hair had continued to curl itself into a tousled look that was very becoming.

"Were you looking for us?" Sherye asked, coming to her feet and brushing off her denim-covered knees.

"Actually, it's Raoul who has called for you a couple of times. The last time I promised I would see if I could find you so that you could call him back."

Sherye felt a cold fear grab her. "What's wrong? Has something happened?"

Danielle looked at her, puzzled. "I don't think so. He didn't sound upset, if that's what you mean. Just determined to speak with you this afternoon if at all possible. I told him I was sure you were around here somewhere, since you never left the château without telling someone where you would be." She looked down at Yvette. "You're turning into quite an exquisite gardener, I must say. Did you plant all those pretty flowers yourself?"

Yvette bobbed her head and immediately launched into a description of her various choices. Sherye bent and scooped up Jules, who was liberally covered in dirt. "I'm not sure I can smuggle him upstairs and clean him up before anyone sees him or not. I don't dare call Raoul until I've found the little boy beneath all this dirt."

Danielle laughed. "Don't worry about him. I'll stay here with him and—"

"Not on your life. He'll have you all smudged and dirty, as well. If there wasn't an emergency, I'll get the children cleaned up before I call Raoul."

Both children were bathed and in bed resting before Sherye called Raoul from the extension in the nursery.

As soon as he answered, she said, "Hi, this is Sherye. Danielle said you wanted me to call you."

"Where have you been? I've called a couple of times this afternoon. Danielle said she'd have you call."

Sherye made a face at his irritated tone. Maybe she should have called him first. "Louise has the afternoon off, the children and I have been working in the garden and, as a result, I had to bring them in and hose them down before I could respond to your message. Is something wrong?"

"Not at all. I wanted to suggest that we go out this evening. We haven't had any time together for several weeks and I thought it would do us both good to get away. I wanted to check with you before I made reservations for dinner."

"Oh!" Sherye was stunned. He'd never made any effort to spend time with her before. "Well, I—uh—"

"When is Louise to return?"

"She'll be back by six."

"Good enough. We'll plan to leave home around eight, if that's all right with you."

Sherye could feel her heart racing in her chest. Why was she being so silly? Hadn't she just been thinking about the man and how little time they spent together? Here he was offering to remedy the situation and she was reacting like a blushing schoolgirl.

"I'd like that, Raoul," she managed to say, her voice sounding hoarse to her ears.

"I should be home before much longer. I wanted to give you time to make whatever arrangements were necessary."

Sherye hung up and checked on the children. They were both sound asleep despite the fact that Yvette continued to insist she was too old for naps and didn't need them any longer. Even so, she was growing up so quickly. Both of them were.

She stood there for a few moments, enjoying the quiet moment before she went in search of Danielle.

As soon as she found her she felt unaccountably shy. Feeling foolish, she said, "I spoke to Raoul. He's making reservations for the two of us to go out tonight, and—"

"What a marvelous idea. I'm impressed that he thought about it. He's practically been living at the winery these days."

"I—uh—I'm pleased. I don't get to see much of him. What I wanted to ask was if you would mind listening for the children for me? I need to get cleaned up myself and I'm afraid I won't hear them if they should need anything."

"Of course. I have some magazines I've been wanting to catch up on. I can read them just as easily in their rooms." Danielle gathered up her magazines and said, "You haven't been out at all in the evenings since you got home from the hospital, have you?"

"No, I haven't."

"Haven't you missed it?"

Sherye grinned. "Not really. It's bad enough whenever we're out during the day and people I don't remember speak to me. Here at home everybody has gotten used to the fact that I feel as though I've only been here for a few weeks rather than six years. When I'm away from here, I'm suddenly confronted with people and situations I don't know how to handle."

"Well, you won't have a problem tonight, not with Raoul with you. He's been working too hard. This will be good for both of you."

Instead of a quick shower, which was her usual habit after working in the garden, Sherye showered to remove the soil, then filled the large tub so she could ease some sore muscles.

Raoul hadn't said what he had in mind for tonight, but she wanted to be rested and prepared. She wished she could stop all the butterflies in her stomach. No doubt she and Raoul had spent many evenings together, particularly before she became pregnant with Jules. It was perfectly natural for a husband and wife to spend an evening together, she reminded herself.

Who was she kidding? There was nothing natural about her relationship with Raoul. They rarely spoke to each other, or saw each other, for that matter. Sometimes she had trouble realizing that they shared this room. By the time she was awake each morning he had showered, dressed and was downstairs. When she arrived downstairs for breakfast, he was already gone to his office.

She closed her eyes, feeling the soothing swirl of water caress her skin. *Stop trying to second-guess Raoul,* she told herself, *and enjoy the opportunity to spend more time with him.*

She didn't realize she'd dozed off until the sound of the bathroom door opening roused her. Raoul stood in the doorway from his bedroom looking as taken aback by her occupancy of the tub as she was at his sudden appearance.

"Pardon me, I didn't realize—"

"Oh! I'm sorry, I—"

They both spoke at once, then paused. Sherye sank deeper in the tub, thankful the swirling of the water from the water-jets had produced so many protective bubbles.

"I must have fallen asleep," she managed to say. "I'm sorry. I'll be out in a moment."

Raoul cleared his throat. "Take your time. I'm in no hurry. I just—" He seemed to run out of words and shook his head. "I should have knocked," he finally said before closing the door.

As soon as the door shut, Sherye climbed out of the tub and grabbed a towel, feeling like a complete fool. After carefully avoiding him for all this time, she'd allowed herself to fall asleep when she knew he would be returning home.

After rinsing out the tub and drying herself, she hurried into her bedroom. Glancing at the clock, she was appalled to see that it was already after six. How could she have lost track of time like that? Would he think she had been in there deliberately? It sounded like something the old Sherye might have pulled. She cringed, hoping he wouldn't be disgusted with her.

She slipped into underwear and walked into the closet, trying to decide what to wear. Tonight she could dress as glamorously as she wished. For some reason she couldn't quite explain to herself, she wanted to look her best. She wanted to remind Raoul that she was his wife.

After discarding several dresses with plunging necklines she let out a sigh of satisfaction and pulled out a sapphire blue gown of layered chiffon and delicate lace that had a high neckline and long, narrow sleeves, while the back was cut down to her waist.

She smiled to herself. A dress with its own surprise. From the tags still on it, she knew it was also a dress that she had never worn. The fitted bodice sparkled with tiny brilliants of the same color, giving a shimmering appearance that would change with every breath she took.

She sat in front of her vanity and carefully applied makeup with a light hand, then pulled her hair up high on her head, allowing it to cascade in back.

By the time she'd completed all her preparations, she felt ready to face the world with her chin held high. A light tap on the connecting door caused her to turn away from the mirror.

"Come in."

Raoul opened the door and she struggled not to show her strong reaction to his appearance. This was the first time she'd seen him dressed in formal wear. The suit had obviously been custom-made, showing off his well-formed body to perfection.

He seemed to be just as taken aback by her appearance. "I don't believe I've seen that gown before," he said slowly.

Since he was looking past her, she realized that he could see the back of the dress in the mirror. "If you don't like it, I can change."

"The dress is lovely. I just hadn't seen it, that's all," he said.

"I must have overlooked it in the closet. It had gotten caught with another dress and fell from the hanger while I was going through the rack."

"You look—I'm certain you must know—quite beautiful, Sherye."

She smiled. "Thank you."

"I'm not certain how, but you look different from your modeling photographs." He came closer, his eyes narrowed as he scrutinized her face. "It must be the makeup or something."

"I've forgotten all the tricks of the trade, obviously." She looked everywhere but at him, feeling awkward.

"Actually, I like you this way much better. You seem more innocent somehow, with a sense of freshness that is very appealing."

"This is the first time I've gotten really dressed up since I've had any recollection of my life." She picked up her beaded bag and nervously dropped a lipstick and comb inside. "I'll admit I feel a little strange, given our circumstances." She forced herself to glance back over her shoulder at him and found him watching her intently, which did nothing to ease her nervousness. She turned to face him, holding her small bag tightly as though she didn't know what to do with her hands. She offered him a rather shy smile and said, "I've been feeling like I'm getting ready for a first date ever since I spoke with you earlier today."

He seemed to relax a little. "I know what you mean. I was feeling the same way when I made my invitation."

For the first time since he'd walked into the room she realized that he wasn't as relaxed as he appeared. "Was there a particular reason why you wanted to go out tonight?"

"Yes, but I'd prefer to wait until later to discuss it."

She couldn't read anything in his expression or his tone of voice to hint at what was on his mind. Gathering her courage around her like a cloak, she said, "All right. I'm ready to go whenever you are."

He offered her his arm and they left the room together, Sherye's heart beating a double-time rhythm to their pace. She wasn't certain she was ready to hear what he had to say, but she also knew that she had to face without flinching whatever topic he wished to pursue.

Chapter Nine

When they reached the bottom of the stairway Danielle was waiting for them with a smile. "What a handsome couple you make," she teased. As soon as Sherye saw her sister-in-law she was reminded of the fact that she had left Danielle to look after Yvette and Jules. How could she have forgotten them!

"I forgot to look in on the children," Sherye said, echoing her thoughts, horror-struck by the omission. "Did Louise make it back all right? Do the children—"

"The children are fine, Louise is here and everyone wishes you a fine evening. Yvette did hope you'd stop in so that she could see you before you leave."

"Of course. I can't imagine how I could possibly have forgotten them." She shook her head with frustration and looked at Raoul. "If you'll excuse me, I won't be but a minute."

"Since I haven't seen the children today, I'll go up with you. Quite frankly, that had been my intent when I came to get you, but, like you, I forgot all about my original intentions when I saw you." He grinned at Danielle. "She looks far from motherly at the moment, doesn't she?"

Sherye knew she was blushing but couldn't help it. She turned away and returned upstairs, hurrying down the hallway to the nursery, Raoul's steps echoing a few steps behind her.

Louise was reading to Yvette when Sherye opened the door. When the young girl looked up and saw her mother, Yvette froze, her expressive eyes going blank.

Sherye hesitated at the door, caught off guard by Yvette's reaction. Her daughter hadn't worn that expression in weeks, not since Sherye had first arrived home. Had Yvette thought she'd forgotten about her, since she was the one who regularly read a bedtime story?

She crossed over to where Yvette sat watching her, still with no expression, and knelt beside the love seat. "I'm so sorry I wasn't here to read to you, sweetheart."

Yvette gave a tiny shrug. "It doesn't matter."

"Of course it does."

Yvette looked at the dress Sherye wore. "You're going out with your friends again, aren't you?" she asked in a low voice.

"Actually," Raoul drawled from the doorway, "your mother and I are having dinner out tonight. I hope that meets with your approval."

The change in Yvette was indescribable. From being a frozen, inexpressive and stilted child, she became animated, her eyes glowing and her smile flashing.

"You're going out *together?*" she repeated, obviously delighted. "You've never done that before!" She scooted off the sofa and gave Sherye a quick hug before darting over to Raoul.

Sherye was caught off guard and speechless. Slowly she rose and turned in time to see Raoul catch his daughter up in his arms, laughing. She felt a sharp pain in her chest—as though her heart was being squeezed—at the sight of Raoul's flashing white smile in his darkly tanned face.

"I want you to be a good girl for Louise, and go to bed as soon as your story is finished, all right?"

Yvette gave a vigorous nod and asked, "Are you and Mama going dancing?"

Raoul glanced at Sherye, lifting one of his eyebrows slightly before returning his attention to Yvette. "Perhaps."

Yvette kissed him on the cheek. "I'm glad, Papa. I like to see the two of you together."

"You do, eh? So. You are pleased with us, is that what you're saying?"

"Oh, yes, Papa. Very pleased." She scrambled down and dashed back to where Sherye stood. "You haven't gotten all dressed up in a long time, not since your accident."

Once again Sherye felt a pain in her chest once she realized why Yvette had reverted to her shell when she first saw her. Yvette was afraid Sherye was going to start staying out at night once again.

"That's true," she replied in a husky voice. "I wanted to wait until your papa could take me, and he's been very busy."

Yvette took Sherye's hand and squeezed it. "You look so pretty, *maman.*"

"Thank you, darling."

"Come," Raoul said briskly. "We must be on our way."

Sherye gave her daughter a hug and a kiss, smiled at Louise and joined Raoul at the door. Yvette giggled when Raoul took Sherye's hand and led her into the hallway.

Sherye could feel herself blushing like a silly schoolgirl and all because her husband continued to grasp her hand as he escorted her down the stairway and out to his car.

They were passing the gates when Raoul spoke. "Is there someplace in particular you would like to go?"

She couldn't seem to keep her gaze off his hands and the way his long fingers looked so capable wrapped around the steering wheel. She glanced up at his face. "Not really."

"Can't remember any of your favorite haunts?"

She stiffened. "Is that why you invited me out tonight, in hopes we can find something that might jog my memory?"

"Hardly. Quite frankly, I realized today that I'm not all that eager to have your memory return if your lack of memory means that you'll continue to behave as you have these past few weeks."

"What do you mean?"

"Oh, come on. You must know how you have the whole household buzzing, wondering what has occurred to make you behave so differently. It's almost as if you're a different person!"

"I feel like a different person," she replied in a low voice. "I continue to have trouble relating to the woman who's been described to me."

"Perhaps the blow to your head is proving beneficial in many ways."

"I take it you prefer me the way I am now?"

The smile he gave her was seductive. "Much."

"Does this mean that you no longer want a divorce?"

His smile disappeared and a small frown formed over the bridge of his nose. "I just know that I'm tired of being married without having a wife. If we're going to continue our marriage, I would like to see some changes."

"Such as?"

"I want more than a wife in name only."

She swallowed. "I see."

"However, I can understand that as far as you're concerned, you've only known me a few weeks, and in that time I've been considerably less than loverlike."

She could find nothing with which to argue in that statement so she wisely remained silent.

"I realized that the only fair thing for me to do in this situation is to spend more time with you and allow you to get to know me once again."

"I take it that you no longer expect my memory to return."

He didn't respond immediately, obviously mulling over her comment. "I have no idea. Neither, from all indications, do the doctors. Consequently we've been living in a state of limbo that is rapidly becoming untenable." He glanced at her before returning his gaze to the roadway. "Everything could come back to you tomorrow. On the other hand, you may never remember anything before waking up in the hospital."

She knew he was right. What surprised her was the realization that her memory loss wasn't as upsetting to her now as it was when she first discovered she couldn't recall anything.

"Perhaps I've been afraid to remember," she murmured.

She could feel him stiffen beside her. "What's that supposed to mean?" he asked.

"I'm not so sure that I want to know why I did some of the things I've been told about. My past behavior has been less than admirable." She smiled to herself, feeling wistful. "All I know for certain is that I have enjoyed these past few weeks tremendously. The children are an absolute delight, I've gotten to know Danielle and feel that we are on our way to being friends. Which reminds me..."

When she didn't say anything more, he prompted her with, "Yes?"

"I've been told by several people that I spent most of my time away from home with my friends and yet I have heard from no one but you and your family since I awakened in the hospital."

"I wondered when you would notice."

"Do you know why I haven't heard from anyone?"

"As a matter of fact, I've been puzzled by the same omission. I would have expected to have them calling you on a regular basis. The only thing I could think was that perhaps you had a fight with someone in the group and they are all punishing you with their silence."

"I suppose that's possible. You did say that I was alone at the time of my accident?"

"Yes."

"A passing motorist found me? A stranger?"

"That's what the police told me. You were already at the hospital by the time I reached you."

She rubbed her forehead. "Perhaps it would be worth remembering just to have some answers to so many puzzling questions."

"There's another question you haven't asked that I've been waiting to hear."

She looked at him in surprise. "What is that?"

"Did I have anything to do with your accident?"

His matter-of-fact statement spoken in a quiet voice shook her more than she wanted to admit to herself. "But you said—I mean, how could you have— You were at the château, didn't you say?"

"Don't you believe me capable of planning such an accident? Looking at it from one viewpoint, I certainly had enough motive to want an end to what had become an intolerable relationship. *Maman* mentioned that she told you I'd spoken to an attorney. I'll admit when you didn't regain consciousness and the doctors were uncertain of the outcome, I could see where a rather solid case could be built against me, given our circumstances."

She stared at the road, aware of the careless ease with which he followed its twists and turns. Was this really happening? Was she riding along with her husband while he matter-of-factly explained why he might want her dead?

She shook her head. "This is ridiculous."

"What is?"

"This conversation. You would not have discussed the possibility of a divorce with an attorney if you'd intended to do away with me. Besides, you told me that I left with very little notice and that you didn't know where I was going. So how could you have possibly arranged an accident?"

"Ah. So you *had* thought of the idea."

The blasted man actually sounded pleased that he was right!

They spoke no more until they reached the restaurant in a nearby city. They were greeted at the door by name with smiles from everyone who seated and served them.

"You must come here often," she commented after they had ordered.

"I bring business associates here on occasion. From the statements I used to receive, I would say that you and your friends spent a considerable amount of time here, as well."

Now that she sat across from him she could better judge his expression. The problem was that he had carefully masked his thoughts and feelings...much the way Yvette had earlier in the evening.

Was he afraid of being hurt? Surely not. Raoul DuBois was much too self-assured to feel anything other than at ease with their present situation.

"So these are familiar surroundings," she said, looking around the room with interest. "I wonder if there's anyone here I'm supposed to know?"

"If so, they're very carefully ignoring us, since you arrived with your husband."

There. Hadn't she caught a hint of feeling in that last remark? A hint of—what? What had she heard for an instant? Sarcasm—oh, yes, there was always a hint of sarcasm in everything he said. Or perhaps it was mockery, although she could never be certain whether his mockery was directed at her or himself.

"The wine is exquisite," she said, hoping to find a more comfortable subject.

"Thank you," he said, lifting his glass in a slight gesture. "I'm rather proud of it, myself."

Her eyes widened. She glanced at her glass. "You mean this is from your vineyards?"

His smile flashed brightly in the dim lighting. "But of course. I would want to order our wine whenever possible, unless I'm checking the quality of our competitors."

She took another sip. How strange to be a part of something so traditional and not to remember anything.

"I keep getting the strangest prompting," she said after a moment. "I'll think of something that I want to mention to Janine before I realize that I can't place her and no one seems to know who she is."

"What is it you wish to tell this friend?"

"Oh, about all of this." She gestured toward the room. "I feel as though this is the first time I've been here, the first time we've been out together, and I want to share it all. I want to tell her about the children, and my gardening and about..." Her words began to slow. "My marriage."

"This Janine would be surprised?"

She nodded slowly. "Yes. Because none of it really exists for me. All of it is just a beautiful dream."

He held out his hand. "Would you like to dance?"

The music had been playing quietly in the background and she hadn't noticed other couples moving toward the dance floor. "But our food—"

"Will wait on us, I'm sure. In any event, we won't be gone long. For some reason I have a strong urge to hold you in my arms." He smiled down at her. "The urge proves to be irresistible."

Once again she could almost believe that she was in a Charles Boyer movie, listening to Raoul's fluent English with just a touch of his native tongue to add a subtle difference.

As soon as he placed his arms around her she caught her breath.

"Relax. I'm not going to bite you," he said, pulling her close to him. He kissed her ear. "I might want to nibble here and there, of course—"

She looked up at him in surprise to find his eyes filled with amusement.

He was flirting with her and she felt totally unaccomplished and vulnerable. He was so sure of himself, so comfortable in the exclusive restaurant and on the dance floor. Shouldn't she be at ease, as well? Wasn't this her life-style—her playground, so to speak?

Why didn't any of it feel natural? Why did she feel so self-conscious? Surely a model would be used to having people stare at her, and she had certainly garnered more than her fair share of looks and whispers tonight.

"Ah, I believe our order has arrived," Raoul whispered, and taking her hand he led her from the dance floor back to where they had been seated. Sherye was glad to returned to their secluded table.

"Why are all those people watching us?"

"You. They're watching you."

"Why?"

"You really don't know, do you? Have you forgotten how beautiful you are? How that dress dramatically displays your assets?"

"I should have worn something else! Something not quite so revealing, something that—" She ran down as she recalled that all the evening wear in her closet was designed to catch the eye.

Raoul reached across the table and took her hand. "Please relax and enjoy yourself. I thought getting out would be a treat for you. You've stayed home for so long."

"It *is* a treat, and I'm enjoying it, but I feel so out of place, nervous that I'm going to do something to make a fool of myself."

He laughed. "You could never do that."

"Wanna bet? I remember the time when I— When—" She stammered to a sudden halt, her mind blank.

"When?"

She shook her head. "I don't know. I had a flash of something but when I tried to explain, it was gone." She touched her fingers to the bridge of her nose. "For a minute there I saw something—remembered something—about school. Perhaps when I was going to school—or—" She waited, but nothing else came. She shook her head. "I can't remember. Whatever it was escaped me."

"Does this happen to you often?"

"Often enough. It's frustrating because the harder I try to remember, the more fleeting the memory."

"Let's enjoy our meal, shall we? I want you to relax tonight. We'll do this more often. I think I have everything under control at the winery. I'll take more time off and we can spend a few hours together each day. I feel as though I'm just getting to know you, too, which is a rather strange sensation. You rarely do or say the expected thing anymore. I find myself sitting back, waiting with a sense of anticipation for what's going to happen next where you are concerned."

She tilted her head slightly, studying him. "You're different, too."

"From what?"

"From the man that came to visit me in the hospital. He was cold . . . and arrogant . . . and sarcastic."

"You don't see me that way now?"

"Not as much. Perhaps you are wary, perhaps suspicious at times, but there are times when I catch glimpses of someone who intrigues me very much."

"Then I would say that we've made a good beginning for one evening, wouldn't you?"

"It's been a lovely evening. Thank you."

"You are most welcome. Now, then, if you're through with your meal, I would very much like to dance with you some more."

His gaze was filled with admiration. There were no shadows of wariness in their depths.

Sherye floated to the dance floor on Raoul's arm, convinced she never wanted this night to end.

Chapter Ten

The moon rode high in the sky on their way home. Sherye was content to lean back against the headrest and gaze out at the landscape brushed with silver light. She was enjoying the companionable silence between them. Raoul had seemed more relaxed—happier—tonight than she had ever seen him before. Without his stern visage he'd looked years younger. And what a dancer! Light on his feet, graceful, easy to follow.

She felt like an adolescent with a crush on a movie hero.

But Raoul was real . . . and he was her husband.

One thing had been evident tonight. He wanted her. He'd made no effort to hide his reaction to her body pressed so closely to his.

She'd been just as aroused. Perhaps both of them needed the long drive home in order to gain some control, although he'd made it clear earlier in the evening that he wanted more from her than their present relationship.

She couldn't think of anything she'd rather have than a workable marriage.

Wasn't it too soon? a small voice kept asking somewhere inside her.

Too soon for what? They had been married for years. Whatever had caused her discontent was mercifully blocked from her mind and her memory.

Perhaps she was being a coward, but she had come to the place in her life and situation where she preferred to keep her discontent at bay.

For the first time since she had awakened in the hospital she was ready to release her need to remember the past. Instead she prayed for her future, one that would include Raoul, Yvette and Jules.

"Shall I let you out at the front door?" Raoul asked as they approached the château.

She wasn't ready for the evening to end. More particularly, she wasn't ready to bid Raoul good-night at the moment, so she shook her head and said, "I'll ride with you to the garage."

He didn't comment, and since he was in deep shadow she couldn't see his expression.

Raoul parked the car with precision and walked around to open her door. He held out his hand and she took it. He made no effort to release her hand when they started across the driveway to one of the back entrances.

A night-light lit the hallway they followed to the front of the house. Raoul paused in the foyer and checked the small table at the foot of the stairway where messages were left for the household. There were no messages.

He turned to look at her, saying as they began to climb the stairs, "Thank you for a very pleasant evening, Sherye. I enjoyed it."

"So did I."

"I must admit that it felt unusual."

"How do you mean?"

They reached the top of the stairs and walked to her door, where he paused, taking both of her hands in his and study ing them as though looking for an answer to whatever was puzzling him.

After a moment he lifted his head and gazed at her. "I'm not certain. As a matter of fact, I was trying to figure out the same thing on our drive home. I believe it's something about your attitude."

She blinked. "You mean it's different?"

"In the past, anytime we were in public I always had the sense that you were very much aware of your image and appearance. Even while we would be in the midst of a conversation I invariably got the impression that you were conscious of the people around us, conscious of their stares, almost as though you were playing to an audience." He gave his head a tiny shake as though he hadn't quite found the words he wanted. "You've always been so conscious of yourself, so aware of your own movements and gestures, so that whenever I was with you I felt as though I was witnessing a well-rehearsed performance."

"Are you saying that tonight I didn't appear to be performing?"

"Exactly! Tonight your focus seemed to be on me, on what I said, on the conversation we were having." He gave a self-deprecating chuckle. "I must admit to feeling quite flattered. It's difficult to remain detached when someone so obviously enjoys my company."

"I *did* enjoy your company."

He grinned. "I suppose that's what made the evening so different. In the past I felt as though I was a necessary accessory to your entrance and evening—I was your escort. I had accepted the role without giving it a moment's thought... until tonight. Tonight I felt as if I was the focus of your evening, a vital, invaluable part." He slid his hands on either side of her jawline and cupped her face. "You made me feel very special tonight," he whispered. "I had never before understood what a touching gift a person's focused attention could be." He brushed his lips across hers, and the words "thank you" wafted between them before he kissed her again, this time with a possessive depth that pulled her into a very heated embrace.

His gentle cupping of her face made her feel treasured and protected while he teased and tantalized her with his lips and tongue.

Sherye leaned against her closed door, needing support for her weakened knees. With seeming reluctance Raoul eased away from her until he was no longer touching her. Her weighted eyelids opened and her gaze met his. His rueful expression caught her off guard.

"I didn't mean to get quite so carried away," he said. "I want to give both of us time to adjust to some of these changes."

She heard his words with mixed feelings. As much as she wanted to make love to him—and she was very aroused by his sensuous kiss—she also felt a sense of relief that she wasn't going to be forced into an intimacy that seemed too new.

For weeks Raoul had avoided her as much as possible, making his attitude toward her clear. Now he'd made a rather abrupt shift. She was having difficulty adjusting to the sudden changes.

Of course she wanted a healthier relationship with him. At one time she must have loved him very much to have given up her career and married him. However, their situation had changed over the years. From all indications both of them had been unhappy with their marriage and each other.

Until she could better understand why she had avoided him, why she had insisted on spending so much of her time with her friends, she wasn't quite ready to disregard totally all that she had learned in the recent weeks.

Raoul leaned around her and opened her bedroom door. "Sleep well, my dear. We have the weekend ahead of us. I am placing my time at your disposal to do whatever we can together."

"I promised the children a picnic tomorrow beside the pond. They're looking forward to it."

He nodded. "As will I." He paused, as though reluctant to leave her. He touched her lips lightly with his thumb, smiled, then turned on his heel and disappeared into the room next to hers.

Sherye entered her bedroom and closed the hallway door, her glance immediately going to the connecting door between their rooms.

The door was closed. She knew that it would remain closed, at least for now.

While she undressed she reviewed their conversations of the evening. She was surprised that he, too, had noticed the lack of visitors for her. How could she have been so socially active before her accident, not to hear from any of her friends afterward?

Another puzzling item to add to the list of mysteries surrounding her accident and loss of memory.

She waited until she was certain that Raoul had finished in their shared bathroom before she went in to remove her makeup and get ready for bed. Even without makeup her cheeks were flushed and her eyes glistening. Physically she was fully recovered; emotionally she was improving rapidly.

Her evening with Raoul had given her a great deal to think about.

Once again in her own room, she slipped into bed, convinced she was too keyed up to sleep, but the relaxing comfort of her bed proved otherwise.

"Papa! Watch me, watch me!" Yvette called, playing keep away from a gamboling puppy as he attempted to grab the end of the rope she trailed just ahead of him.

Raoul had been watching her all the while Sherye gently rocked Jules in her arms. Their picnic had been vigorously enjoyed, and the combination of a full tummy and the warm summer air had contributed to Jules's sleepiness.

Raoul had brought the adults a pair of folding chairs and after their picnic on the blanket he and Sherye had gotten more comfortable by sitting in the chairs.

"I'm so glad she's enjoying the puppy. She'll learn a great deal about responsibility now that she has something to look after," Sherye said softly so she wouldn't disturb Jules.

Raoul had been amazed earlier today when Sherye had appeared with the puppy in her arms. She had asked him if he would bring the children outside while she went to pick up a surprise she'd gotten for Yvette.

"That's true. She's repeatedly asked for a dog these past few months," he admitted.

"I think every child should have a special pet to love."

He made a sound of agreement while his thoughts raced. Could a lack of memory make such a profound difference in a person? On closer observation Raoul found more and more discrepancies between the Sherye he knew before the accident and afterward. It was almost as though she was an entirely different person.

How could that be? Of course she was his wife. Unless Sherye had a twin sister who could have stepped into Sherye's life at a very opportune moment, this *had* to be the woman he'd married.

The differences, mostly in attitude, continued to surprise him.

Take the puppy, for example. The woman he thought he knew had ignored Yvette's pleas for an animal, insisting she didn't want a dirty, messy, noisy pet around the place.

Now today she surprised Yvette with a Brittany spaniel, having gone to considerable lengths to find one.

The way she treated their son was another radical change. After ignoring him most of his life, she now seemed to know what he needed before Jules did. She fed him, changed him, coaxed him to rest, all with the minimum amount of fuss, as though she'd spent all of his life by his side.

The changes in her appeared permanent, and to her they were quite unremarkable since she could remember no other behavior. At times like today, Raoul wished his memory could be wiped clean as well, so that he could enjoy his time with his family without questioning what was happening.

The children had already grown used to picnics and playtime with their mother. He could tell from their conversations that today was a routine occurrence.

The day was a revelation to him.

His eyes met hers and she smiled at him. "Would you like me to hold him for a while?" he heard himself asking. "He looks heavy."

"He's fine," she whispered. "I enjoy holding him, even when my arm goes to sleep. He's growing up so quickly. I can already see so many changes in him, just since I arrived home from the hospital."

Even the dullest person would be able to see how much she loved her son. If for no other reason, Raoul admired her for the changes she had made in the children's lives.

"What would you like to do this evening?" he asked.

"Oh, I haven't given it any thought."

"Would you like to go out somewhere?"

"Not particularly. I mean, of course I'll go if you'd like, but I'd just as soon stay in tonight."

He grinned. "All right. How about a game of chess?"

She frowned. "Do I know how to play?"

"A little, but you've never cared for it. I was going to see if that attitude had changed, as well."

"Ah, a trick question, I see."

"All right. You think of something we can do together."

He watched her cheeks darken to a rosy glow and fought to disguise his reaction to what she was obviously thinking. Perhaps he *was* being too reserved where their love life was concerned. For whatever reasons, Sherye was unable to articulate her willingness to resume their marital relationship, but she couldn't hide her interest in and awareness of him.

Every time she looked at him, his body reacted to her gaze as though she had physically touched him. Sherye had always been a passionate woman, using her beauty to get what she wanted. Her manipulative technique was another piece of her personality that seemed to have been lost among other misplaced memories.

Raoul found the nonmanipulative role she'd adopted since her accident more arousing than he could have anticipated. Her direct gaze withheld nothing, it seemed. Clearly she found him attractive. Equally clearly she had difficulty keeping her eyes off him.

What man could resist such a message?

What man would want to resist?

Now it was time for him to let go of his resentments toward her past behavior and accept the changes in her. He couldn't deny his hope that the changes would be permanent. Even if her memory returned, perhaps she would be willing to discuss the difference in her behavior.

Raoul vowed to be more understanding in the future. He wanted to rebuild the relationship he'd been ready to jettison. From all indications, Sherye was willing to help.

Sherye ran the brush through her hair while gazing at her reflection. She'd slipped on her nightgown after her shower and had intended to read in bed until she became sleepy. Unfortunately she was too restless to climb into bed.

She studied the woman in the mirror of her vanity dresser, wishing she knew her better. She could objectively note her assets and understand why people noticed her. The flaming red of her hair demanded notice. The color seemed to accentuate her fair complexion and call attention to the vivid hue of her eyes.

What puzzled her most was Raoul's seeming indifference to her particular charms. Remembering his physical reaction to their kiss last night, she amended her thought slightly. He was a healthy male and his body had certainly reacted to her, but it was his mind that made decisions for him.

Mentally he had rejected her.

She had no idea how to change his mind. She only knew that she wanted to . . . very much. Now that he had decided to spend more time with her, she was painfully aware of how attracted she was to him. Her heart beat faster, her need for air seemed to come more quickly and even the surface of her skin seemed to tingle with awareness of him.

Her problem was that she had no idea how to let him know, which was one of the reasons she was so restless tonight. She felt as if she was supposed to know how to go about seducing the man, but she didn't! What kind of femme fatale had she become since her accident?

A very inept one, to be sure.

She sighed, placing the brush on the small table, and stood. She turned toward the bed, and it was only then that she became aware of Raoul leaning against the jamb of the door between their rooms. From his relaxed position, with his hands in the pockets of his robe, he looked as though he'd been standing there for some time.

She could feel her embarrassment overtake her, even though she knew there was no way he could possibly know what she had been thinking. She fought to contain the wave of heat that seemed to engulf her. "I'm sorry," she said, her voice sounding rusty in her ears, "I didn't realize you were there."

He slowly straightened, his gaze seeming to go through her thin gown to the rosy skin beneath. "I'm the one who should apologize. I should have tapped on the door first."

She gave a nervous chuckle. "Nonsense. There's no need for such formality between us. Did you want something?"

The grin he gave her caught her totally unprepared. His expression was filled with mischief as well as a carnal awareness of the tension between them.

He moved toward her, his eyes focused on her face as though watching her expression for a clue to what she was thinking. Unfortunately her brain seemed to have rolled over in a dead faint as he approached her, leaving her feeling more vulnerable than she could ever before recall.

"Raoul?" His name seemed to singe her lips, the words coming out in a choked whisper.

"Hmm?" He paused in his approach, less than a hand reach away from her.

She attempted to swallow around the lump that had suddenly lodged in her throat. When she didn't say anything more, he tipped her chin up with his forefinger and placed a gentle kiss on her lips.

She shivered at his touch. She felt out of her depth with this sophisticated man who was her husband. She wanted to cling to him and to plant kisses all over his taut, well-hewn body. She wanted...

Everything with this man.

She flowed against him like melting wax against a contoured surface, molding her curves against him. Her unconditional response gave him all the encouragement he needed. With economical movements he swept her up in his arms and strode toward the bed nearby.

Sherye felt frantic with need. She'd waited so long, too long, for his touch and possession. She clung to him when he began to lower her onto the bed. He followed her down without interrupting the kiss. She made a low noise of pleasure deep in her throat as she felt the weight of his solid body on top of her.

Feverishly she brushed away the folds of his robe, eager to find him. Her touch made him lose any semblance of control he'd attempted to exert over his reactions to her. Raoul lifted the hem of her gown and ran his fingers along her inner thigh.

She couldn't lie still. She felt as though she was on fire. When he shifted she opened herself to him. He needed no further invitation.

With a tiny cry of triumph Sherye wrapped her arms and legs tightly around his muscular body as though reassuring herself he wouldn't leave her.

There was no chance of that, at least not for any time soon. Raoul fought for some semblance of control, not wanting to hurt her, not wanting their coming together to end too soon, but there was no way to slow the momentum of their coming together.

He felt as though he was burning up in the flame of her response to him. With a short groan of relief he gave himself over to an incendiary rhythm that guaranteed an almost immediate explosion. He fought to hang on but it was way too late for any attempt at control. Just as his body took over he felt the marvelously erotic contractions deep inside her that signaled she was with him—as she had been with him—every step of the way.

Raoul was still trying to come to grips with his unaccustomed loss of control when he became aware that he was still lying on top of her and that they were stretched across the bed sideways.

He hadn't been able to get them into bed properly before he claimed her. Not that there had been anything particularly proper in his behavior.

He wasn't at all certain that he was going to be able to move again, but he attempted to relieve her of some of his weight by shifting his arms to rest on his elbows.

Her arms tightened around him, holding him in place.

He tried to laugh, but was too weak. Fighting for breath, he managed to wheeze, "I'm too heavy for you."

"No."

She brushed her mouth against his ear, causing him to shiver. She nibbled on his earlobe and he felt the ripple of goose bumps race along his spine and over the backs of his arms and legs.

Still holding her as tightly as she held him, Raoul eventually managed to roll onto his side, amused to discover that despite his sated condition he was already more than half aroused again and still buried deep inside her.

He wasn't used to such a strong response, either in her or in himself. At the moment he was too involved with what he was feeling to attempt to analyze the differences he'd peripherally noted during the recent firestorm—a firestorm whose embers were already being fanned by the kisses she continued to lavish on whatever part of his body she could reach.

This time he tried to set a slower pace. Unfortunately, once control was lost it was tough regaining it, and Sherye wasn't helping in the slightest.

He cupped one of her breasts and nuzzled it, flicking his tongue across the pebbled peak, pleased to see the shimmer of awareness rise in her, as well.

She arched into him, causing his flesh to instantly harden within her. After that, neither could resist the rhythmic move of hips that increased the pleasure of being joined.

He kissed her, his tongue keeping the same inexorable rhythmic pace, steadily increasing the surging, life-giving movement that tossed them back into another explosion of mind-destroying pleasure.

This time they lay collapsed, side by side, their lungs gasping for air, their bodies slick with a film of perspiration. Raoul knew that they needed to move. They would grow chilled once their bodies cooled down, but at the moment all he could do was to lie there with Sherye in his arms and allow himself to drift into a pleasant space of satiated unconsciousness.

He had no idea how much time had passed when he opened his eyes again. The small bedside lamp was still lit and Sherye was curled beside him, her arms and legs still entwined with his.

Raoul couldn't remember a time in his life when he had felt so truly whole and complete. What had happened between them tonight was nothing short of a miracle. Never had he felt such a tenderness toward his beautiful and willful wife.

She'd shared her unabashed needs without shame, all the while making him feel as though he was the only man who could satisfy those particular needs. He lifted a long strand of her hair and watched it curl around his finger.

"Are you cold?" she asked.

He'd thought she was still asleep until her long lashes had lifted from her satiny cheeks. Her eyes were fuzzy with sleep.

"A little," he admitted with a half smile.

"We could get under the covers, if you'd like."

"We could." He didn't move.

She grinned. "Are you too comfortable to move?"

"Something like that."

She slid the leg she'd tucked between his thighs a few inches up... then a few inches down... his leg.

He tightened his arms around her. "I have an idea," he whispered.

"What's that?"

"We could go shower, then sleep in my bed for the rest of the night."

"Mmm."

"Is that a yes or a no?"

"Oh, I think it could definitely be considered a yes."

He sat up, pulling her up with him. Once on his feet he lifted her in his arms and carried her into the bathroom. There he allowed her to stand while he adjusted the spray of the water, then guided her into the shower with him.

With careful strokes Raoul lathered her entire body, blocking most of the water with his back, then stepped aside to allow her to rinse. Dutifully she took the washcloth and mimicked his ministrations until she had him so stiff he had to grit his teeth to keep from lifting her onto him right then and there.

He forced himself to turn his back and hurriedly rinse. Then he stepped out of the shower, grabbed a towel and in record time dried both of them off. This time he was determined to make it to bed and beneath the covers.

He made it, but just barely.

This time he placed himself on the bed and urged her to move over him. With a mischievous grin she knelt over him and soon had him gripping the sheets and clenching his jaw to stop himself from groaning at her exquisite touch.

When she finally eased herself down over him, engulfing him with her velvet-lined sheath, he was too far gone to do anything but grab her hips and encourage her to ride him fast and hard until she collapsed on his chest after they had once again reached their peaks together.

Raoul went to sleep with her bonelessly sprawled across him.

He was so soundly asleep that he couldn't seem to figure out how to quiet the jangling noise that impinged on his consciousness. The steady *brriinng* nearby wouldn't go away. He didn't know how long the noise had been going on before he was awake enough to recognize the sound of the phone.

Sometime during the night Sherye had curled up on her side, and he was tucked spoon-fashion beside her. With a groan he rolled away from her and reached for the phone.

"Yes?"

"Sorry to bother you," the housekeeper said hurriedly, "but you have a phone call from Perth, Australia. They insisted on speaking to you right away."

Perth, Australia? He had no business contacts there. Raoul shoved his hair out of his face, rubbed his jaw and said, "All right. Put it through, please." He glanced over at Sherye and saw that she was still sound asleep. No wonder, he thought with a grin of purely male satisfaction. He was already thinking of some fairly inventive ways he could wake her up a little later when another voice came on the line and he said, "This is Raoul DuBois."

Chapter Eleven

Sherye wasn't certain what caused her to awaken. She heard a low murmur nearby, then a sharp questioning sound that somehow broke through her wonderful dream and caused her to surface into awareness of her surroundings.

She blinked, surprised to see that she was not in her own bed before the events of the previous night rushed into her mind. She stretched, then winced as certain achy spots on her body forcibly reminded her of recent activities.

Smiling, she rolled over and reached for Raoul.

He was sitting on the side of the bed, obviously listening to someone on the phone. Unable to resist the temptation of that smooth, bare expanse of muscle, she placed her hand on his back.

He jerked away as though she had burned him and looked around at her with a grim, shocked stare. The combination of his expression and instinctive withdrawal sobered her.

What happened to the warm, loving, passionate man from the night before?

She stared at him in confusion. The tender lover of last night had disappeared as though he'd never existed. In his place was the cold, hard, aloof man that had been waiting beside her when she first opened her eyes at the hospital.

She could have wept if it would have done any good. What was wrong? What had she done? Was there some etiquette about sharing his bed that had been lost along with so many of her other memories?

Sherye forced herself to listen to his end of the conversation, for the first time wondering if the phone call had anything to do with his inexplicable change of attitude.

She couldn't tell much from his side of the conversation. He was asking short questions and receiving lengthy answers. Afraid to do anything that might further distract or annoy him, she lay quietly and waited for him to get off the phone.

When Raoul hung up and looked at her she knew that whatever information he'd received would affect her. She could feel a trembling beginning somewhere deep inside. She fought to control her reaction to the implacable mask Raoul now wore.

"What's wrong?" she finally asked when he didn't speak but continued to stare at her.

"I would say just about everything," he finally responded. He got out of bed and strode into the bathroom, closing the door quietly behind him.

By now the trembling had taken over her entire body. She knew that she needed to get up, to put on some clothes so that she wouldn't feel quite so vulnerable, but at the moment she was shaking too much for her knees to support her.

Within moments Raoul reentered the bedroom and, without looking at her, began to dress.

"I heard you say you'd be there as soon as you could. Is there an emergency at the winery?"

Once dressed, he walked over to the bed and stood at the end of it. He was studying her as though she was someone he'd never seen before. His stare unnerved her.

"Raoul?" she whispered, feeling as though her world was suddenly spinning out of control. How could she hope to adjust to such a wide range of moods as he'd exhibited in a few short hours? Was that why she'd ended up distancing herself from him in the past?

His first words wiped all speculation from her mind.

"The doctors and I should have listened more closely to you when you first regained consciousness."

She stared at him in confusion. "I beg your pardon?"

"During those first few days you kept talking about your home in Dallas, about your friend Janine, about seeing yourself in a classroom."

"Dr. Leclerc felt those images could be explained," she reminded him when he didn't say any more.

"Of course. Based on the fact that I identified you as my wife."

"Well, yes, that's true."

"But you didn't believe me. Or him. You were shocked to see that your hair was red. You were not comfortable with the clothes, you didn't recognize the children, the château, or Danielle and *Maman.*"

"But I thought you said you no longer cared about my memory loss. You said—"

He made a chopping motion with his hand. "Forget what I said. Forget everything you've been told."

"But I—"

"I have just been informed that my wife—that Sherye DuBois—is presently in a coma in a Perth hospital. That she has been there for several weeks without identification. There would have been a more timely identification if there had been a missing persons bulletin out on her." He leaned closer. "But of course there would not have been a missing persons report filed, since I believed Sherye DuBois was living at home, showing an unusual amount of interest in my children, in my home and in my life."

He turned and began to pace.

"I should have known. You were too different from Sherye despite the physical resemblance between the two of you. If I'd been thinking at all last night I *would* have known. You are nothing like Sherye in bed . . . nothing! But I was so caught up in passion that I ignored all the evidence."

She felt stabbed by his offhand comment. She couldn't have said anything if her life had depended on it.

He stopped pacing and stood at the end of the bed once again. "The only thing that I do believe is that you haven't faked your memory loss. You were tested too vigorously to have faked such a thing." He ran his hand through his hair and frowned.

"I don't have time now to deal with who you are and how you came to be driving Sherye's car. I've got to fly to Perth and bring her back here."

She couldn't deal with what he was saying. She simply couldn't. One shock was falling on another. She wasn't Sherye? She wasn't married to Raoul? She wasn't the mother of Yvette and Jules?

"I—" She stopped, unable to go on.

He came around the bed and flipped the sheet away from her body. Instinctively she grabbed for it, but too late. He ran his hand over her smooth abdomen. "I bet you've never had a child. There are not stretch marks, something I didn't notice last night, but Sherye had several, here—" he ran his hand along her pelvic bone "—and here." He touched the curve of her hips.

Everywhere he touched her, her skin tingled, as though remembering his touch during the long, heated hours of the night. She tucked the sheet around her, pulling it high on her chest.

"It's a little late for modesty, don't you think?" he drawled.

"Why are you being this way? Do you think I've done this on purpose? Do you believe that—" she choked on the words "—your wife and I planned this?"

He spun away from her and began to pace once again. "I don't know what to think... or believe. All I know is that I must leave right away and you—" He paused, and when he didn't go on, she prompted him.

"Yes? I what?"

"There's nothing else you can do but to stay here until we can find out who you are and how the hell you came to be here." He started pulling clothes out of his closet along with a bag. "I'll hire a private detective to see what he can find. I'll have him come here and interview you to see what you can dredge up from your memories that might give him some place to begin his search."

She rubbed her hands over her face. She was dreaming, that's all. This was some kind of nightmare. Any moment now she would wake up and she and Raoul would be able to laugh about her silly dream.

Tears slid down her cheeks. She couldn't seem to control them. They rolled faster and faster and she caught her breath in a sob.

He looked up from his suitcase, then slowly walked over to her. Sinking onto the side of the bed, he said, "Look, I'm sorry I'm not handling this very well. I should have realized the shock would be as great to you as it is to me, given our circumstances."

She wiped her cheeks with the heels of her hands. "I don't even know my name," she whispered.

As though he couldn't stop himself, Raoul took her hand and massaged the knuckles with his thumb. "We'll find out."

"I don't belong here."

"But you'll stay here until we find out where you *do* belong."

The confusion as well as the unexpected kindness in his voice was her undoing. She could no longer hold back the pain.

* * *

The first thing she noticed when she opened her eyes was that she was back in her room. No. That wasn't right. She was in *Sherye's* room.

Dear God! This was even worse than the first time when she had awakened in the hospital. Now she had memories of a different sort, memories that shouldn't have been hers at all because she wasn't Sherye DuBois. Instead she was some nameless person who looked like the famous model.

Listlessly she turned her head on the pillow, aware for the first time of the lengthening shadows in the room. Raoul had given her something, hadn't he? She vaguely remembered a prescription for medication the doctor had sent home with her. Something to soothe her if she became too agitated. Raoul had offered her a tablet with a glass of water and she had been willing to escape into oblivion in order to avoid the pain of the moment.

Now she felt sluggish, her mind disjointed from her body and her surroundings. Raoul must be gone by now, gone to Australia to find his *real* wife.

She felt removed from the whole idea of Raoul and his wife who was in a coma. There was something to be said for being in a coma. At least Sherye could escape from a world she hadn't been able to face.

"Are you feeling better now?" Danielle asked, stepping closer to the bed.

"Oh. I didn't see you."

"Raoul asked me to stay with you. He didn't want you to wake up alone."

Not only had he placed her in her own bed, he had also slipped a nightgown on her. She closed her eyes, not wanting to remember the night they had spent together. Nor did she want to remember what he had said about their lovemaking. But she couldn't forget that he had known she was a fake. She hadn't been able to compare to Sherye when it came to making love with him.

Here was another humiliating aspect of her present situation. Not only did she not know who she was, she hadn't been able to successfully be someone else.

Her fairy-tale life had ended. Somehow she would have to pick up the pieces and go on from here.

Danielle took her hand and gently squeezed it. "Raoul explained that we were wrong about your being Sherye. I'm so sorry all of this has happened. I've grown to love you very much during these past few weeks."

She tried to smile, but she wasn't certain of her success.

Danielle continued. "Raoul contacted an investigator, who wants to speak with you as soon as you feel up to it."

"Yes. I need to do whatever I can to find out where I belong."

"In the meantime, we have to find a name to call you. Can you think of one you'd like?"

She shook her head and Danielle didn't push. After a moment Danielle asked, "Are you hungry? I could order a tray for you."

"I'm not particularly hungry but I know I need to eat." She tried to think. "Am I supposed to call the investigator to set up an appointment?"

"Why don't I call him and suggest he meet you here at the château in the morning?"

She nodded. "Thank you."

"We'll get through this together. You don't have to go through any of it alone. I may not know your name, but you are my friend and will always be my friend. Try not to fret. I'll be back with something for you to eat."

Once she was alone again, she slipped out of bed and went in to shower. She wanted to dress and feel more in control. She had to face the situation head-on and find the answers. Obviously Raoul had his hands full with this most recent news.

She stood in the middle of the room the two of them had shared since her memory began and thought of the man who had played a major role in her new life.

Raoul...who was no longer her husband...who had never been her husband.

Raoul... the man she loved.

Raoul leaned his head against the airline seat and closed his eyes. He'd managed to make good connections, but he had several hours of flying time before he would reach Perth on the western coast of Australia.

Perhaps during the ensuing hours he would be able to come to grips with this latest devastating news. The shock of the early-morning call had forced him to put all of his feelings on hold while he dealt with the practical details of the unusual situation in which he found himself.

For weeks he'd been living with a woman who wasn't his wife. The irony of the timing of the phone call hadn't escaped him. Twenty-four hours earlier and there would have been no intimacy between him and the woman he'd thought was Sherye. He could have apologized for his role in the misidentification, helped her find out her true identity and, perhaps, felt a touch of sadness that the woman he'd come to know—the kind, gentle, caring woman—was not, after all, a new incarnation for his previously shallow, self-centered wife.

Unfortunately he had been given that twenty-four hours, which had compounded the inherent problems in the situation and added a distinctly painful side effect to everything that had happened.

He couldn't run away from the fact that he was in love with a woman with no memory of who she was. The only thing known for certain was that she was not his wife.

The authorities in Perth had made certain their proof of identity was incontrovertible before they had called him, not wanting to be held responsible for any possibility of a mistake.

Now he had to find some way to blot out the multitude of discoveries he'd made while making love to the woman he'd believed was Sherye—discoveries about how differently he viewed himself and his feelings and abilities to relate to others.

He had given himself in a way he'd never done before. He had shared all of who he was and accepted all of who she was...the woman who now held his heart in the palm of her hand.

He had seen her shock and emotional distress and had wanted nothing more than to stay beside her, holding and comforting her, reassuring her that somehow, some way he would make things work for them.

But he'd known better. He'd known from the time the authorities confirmed the identity of the woman in Perth that all the joy he'd discovered, the sense of unity he'd felt with another, his insight of how love transcends all boundaries would not matter now that he knew about the mistaken identity.

It could not matter. It must not matter because he had a duty to deal with life as it was, not the way he wanted life to be.

Hopefully the investigator he'd hired would soon be able to return the woman he'd left to her rightful life.

It was early evening, local time, when Raoul stepped off the plane in Perth. Passing through customs was a relatively simple matter and in a short while he was in a taxi on the way to the hospital.

He'd lost track of time. He didn't know if this was the same day he'd received the call about Sherye or the next one. He couldn't remember the last time he ate. He'd forced himself to nap on the plane, knowing he had to keep his wits about him. Despite his resolve, he could feel the bone tiredness pulling at him when he stepped out of the taxi in front of the local hospital.

Raoul paused at the front desk and asked for Dr. Parkinson, the name he'd been given by the police investigator who had placed the call to him. He was directed to the medical section—as opposed to the surgical or obstetrics section—of the hospital and told to ask for the doctor there, since he was logged in at the switchboard as still making his rounds.

When Raoul reached the proper area he paused at the nurses' station and identified himself to one of the nurses on duty.

The woman grew flustered when she discovered who he was. She quickly rushed into speech, assuring him she would find Dr. Parkinson right away and have him meet Raoul in Sherye's room. She escorted him down the silent hallway and paused in front of one of the doors, pointing out Sherye's room to him.

Raoul felt a sense of déjà vu when he pushed open the door and saw Sherye lying so still in the bed, hooked up to various tubes and machines. A creeping sense of unreality washed over him as he moved closer. Would this Sherye open her eyes and admit to having no memory of him?

There were differences, of course, in the layout and the lack of luxury in the room. What he hadn't expected was to experience the oddest feeling that the woman lying there appeared to be more of a stranger to him than the woman he'd recently left.

Her hair looked dry, faded and lifeless; her skin looked gray and dehydrated. Sherye had always been in control of her weight because of her profession, but Raoul knew he had never seen her this thin—almost gaunt.

He also knew he was witnessing more than an extended bout of unconsciousness, such as he'd seen with the other woman in France. He felt a chill of unease as he studied Sherye's unnaturally still body.

One of her hands lay on her chest on the sheet covering her, while the other rested by her side. Her long, graceful fingers appeared almost transparent. Her nails looked brittle and unkempt.

Raoul couldn't be certain that he would have recognized her if he hadn't known who she was.

Whatever was wrong with her, it was damned serious.

He paced the room while he waited for the doctor to appear and thought about the information he'd been given during that traumatic phone call.

Now that he had seen her condition, more and more of the information he'd heard while in shock came back to him. For a little while he could distance himself from the emotional reaction. He'd had time to adjust to the intial shock.

While he paced, Raoul focused on what he could remember of the information he'd received on the phone.

Sherye had been brought to the hospital by two unidentified men. They told the doctor on call in the emergency room they thought she might have overdosed on drugs.

While one agreed to stay and answer questions for her admission, the other explained that he needed to move their car out of a no-parking zone and that he would return in a few minutes.

According to the report later given to the police who were investigating Sherye's case, the emergency room that day was filled with a miscellaneous assortment of injuries, including two heart attacks and a young boy injured in an automobile accident. These emergencies were brought in within the same hour as Sherye.

The nurse who was to get the information for Sherye's admitting form got called away before she'd had a chance to do more than jot down the words *Sherye* and *possible overdose* on a piece of paper.

After an absence of ten minutes or so—she'd later sworn it was no longer than that—the nurse returned to the desk and discovered that the first man had never returned and the second man was gone, as well.

Neither man had been seen again, nor were the police subsequently able to find them.

Raoul was told that in the weeks since she'd been there, the hospital staff had managed to stabilize Sherye's condition. However, up to the time of the phone call notifying him of her whereabouts, she had never regained consciousness.

After the inquiries into the whereabouts of the two men turned up nothing, the local police sent notices to enforcement agencies throughout Australia giving Sherye's first name and a general physical description as a possible missing person.

When the police saw that the first notice didn't produce any results, the crime lab came to the hospital, took photographs of Sherye and forwarded copies to every agency on the continent.

Because of the drug overdose, which had been confirmed at the hospital, the police decided not to take the usual missing person procedure of going public and flooding the newspapers and television with her picture, which the officer who called him had admitted hampered the progress of the investigation.

What they did do was consider the possibility that she was a tourist, visiting the country. Not knowing her nationality, they ran a check on every visa request for the past six months. In addition, they showed her photograph at every transportation terminal in the city.

No one recognized her.

According to the officer, one piece of luck in their favor was the city's relatively isolated position on the continent. A visitor to that part of the country would have limited access to it.

Although no one claimed to have seen her, the investigation turned up the seemingly irrelevant piece of information that a private, unidentified yacht had been spotted in the harbor at Fremantle, a seaport near Perth, on the same day Sherye had been brought to the hospital.

By the time the police decided the coincidence might be worth checking out, the yacht had been gone for some time without a trace.

The investigation had gotten stalled at that point.

Through sheer, unexpected luck, one of the female dispatchers in the Alice Springs police department kept looking at the picture they'd received—Sherye looked familiar to her. She went home and dug through several old magazines she'd saved. Ironically, she didn't recognize the famous model from any of her glamour shots. Instead she'd vaguely recalled seeing a candid snapshot of Sherye taken on a beach when she wasn't working. She'd worn very little makeup—and the photo was a close-up to verify the model's beauty in its most natural state.

For whatever reason, that photograph had stuck in the dispatcher's mind. As soon as she spotted it again, she knew she'd found the Sherye everyone was looking for.

The investigation had moved forward once again until it reached Raoul in France.

Looking at her now, Raoul was even more amazed that they had recognized her. Raoul reached out and touched her hand. "Sherye?"

There was no movement or sign of life other than the slight rise and fall of her chest when she breathed.

The door opened behind him and he turned to see a tall, middle-aged man walk in.

"Mr. DuBois?"

"Yes."

The older man held out his hand. "I'm Wil Parkinson. Sorry to keep you waiting for so long. I wanted to clear my schedule so that I'd have all the time we needed."

The two men shook hands. The doctor was the first to speak. "Although I'm sorry we have to meet under such sad circumstances, it's been a tremendous relief to all of us—police and hospital staff included—to finally locate Sherye's family. I want you to know that we're grateful that you responded so quickly. I can appreciate the fact that this is difficult for you."

Raoul nodded. "It's been a shock," he said, returning his gaze to Sherye.

"You must be concerned about her condition."

"Yes, I am."

Dr. Parkinson looked at the chart he held, flipping through his notes. "We have verified that her initial condition was brought on by a drug overdose. When we examined her, we found signs that she has been using drugs intravenously for some time."

Raoul spun away from the bed, feeling the jolt of shock-produced adrenaline hit his system. "You're positive of that? I mean, is there a chance you could be mistaken?"

Dr. Parkinson reached over and picked up Sherye's arm that rested by her side. Then he gently rolled the one on her chest until her inner arm was exposed. There were signs of old bruises on the inside of her arms from her wrist to her elbow, as well as needle tracks.

"I assume from your reaction that you weren't aware of her drug habit."

Raoul stared at her arms in horror, unable to reconcile what he was hearing and seeing with the woman he thought he knew. "She once mentioned that she'd become addicted to drugs when she was fourteen, but she saw what they were doing to her and after a couple of years managed to stop. I've never seen any signs of drugs since we've been married."

The doctor rested his hand over Sherye's. "I believe the evidence speaks for itself. She was in poor physical condition when she was brought in—underweight, dehydrated and anemic. While the police pursued the search for her identity we first worked to stabilize her vital signs and then began a form of therapy to stimulate her by various methods in the hope of bringing her out of her coma." He smoothed his hand over her hair in a comforting gesture. "As you can see, we haven't been successful, thus far."

"When was she brought here?"

The doctor checked his notes and quoted a date three weeks ago. "I know I'm being personal and I'm sorry to appear as though I'm prying into your personal life, but I've wondered how close you are to your wife. I believe the officer who called you explained that one of the obstacles they ran into in tracing your wife was the fact that there was no missing persons report filed on her."

Raoul contained his irritation despite the implied criticism of his behavior. "I can understand why this situation seems peculiar to you. I'll admit that I'm at a loss to explain some of the recent events, myself."

The subject had moved subtly from Sherye to Raoul. With that shift he realized that he could no longer hold on to his hard-earned objectively. His emotions surged suddenly despite his strong will to suppress them.

He disliked discussing his personal life with outsiders. Hadn't he already gone through this, for God's sake? First at the hospital in France and now here in Perth. He was being pressed and prodded to explain . . . to expose . . . to analyze an area in his life that had gone sour.

He knew he was oversensitive regarding the failure of his marriage. However, in recent weeks—up until the phone call he'd received several time zones ago—he'd believed that he'd been given a second chance, a chance to rebuild a shattered, hopeless relationship into something healthy and strong, a chance to resurrect a relationship and fill it with love and friendship, a new tenderness and understanding, a shared love of their children.

With one phone call, his life and his perception of his life, his values, his basic belief in himself—all of the pieces that formed the foundation of who he was—had been tossed into a chaotic swirl of events where the impossible had suddenly become not only possible, but had happened.

Raoul knew that he owed this doctor no explanations about his marriage. He also knew that sometime in the near future he would be facing a barrage of probing, in-depth questions from the local police if Sherye didn't regain consciousness soon in order to answer them herself.

He had no way of knowing how many laws—local and international—she had broken on her way to her capricious rendezvous with fate here in an Australian hospital, alone and unconscious. Just for starters, she hadn't cleared customs before entering the country. The evidence of habitual drug use was another red flag that would be investigated.

He had a hunch there was a much longer list involved.

Raoul realized that he had been standing beside her during his battle to override and suppress his emotions once again. He tested his control by looking into Sherye's expressionless face.

She knew all the answers to their questions. She was the one who could explain reasons, motivations, schedules, plots. She was the one who could explain why another woman was found with her car, her papers and wearing her clothes.

It was typical of Sherye to avoid confrontations that might lead to any unpleasantness. She'd always been skilled that way. She'd never been willing to assume responsibility for her behavior, either past or present.

Was her overdose an accident or had too many of her recent decisions produced a situation that got out of control? Had the consequences of her actions begun to catch up with her?

Knowing Sherye as well as he did, even if she were to regain consciousness he knew there was no guarantee that she would answer questions posed by the police.

On the other hand, she might find it amusing to play along, but then she'd never seen a need to tell the truth if a lie would better serve her.

No. He wasn't going to be able to ignore what he was feeling.

Raoul needed to talk to someone about all of this. Perhaps in the telling he would be able to make some sense out of what seemed to him at this moment to be an incomprehensible series of events, possibly orchestrated for nothing more than Sherye's own amusement. She'd carelessly played with all of their lives before blithely going her own way.

He turned away, unable to look at her without feeling his anger and frustration build. He was more than weary. He was exhausted. He didn't have the energy to deal with his roiling emotions on his own.

Dr. Parkinson had been quietly watching Raoul wrestle with the conflict between reason and emotion within him, reading him fairly accurately as a result of his own wide and varied experience of dealing with people in crisis. He saw the moment that Raoul decided to trust him enough to share a part of himself.

Raoul looked around the room blankly, suddenly conscious of his need to sit down before he collapsed. As soon as he stiffly lowered himself into one of the well-padded chairs that furnished the room, Dr. Parkinson sat in its mate, leaned back and waited for Raoul to begin—at his own pace and in his own way—to discuss what must be a very painful and difficult subject for him.

"For the past year or more my wife and I have been having marital difficulties—since around the time our sixteen-month-old son was born. Approximately six weeks ago Sherye left our home, insisting she would be back the next day. The following night the police called and informed me that my wife had been in an automobile accident and had been taken to a hospital just outside Paris, where she was listed in critical condition."

Dr. Parkinson had started making unobtrusive notes soon after Raoul began. He looked up from them now with a puzzled expression. "I'm afraid I don't understand." His gaze strayed to where Sherye lay. "You mean she was already under a doctor's care weeks before she—" He paused, searching for words that might clarify what he thought he was hearing.

"No. What I am saying is that the woman found at the scene of the accident that night after Sherye left our home looks exactly like Sherye. She had the same hair and eye color, and the same physical statistics and features.

"There was never any doubt in my mind when I first saw her that she was anyone but Sherye. In addition, she was wearing Sherye's clothes, carrying her purse, driving her car.

It was through the identification she had with her that the police were able to locate and contact me."

He could feel his body beginning to relax. He rubbed the back of his neck in an attempt to ease the tightness there. "No one thought it necessary to check her dental records, which I was told the police did as a final step in their positive identification of Sherye before they called me."

Dr. Parkinson had stopped writing and was staring—slack jawed—at Raoul. "This woman told you she was your wife?"

Raoul shook his head. "She couldn't tell anyone anything. Like Sherye, she was taken unconscious to the hospital. She'd received a severe blow to the head and remained unconscious for several days." He nodded to Sherye. "Ironically, the situations are quite similar except for the problem with her identity. That is, there was no problem of that nature until she regained consciousness and didn't recognize anyone.

"Unfortunately she couldn't identify herself, either. The doctors assumed her condition was the result of the blow to her head she received at the time of the accident. Her lack of memory was an unfortunate side effect to the accident, but the situation appeared staightforward enough."

Raoul's body was finally protesting the long hours and unbearable tension he'd been under. His head felt as if a tight band encircled it, and it continued to tighten as the minutes ticked by.

He leaned forward, placing his elbows on his knees and resting his head in his hands, which gave him some relief.

These were the painful memories, the ones that seemed to stab him in his gut. In a hoarse voice he said, "I thought I was bringing my wife home from the hospital last month. Until the phone call about Sherye, I'd been given no reason to doubt that the woman currently living with me was my wife."

He knew he was lying, even as he heard the words. Some instinct deep within him had known that no one could make such a tremendous shift in her personality, beliefs and value system, but because he'd wanted so badly to accept and embrace all the positive changes in her, and because he knew there was no way she could be anyone but Sherye, he'd deliberately disregarded the wall that he and Sherye had placed between them so many months ago. He'd believed what he wanted to believe.

So what kind of person did that make him?

Dr. Parkinson had started making notes again, leaving Raoul the necessary space to deal with the pain as it surfaced. As the silence lengthened, the doctor finally accepted that he would have to help the man deal with the pain.

He glanced up from his notes and said in a casual voice, "I would say that your story certainly explains the lack of a missing person report, but it certainly raises a great many other questions that demand answers."

"Yes, it does."

"You've been subjected to several bits of shock-provoking news in a very short time. Taken altogether, it's no wonder you've been severely shaken."

"Yes." Raoul gestured toward the marks on Sherye's arm. "How could I not have known that she was so heavily involved in drugs?"

"Oh, that part isn't so unusual. Addicts are extremely clever at covering evidence of their use, at least in the early stages. If, as you mentioned, there was some discord between you, I would imagine she had little difficulty in hiding her addiction from you."

Raoul stood, needing to move, needing some privacy to deal with the turmoil inside him. He walked over to the window, sticking his hands into his pockets in an unconscious desire to hide, and stood there for several minutes in silence before Dr. Parkinson spoke once again.

"Do you know how your wife came to be in Perth?"

Raoul shook his head without looking around.

"Did the police tell you that there was a yacht seen in a nearby harbor close to the time she was brought in? No one on the ship contacted the port authority or immigration officials for permission to come ashore, so there was no official registration of their being offshore. Despite their efforts, the police could find no one who happened to observe or remember the name." He studied Raoul's shadowed figure, judging from his physical stance where he stood emotionally at the moment.

The man was almost reeling, he was so tired. Dr. Parkinson decided to press on. "Do you suppose it possible that she was on board the yacht? It's rather a long shot, but nothing else has turned up."

Raoul turned away from the window and leaned his shoulder against the wall, facing the doctor. "It's possible, I suppose," he mused, sounding a little more relaxed. And why not? The subject had veered away from him. His reactions were typical of most people, the doctor noted absently. He listened as Raoul continued without being prompted. "There has to be some explanation for her turning up here. I suppose that one's as good as any. I don't know many of her friends. Those I have met seemed to have enough money to afford to do pretty much as they pleased." He shrugged. "Whether one of them has a yacht is anybody's guess. I'm sorry. I wish I had more information for you."

Dr. Parkinson made several more notes before he looked up, shaking his head in amazement. "I don't believe I've ever heard of a situation like this before."

"Me, either." Raoul wearily rubbed his forehead in an effort to concentrate. "There is one thing that I thought of while I was on the plane coming over. It's something I'd forgotten about at the time of the automobile accident. I don't know that it's particularly helpful, but might suggest Sherye's plans if she thought she had managed to work out a plan where she could disappear without anyone suspecting."

Raoul walked back to the chair and sat down. "I came home early the day she left and found Sherye packing resort wear into a rather large bag. As I recall she was surprised to see me because I rarely get home that early. Perhaps she had hoped to be gone before I arrived. Now that I think about it, I'm sure she hadn't intended for me to see that bag."

"Yes, that makes sense. Why pack a large bag if she's only going to be gone overnight?"

"My question to her, exactly."

"What did she say?"

"Nothing. She ignored the question and left, which is customary behavior for her."

"Did the bag show up at the scene of the accident?"

"No, but at the time I gave it no thought, since she was thrown—or, rather, I should say the other woman was thrown out of the car before it went over an embankment and exploded into flames. Had I thought about it, I would have assumed her luggage was in the car when it went over."

"Is it possible the woman pretending to be your wife is feigning her loss of memory? Could she, in fact, be related to your wife in some way and agreed to take her place?"

"Anything is possible, doctor. I wouldn't begin to guess at the truth at the bottom of all of this. If the woman was part of the deception, something must have gone wrong in the plan because she was seriously injured. Since I was suspicious of what I considered to be a convenient memory lapse, I specifically asked the doctors to test her extensively in hopes of catching her out. It was their expert opinions that she was not faking her memory loss. Having seen the injury, I know that it wasn't faked.

"As for the possibility of their being related, all I can say at this point is—who knows? According to Sherye, she was raised by a single mother who had no living relatives. She never knew her dad. Sherye has never mentioned anyone in her family other than her mother, either when talking about her childhood or as she grew older."

"Would her mother be able to—"

"Her mother died when Sherye was in her early teens."

"Unfortunate at any time, but particularly devastating at such a vulnerable time in a person's life. I would hazard a guess that it was about that time that Sherye began to experiment with drugs."

Raoul looked at him in surprise. "Now that you mention it, I wouldn't be surprised if the two events were tied together. Getting back to the almost eerie resemblance between the two women, I took the time before I left home to hire a reputable and quite effective private investigator. I asked him to speak with the woman I thought was Sherye while I'm gone to see if some of her unusual and confusing memories would make more sense now that she knows she isn't Sherye DuBois."

"How did she take the news?"

Raoul attempted to block the brief flash of memory of the last time he saw her from his mind, but it was already there. He had held her in his arms and wiped away her tears. Since the doctor had cautioned him about the importance of not allowing her to get upset, Raoul had finally given her some of the medication the doctor had sent home with them.

He'd held her in his arms until she'd fallen asleep, then he'd searched out and found a new gown to put on her before carrying her back to her own room. There was no reason for anyone to know that she had spent the night in his room.

He knew that was one of the reasons she'd been so upset. Perhaps it was the only reason, given the circumstances. After all, the feelings she'd openly expressed toward him were perfectly natural toward a husband. Like him, she'd probably hoped to ease the tension between them. Fully believing they were married was grounds enough for her to have met him halfway in order to eliminate the strained atmosphere between them—despite the fact she had no memory of marrying him.

Whether she'd been a party to the deception or not, her lack of memory placed her in the role of victim. Unfortunately he had perpetuated her role by his foolhardy and premature behavior toward her.

He hadn't known, damn it! How could he have known? Wasn't he the planned victim in the scenario? The dupe? The unsuspecting, insensitive husband who wouldn't be able to tell the difference between his wife of six years and a total stranger?

The worst part of it for him was that it had worked... up to a point. Making love to the woman he'd brought home from the hospital had clearly shown him there'd been some kind of mistake, and he had made it. What gnawed at him was the question of whether—in his totally besotted condition—he would have had the integrity to admit to himself, to her and to the family that she couldn't possibly be the Sherye DuBois he'd married. Then he would have been expected to explain why he had waited so long and what had prompted his discovery.

It was a test he hadn't had to face. The early-morning phone call had rescued him. Now he didn't know what his choice would have been.

Sherye, and possibly this unnamed woman, had placed him in a position where he'd had to face parts of himself that had never been tested, parts that he'd never wanted to face.

He wasn't sure he'd ever be able to forgive either one of them because of it.

"The other woman," Dr. Parkinson repeated when Raoul didn't immediately answer him. Obviously he'd managed to touch on another painful part of the saga. "How did she take the news?"

"She was upset, which was a natural reaction. With no memory of her own, she accepted another woman's life. Now she has to start all over in an effort to find out who she really is. Since I have a strong desire to know as well, I fully intend to pursue the matter."

"Well, you certainly have a mystery on your hands. I don't envy you the task of unraveling it."

"My immediate concern is how to have my wife returned to France. Will she have to stay here until she regains consciousness?"

"If it was that simple, I would say yes, because she would then be able to answer some questions from officials. If she was brought into the country in her present state, she can't be held accountable for anything other than not having a passport and visa."

"You say 'if it was that simple,' meaning what?"

"Mr. DuBois, there is a better-than-average chance that your wife may remain in the coma for years without regaining consciousness. There's ample medical evidence to support the possibility that she could live out her natural life as she is now."

Raoul approached Sherye's side once more. She looked peaceful lying there.

Perhaps she had intended to die.

Perhaps she had accidentally overdosed herself.

Unless she was aware enough to answer, he might never know the truth.

Whatever the truth, Sherye had made good on her vow to prevent him from ending their marriage.

Once again Raoul faced the dark test of his belief in his own integrity. He knew that he could never divorce Sherye as long as she remained in her present condition because he wouldn't be able to face the knowledge that he could abandon her when she was helpless to care for herself. He took his marital vows quite seriously.

He'd promised to love and honor her. He'd been unequal to the task and he had failed.

He'd promised to love her in sickness and in health. Somehow, he would have to make up for his lack in other areas by caring for her now.

Chapter Twelve

"All right, Madame DuBois," Claude LeBeau, the private investigator, began once introductions had been made. "If you will, please tell me anything that you can remember prior to the accident, anything at all, so that I might gain some idea where to start my investigation."

"I'm not Madame DuBois," she replied in a quiet voice.

The two of them were seated in the salon. LeBeau had arrived promptly at nine for their interview, obviously eager to begin his assignment.

He looked pained by her response. Impatiently he waved his hand and said, "Yes, yes, of course. I quite understand the complexities of the matter. Nonetheless, we are faced with the problem of giving you some sort of address until we can ascertain exactly who you really are."

She looked down at her hands for a moment. "We call them Jane Does," she murmured, more to herself. LeBeau's hearing was acute. He leaned toward her intently.

"We?"

She looked up. "Oh. In Texas—in the States."

"Ah! There, you see. We have already discovered something important. You are an American, most probably from Texas, if that is the state that first popped into your mind."

She'd awakened with a headache this morning, fighting to resist the familiar sense of confusion and dismay that had accompanied her during these past few weeks. "Perhaps, but I was also told that Sherye was born and lived in Dallas when she was a child. Since I'd accepted the fact that I was Sherye I'm not certain how much of my thoughts are based on what I was told about me and how much are part of the life I led before the accident."

LeBeau made some notes, then tapped the head of the pen on the notepad several times. He spread several photographs of Sherye in a fan across the pad, looking at them, then at her, carefully comparing features.

"The one amazing coincidence in all of this," he mused, "is the astonishing resemblance between you and Madame DuBois. Is it possible that you are related?"

"I've been told that Sherye was an only child."

"Hmm." He made some notes. "I will have to follow up on what we know about her early life, as well. Perhaps we will discover a common thread." He looked at her for a moment in silence. "Do you remember if you knew her before the accident?"

"No."

"What do you remember? Anything? Anything at all?"

She tried to focus back to those first few days after she regained consciousness, before she had accepted her new life and become absorbed in the routine of the château.

"For a while I would get flashes of pictures—rapidly moving pictures—mostly with no sound. I couldn't make much sense of them without some context in which to place them."

"Did the doctors work with you to help you recall anything?"

"They worked with me, yes. However, they were trying to assist me in remembering someone else's life, although none of us recognized that at the time."

LeBeau rubbed his chin thoughtfully, pondered his notes, then asked, "May I make a suggestion?"

"Of course."

"A trained medical person might be able to work with you under hypnosis and further clarify some of these images for you, perhaps opening up memories that haven't surfaced in the course of natural events. Would you consider getting help in such a way?"

She was astonished to hear an obvious solution to a situation that had seemed almost hopeless to her for the past twenty-four hours. "Why, that's a wonderful idea! I wonder why no one suggested hypnosis before?"

"You must remember that there was no question as to your identity before, therefore there wasn't as big a need for you to explore your subconscious. Your identity had already been established, and no doubt the professionals felt it merely a matter of time before your forgotten memories would surface." He closed his notepad. "Now, you see, it is mandatory that we find out everything we can regarding your life prior to the accident. So. We delve deeper than we were willing to go before."

She nodded. "Yes. Of course you're right. I'll call the hospital where I recuperated. I'll explain to the doctors what has happened and see if they will work with me once again."

The investigator stood. "Fine. In the meantime, I will see what I can discover about Sherye DuBois's birth and her early childhood in Dallas, as well as look for any other information that might validate your own belief of having lived there." He held up a camera. "Before I go, I would like to take some photographs of you, if you will be so kind." He touched the professional modeling glossies. "These are a good likeness, but rather glamorous compared to the way you look this morning."

With a minimal amount of makeup, a shirtwaist dress and her hair pulled back from her face, she knew she presented an entirely different image from the pictures LeBeau held. "Of course," she replied with a nod, touching her hair. "I'll just— Oh! I just remembered something!"

"Yes?"

"When I first regained consciousness I was shocked to discover that my hair was red. I knew that my natural hair color was a very pale blond. Raoul said that Sherye was a natural blonde who kept her hair tinted."

"Ah. You were both natural blondes and you think you had kept your hair its natural color."

"Yes."

"Perhaps I can doctor a couple of these photographs of you today and see what difference that makes in your appearance." He reached into his pocket and gave her his card. "If you have any more thoughts on the matter, call me at this number. My associates will be able to reach me wherever I might be."

She walked with him to the door and paused on the front steps with him.

He looked around the grounds with appreciation. "It must be a grave disappointment for you to discover that you do not truly belong here."

"Somewhere deep inside of me I think I've always known that this wasn't really my home. I think I've been pretending for weeks to accept my place here. But you're right. I'm going to miss living here, miss everyone I thought was part of my world." She blinked back the tears, determined not to shed one more drop of moisture for what couldn't be helped. "Thank you for being so prompt. I'm sure Raoul will be grateful for your swift response to his request."

He took her hand. "Please keep in touch. Tell Monsieur DuBois that I will contact him as soon as I have something."

She stood at the top of the steps and watched the investigator get into his car and drive away. She thought about their discussion, reviewing his suggestions and comments. Yes. She would call the hospital this morning. If they would accept her, she would leave the château, making a clean break between the life she had been living here and whatever might lie in her future.

She had discussed the matter with Danielle last night and they had both agreed that the children were too young to understand what had happened. She would spend this morning with them—one last morning that she would give to herself as a farewell present. Then she would explain to them that she would be making a trip.

Once Raoul returned with Sherye, the two of them could explain what had happened if they chose. She knew it wasn't her place to say anything.

With a sigh she turned back to the château to face another series of challenges that she wasn't at all certain she could handle with the dignity and courage she knew she needed. A betraying thought flitted across her mind—if only Raoul could be here to ease her through the next few days and weeks, as he had been there in the background when she'd first opened her eyes to a world that belonged to Sherye DuBois.

She'd been at the hospital a little over two weeks when the soft sigh of the door to her room pulled her attention away from the book she was reading. She looked up and saw Raoul standing in the doorway.

His unexpected appearance almost took her breath away. Each day she had been at the hospital had been filled with consultations, hypnotic therapy, journaling and learning to live in the limbo state of her present existence.

She'd done her best to block out memories of the château and her life there—focusing instead on memories that were trickling back into her head.

Despite all her efforts, Raoul seemed to linger in the background of her mind at all times. Seeing him now, she thought her yearning to see him had conjured up his presence.

He crossed the room to where she sat and pulled up the chair beside her.

Seeing him up close she knew that their weeks apart had been as stressful for him as for her. His eyes were deeply shadowed, his expression grim.

She placed the book on the table beside her and instinctively reached out to touch him. Realizing what she had done, she paused with her hand hovering between them. "Hello, Raoul."

He grasped her hand like a drowning man and held it tightly, his gaze scanning her features. "How have you been?" he asked, his voice sounding rusty from disuse.

"I'm all right. How is Sherye?"

He gazed at her bleakly. "There's no change in her condition. I've spent every day of the past two weeks dealing with the Australian legal and hospital systems in an effort to have her released to my care. The red tape was indescribable. They could fill a thick book with transcripts of the multitude of interviews and interrogations I went through." He shook his head. "I never want to go through anything like that again."

"Where is she now?"

"I placed her in a hospital near the château. The doctors there have reviewed all her medical information. They refuse to make any predictions about the possibility of a full recovery." He shifted in the chair although he continued to hold her hand. She needed that small contact with him. His touch had always been able to soothe her.

"Do they know what caused the coma?"

He'd been absently studying her hand, and looked up at her question. "Oh, yes. She suffered a drug overdose. It seems someone was keeping her well supplied."

"Did you find out how she came to be in Perth?"

Once again he nodded. "We found out for certain a few days ago. It seems that she and a group of her friends were invited to spend the summer on a friend's yacht. They were under the impression that I knew where she was and didn't care. It's possible that she at least implied by her behavior that our marriage was over. I've spoken to Ted Andrews, one of the men who helped to get her to the hospital. He had to face police questioning once they found him because of the way Ted and the other man abandoned her at the hospital. By the time the police finished with Ted he was quite shaken. When I spoke with him and explained her present condition and my lack of knowledge regarding her whereabouts, he reluctantly agreed to tell me as much as he knew.

"He was understandably embarrassed to discuss the matter with me. I understood why when he explained that Sherye had boarded the yacht with a man she introduced as Mario, claiming that he was an old friend of hers and that she'd brought him along as her guest. It quickly became apparent to all those on board that she was flagrantly indulging in a flaming affair with him. None of them had ever seen him before and didn't know what to think of her behavior.

"When Mario found Sherye unconscious and reported it to the others, the ship's captain took them to the nearest port, which happened to be Fremantle. To avoid having to answer questions, Ted and Mario slipped ashore with Sherye without going through official entry procedures. They flagged down a taxi and got her to the hospital.

"When Ted heard Mario tell the nurse he was going to move their car, Ted realized Mario's intentions and that he would be left to answer any questions about Sherye's condition. He admitted to me that he panicked and got out of there as soon as he could."

Raoul stated the facts and events coolly, giving no indication that he was emotionally involved with the woman he was discussing. She wondered how he could be so objective in the telling of what had happened.

Perhaps he still intended to divorce Sherye. She had certainly given him ample provocation. She reminded herself that it wasn't any of her business what he did. The DuBois family was no longer her concern. Not anymore.

"Have the police spoken to Mario?"

"No. They can't find him. He never returned to the yacht, not even to pack his belongings. I understand the owner of the yacht received a note requesting his things be shipped to a post office address in France. When local police checked, the box was no longer in use."

"Are you going to try to find him on your own?"

"It would be difficult, since they aren't certain he used his real name. I believe it would be a waste of time at this point. I have no reason to speak to him. According to Ted, he and Sherye spent most of their time on board away from the others. I think one of the reasons he bolted was because it's a good bet he was the one supplying her with drugs. If that's the case he's going to make sure his tracks are covered. He can't afford to be questioned."

"Do you have any idea how I became involved with all of this?"

He shook his head. "I'm afraid not. Only Sherye and possibly this Mario can explain how you came to be in her car. The authorities are now checking into the possibility that your accident may have been faked, that you might have been drugged and placed there. If so, whoever hit you on the head didn't know his own strength. That blow alone could have killed you."

"Drugged?" she repeated faintly.

"Yes. There were traces of a chemical in your bloodstream when you were first admitted that may have been an experimental drug currently being tested. LeBeau has been asking questions of the doctors, trying to find out more about it. He spoke with chemists and other scientists, who've concurred that the drug could have created lapses in your memory."

She shivered. "An experimental drug. How awful. I could have died there at the scene. Did whoever planned this scheme consider that? Did they care? What were they hoping to accomplish?"

"LeBeau and I have been trying to find a workable theory that covers all the facts we've gathered so far. One theory is that Sherye wanted to cover up the fact that she was going on that cruise. Her behavior these last several months has been increasingly difficult to deal with. We rarely saw each other. When we did, we ended up arguing. On one occasion I told her I wanted a divorce. She threatened to create a scandal if I pursued the idea. She didn't pretend that she wanted anything other than my money and social standing, but that was enough for her. However, she took me seriously and for a while her behavior improved to some degree. I believe that she wanted to go on that cruise and she knew I wouldn't tolerate the idea. That I would divorce her, despite her threats. Somehow, some way, she came up with an idea that would create a smoke screen to cover what she was really doing by providing someone who would be mistaken for her—at least on a temporary basis. Knowing Sherye, she probably expected to get away with it."

Such a mess and there seemed to be no end to it. She felt so helpless, knowing there was nothing that she could do to make things any easier.

"The part that has been so confusing for me," she said, "is how Sherye got me to participate in the plan. I can't imagine ever agreeing to pretend to be someone else. Even if I had, what assurance did she have that I wouldn't change my mind and tell you the truth?"

"You'd have to know Sherye to understand the way her mind works. She makes up her own rules, changing them to fit her whims. If she got caught, she probably figured she could talk her way out of any problem it might have caused. She has a history of being able to get her own way. She probably enjoyed the challenge of trying it in order to see if she could get away with it."

"I'm beginning to understand your attitude toward me when I first recovered consciousness."

"LeBeau thinks you were given a drug that would induce at least a temporary amnesia to lessen the odds against my finding out that you weren't Sherye."

"You mean she counted on my not being able to remember anything?"

"Or at least you'd be confused and disoriented, which could be attributed to the injury you'd supposedly sustained as a result of the accident. All of it would buy her time."

She shuddered. "To go to such extremes just to have a few weeks away from her family. Such an elaborate ruse doesn't make sense."

"Not to me or you, perhaps. Remember, that's just one of the theories. There are others. We'll have to see what additional facts turn up in the investigation." Still holding her hand, he touched her cheek with his other hand. "Enough about Sherye. I came to see you to make certain you were all right and to tell you how sorry I am that I couldn't stay with you the day I received the phone call from Perth."

"I didn't expect you to stay with me! Of course you had to go. She's your wife. The shock had to have been as great for you as it was for me." She looked down at their clasped hands, feeling his warmth and concern for her, fighting the almost overwhelming desire to throw herself into his arms and cling to his strength.

"We need to talk about what happened between us," he said in a low voice. When she didn't look up, he brushed his knuckles under her chin and raised her head until she was forced to meet his gaze.

"What is there to say?" she managed to say. "It happened. You thought you were reconciling with your wife. At least," she added with a tiny shrug of feigned indifference, "you discovered the difference once I was in your bed." She could feel the heat of her embarrassment sweep over her body.

His eyes darkened. "Yes. Given time to think about it, I would have known you couldn't possibly be Sherye."

She fought to hang on to her composure—determined not to let him know how much his words hurt—until she realized what he was saying to her.

"You were too open, too honest in your responses to be Sherye. You wrapped me in your flaming warmth and showed me what lovemaking could be—a free expression of pleasing and giving pleasure. You set me on fire and I lost all control but it didn't matter. I'd never experienced anything like it before. Sherye never had that effect on me, even at the beginning of our relationship."

He touched her cheek with his thumb and wiped away a tear. "I didn't mean to make you cry."

"When you told me that morning that you knew I wasn't Sherye when you made love to me, I thought I'd disappointed you. I—"

"On the contrary, you showed me what real lovemaking is all about. I woke up the next morning knowing I'd learned something valuable about myself and about you. I couldn't wait for you to wake— But then the phone rang and I discovered the new life I thought I'd discovered was an illusion. Nothing had been real. Except you."

She saw the pain he'd tried to mask and she ached with the need to hold him, to tell him how much that night with him had meant to her. She was touched beyond measure that he had shared his feelings about that night with her. He didn't owe her any explanations, but hearing them made such a difference to her bruised heart.

"Thank you for telling me this, Raoul. It helps, somehow, to know that what I felt that night wasn't one-sided."

They'd had one night together, a night that had opened her eyes to all that she felt for this man. She didn't regret it, not for a moment, but she knew that because of the circumstances, he didn't want to be reminded of what had happened. She cast around in her mind for another subject.

"How are the children?"

"Confused."

"Yes. Of course they would be."

"It's difficult to explain to them what happened and why, since we don't have many answers. It's particularly difficult when they ask questions, since we know so little about you."

"Not even my name or how I came to be in France."

"LeBeau is working on that."

"Yes. He calls almost daily to check with me and see what more I might have remembered."

"You must have friends somewhere who are frantic to know what happened to you."

"I can only recall the one name—Janine."

"Do you think there's a possibility that it's your name?"

"Danielle and I discussed that, but I really don't think so. I see a face, a laughing face, whenever I think of the name."

"I wish there was something more I could do for you."

She forced herself to smile and say, "You're paying for my stay here, which is very generous of you, considering that I was part of a plan to dupe you."

"An unwilling part, I'm sure."

"How can you be so sure? Perhaps Sherye paid me to pretend, then later made certain I wouldn't betray her."

"That possibility has already been offered. I'm ashamed to admit that I briefly considered the idea, but I know better."

"But how? You know nothing about me."

"During the past two weeks I've had a great deal of time to think about all that has happened. It's true that I don't know your name, nor do I know how you became involved. What I realized was how much I've learned about you during the weeks we've been together. I watched you very closely, remember, convinced at first that you were putting on an act for reasons of your own. Gradually, however, I began to see how your mind works. Had I been completely honest with myself I would have admitted—at least to myself—that you couldn't possibly be Sherye. You are incapable of deceit."

"Then you know me better than I know myself." She looked away from him. "I've lain awake nights wondering not only who I am, but what kind of person I am. How could I be a part of something so shameful, involving the children, and Danielle and Felicity, not to mention the problems all of this has caused you? It's so scary, this not knowing."

"Let me reassure you, then. Your name doesn't matter. What matters is how you live your life. I watched you day after day being gentle and kind to those around you who were being harsh and unkind to you. You accepted everyone in the family despite their strong judgments of you. You were not only recovering from a physical and emotional setback, you were attempting to find your way around an alien life-style, if we'd but known, and yet you never took your frustrations out on any of us."

She didn't know what to say.

"I don't know who you are, but I know that during the weeks I spent with you I came to admire you very much. You've become a part of me, a very special part. Regardless of what happens, I want you to know that I will always be your friend. If you ever need anything...anything at all...I want you to contact me. You've taught me and you've taught my children to embrace life with open arms, to enjoy each and every day. Having you with us has been the only bright spot in our lives for a long while. There's nothing that I could do that would adequately repay you. I can only offer you my thanks and my friendship."

"Oh, Raoul," she said, her voice breaking.

He reached for her and pulled her into his arms, holding her tightly. "I didn't mean to upset you. I just wanted to assure you that whatever happens, I don't want you to feel that you have no one to turn to. We want to be your family."

She pulled away from him, holding his hands in hers in an attempt to control her emotionally intense reaction. She couldn't handle being so close to him much longer without giving in to her need to cling to him. She did not have that right. She was not his wife. She was the impostor.

"Thank you for coming to see me, Raoul," she said in an attempt to bring his visit to a close. "It was quite a distance for you to come and I appreciate it."

"So you're sending me away," he said ruefully.

"Yes, because you have other responsibilities now. I don't want to be another one. I appreciate more than I can possibly tell you the fact you came to see me in the midst of getting Sherye settled and dealing with the aftermath of all that has happened. I, too, am grateful to have had the time with you and your family. All of you have added so much to my life. I will never forget you."

He squeezed her hand and reluctantly stood. She followed his movement, not realizing until she stood beside him that she was much too close to him. Hastily she stepped back before she made a fool of herself.

She clasped her hands in front of her. "Take care going home. Give the children my love. I miss them very much."

He stuck his hands into his pockets. "I'm in daily contact with LeBeau, so I will be able to keep up with the way his investigation progresses. In the meantime, please remember—if you need anything...anything at all...call me."

He started toward the door, paused for a moment with his back to her, then turned and in a couple of steps was back in front of her. In an achingly familiar gesture he placed the palms of his hands along her jawline and tipped her face up to his. Disgusted with her lack of willpower, she closed her eyes and allowed herself to savor the touch of his lips on hers for one last time.

With a muffled sound she curved her arms around his waist and held him while his gentle kiss deepened and changed into a searing statement of their explosive emotions.

When he stepped away from her, she was visibly trembling. She caught her bottom lip between her teeth when he brushed a wisp of hair behind her ear.

"Take care of yourself," he murmured.

"I hope Sherye's condition improves soon. I know you'll help her to heal, just as you did me."

She watched him walk out of the room and knew he was walking out of her life, as well. It was necessary. It was the only thing to do. At least they'd had this chance to meet once more, a chance to give their relationship a sense of closure.

She was the only one who knew that when he left, he took her heart with him.

Chapter Thirteen

Her name was Alisha Conrad. She lived at 412 Apache Way in Dallas, Texas. At the moment she was somewhere over the Atlantic, flying to New York with connections to Dallas.

Alisha sighed, wishing she could sleep, tired of thinking about all she had learned about herself in the past few weeks.

The continued regime at the hospital had helped her, but it was Claude LeBeau who had established her missing identity.

His search regarding Sherye DuBois's early childhood had netted as many questions as it had gained results. Convinced it was no mere coincidence that two women could look so startlingly alike, he had gone back to birth records, looking for twin births, adoptions, anything that would give him reasons to suppose that the women were related.

There were no twins born on April 10 of that year, but he had found Sherye's birth certificate easily enough. She'd been born at home to Thelma Hopkins. In the space listed for father's name was the word *unknown*.

What caught his attention was the mother's listed occupation—midwife.

He had systematically followed the records of every baby girl born on or about that date in Dallas County, hiring researchers to follow every lead until they found similar statistics and descriptions.

Eventually they had found that Michael and Anna Matlock had had a daughter they'd named Alisha Marie Matlock. Alisha had been delivered at one of the local hospitals by a doctor whose name was signed at the bottom of the certificate as attending physician. Her vital statistics were similar to Sherye's, but her birth date was listed as April 11.

Because of the time constraints, LeBeau had made no more effort to follow up on a possible connection between Thelma Hopkins and Anna Matlock. Instead he had traced Alisha's records in an attempt to establish whether or not she was the woman they hoped to identify. He'd followed a paper trail through her childhood, her school years and marriage to Dennis Conrad.

Dennis.

As soon as she'd heard Dennis's name, memories had crashed down around her. Dennis had been the key to unlocking her past.

She'd met him during her senior year at SMU. They'd married two weeks after graduation. Four years later he'd been killed when a commercial airline tried to bring a crippled plane in to land at the Dallas-Fort Worth airport. Dennis had been one of twenty passengers killed.

When her memories returned, the pain of her loss felt new, as though she were reliving that time in her life.

It was Janine who had been there for her, Janine who had stayed with her day and night those first few weeks. If Janine had not been with her, Alisha might have died the night she'd miscarried her twelve-week fetus and begun to hemorrhage.

The double loss had been more than she could bear, or so she had thought at the time. Why couldn't she have permanently forgotten that terrible time in her life? What was wrong with having selective amnesia?

At least she would soon be able to see Janine again.

She remembered most of her life now. She remembered when she and Janine had met, both of them freshly out of school, Alisha newly married. They had become instant friends, and the friendship had deepened over the years.

What she couldn't remember was how she had come to be in France, although there was a certain amount of logic in the idea that she might have chosen to spend her summer vacation in the country whose language she had majored in and presently taught.

The problem was, she couldn't remember. There was a gap in time, no more than a week or so, when she could remember nothing. She recalled the last few days of school, when she and Janine were looking forward to having time to themselves.

Janine had been invited to join a group that was going to tour Scotland for the summer months. Alisha had been invited to go, but she'd decided not to travel that year.

What had changed her mind?

So many questions, and so few answers.

Now it was the middle of August. She'd been found near Sherye's burning car the first week in June. The school was closed for the summer. Everyone employed by the school had scattered to enjoy their well-earned summer vacation.

If Janine had followed her itinerary, she should be arriving home within a few days of Alisha. Perhaps Janine could help her reconstruct some of those missing days.

On the other hand, maybe she couldn't.

Alisha knew that she had to find out.

In addition, Alisha intended to do some investigating of her own. She wanted to know more about Thelma Hopkins, the midwife who had given birth to Sherye.

She wanted to find out why the two of them were born in the same city only a day apart to different parents, although they looked like identical twins.

Alisha knew that she had to focus on something to blot out the loss of the family she had acquired in France.

Most of all, she had to forget Raoul DuBois, whose presence in her life had taught her how to love again.

When the taxi let her out in front of her condominium, Alisha felt a sense of anticlimax. She carried only a small bag, having left all but essential toiletries in France.

Everything looked the same and she wondered how she could possibly have forgotten the place she had lived for the past three years. She and Dennis had been renting an apartment when he'd been killed. After she'd lost the baby she had decided the only way she could face each day was to begin somewhere else.

With part of the settlement from the airline and Dennis's insurance, she had bought the condo, determined to make a home for herself, determined to get on with whatever life remained to her.

When she unlocked the door and opened it she found scattered across the floor an enormous stack of mail that had been dropped through the mail slot. She stopped, gathering up the envelopes and magazines, and carried them into the dining room, where she placed them on the table.

Her poor houseplants were dead and there was a film of dust over everything. She wished she could remember leaving here.

She checked the refrigerator and found it empty of anything that might have spoiled. She must have made preparations to be gone for a while.

After stepping out into her small enclosed patio area where the grass seemed to have grown a foot, Alisha felt a little overwhelmed with all that needed to be done. The heat and humidity drove her back inside. She was tired, that's all. Once she got a good night's sleep she'd be ready to tackle the dust and the grass. She'd be glad to have something to keep her busy until it was time for the school year to begin.

She decided to go upstairs and lie down for a while. There was nothing that needed to be done right away. Then she'd make a list of groceries and go out a little later to shop.

Halfway up the stairs the sudden ringing of the phone startled her, causing her to jump. She ran up the rest of the way. Her hand was shaking when she lifted the receiver.

"H'lo?"

"Ah. Then you have arrived safely."

Her knees buckled and she sank onto the side of the bed. What was it about a Frenchman speaking English that was so provocatively sexy? Her pulse rate doubled and she fought to take a calm breath.

"Hello, Raoul."

"When did you arrive home?"

"I've only been here a few minutes." She glanced at the bedside clock. "Maybe half an hour. How did you know when to call?"

"I didn't. The hospital told me you left yesterday and they weren't certain of your travel plans, so I have been calling off and on all day.

"How is Sherye?"

"There is no change."

"I'm sorry to hear that."

"And you? Does everything in Dallas look familiar to you?"

"Oh, yes."

"The doctors say that you've regained most of your memory."

"Yes, except that I can't remember anything about going to France. The last I remember I had intended to spend the summer at home. I don't know why I ended up over there."

"Have you spoken with your friend, what's her—oh, yes, Janine?"

"No. I remembered that she had plans to spend the summer out of the country. She should be back in a few days."

"Perhaps she can help with some of the blank spots that are left in your memory."

"Perhaps."

He sounded so close. She could almost feel his presence. She squeezed her eyes shut, fighting for composure. He didn't need to know how much she missed him.

"I, uh, want you to know that the doctors are preserving your confidentiality. Now that they know we are not connected in any way, they referred me to you if I had any questions. LeBeau gave me the information he'd turned up on you."

"I don't mind your knowing about my life, Raoul."

"I was sorry to hear about your husband. It was very sad how he died."

"Yes. Yes, it was."

"It makes me very angry that you had to go through so much this summer, in addition to what you've had to face in the past."

"It wasn't your fault. Besides, I didn't remember any of it then, and I don't regret my summer in France." Her throat closed and she swallowed. "I will cherish the time I had with you and the children. It was very, very special to me."

"You are certain that you are all right now?"

"Yes. Please don't concern yourself with me, Raoul. I'm a survivor. I'm used to being on my own."

"Of course. I forget about the independence of the liberated American woman."

He was teasing her! She hadn't heard that tone in his voice for such a long while. She laughed, but her laugh caught on a sob.

"Has there been any luck tracing Mario?"

"The police in France and Australia are investigating his role in the matter. As far as I know, he's still being sought for questioning, but I have heard nothing more about the investigation. Until Sherye improves enough to be questioned, there isn't much we can add for them."

"How are the children?"

"They miss you very much. They have accepted that your name is Alisha and that you only look like their mother. Because of your accident, you were told you were their mother. Yvette speaks of you often and asks about you. Jules is too young to understand why you aren't here, of course."

"Give them my love. I'll send them some colorful postcards to let them know I'm thinking of them." She bit down hard on her bottom lip. "This phone call must be costing you a fortune. I appreciate your concern, but I'll be fine now that I'm home. School will begin in a few weeks and I'll soon be back into my regular routine."

There was a silence on the line. She couldn't deal with his feelings as well as her own.

"Goodbye, Raoul," she said in a polite tone of voice. "Thank you for calling. I really must go."

She placed the phone back on the receiver and stared pensively at her last connection to Raoul.

Just as she had expected somewhere deep inside, the château and all those who lived there had been a wonderful dream, one that couldn't last. She was awake now and her real life had to go on just as before.

Three days later the doorbell rang. Alisha already knew who it was because Janine had called earlier to make sure she was home.

There had been several postcards from Janine in the stack of mail waiting for Alisha. She had put them in order by date to get an idea of the places Janine had visited.

Alisha opened the door and smiled at her friend, who seemed to be vibrating with energy and excitement. Janine was already talking as Alisha swung open the door.

"Gawd! But it's great to be home. Boy, did I get homesick. I can hardly wait to—" She had dashed by Alisha and spun around, her words jumbled together in one long rush until she looked at Alisha and came to an abrupt halt, her eyes widening. "What in the world have you done to yourself!"

Alisha frowned. "What? Do you mean my weight? I don't think I've—"

"No-no-no, not your weight. Your hair! What have you done to your hair! It's gorgeous, and the style looks marvelous on you. I've never seen you wear your hair down like that. You look downright glamorous, like some movie star or model or something."

Alisha grinned and shook her head. "C'mon, I'll pour us some iced tea and we'll go catch up on each other's summer."

Janine followed her into the kitchen, still staring. "But it's something else, isn't it? There's something else that's different. I just can't quite put my finger on it. You have a different look about you—softer, maybe. Almost a glow or—I've got it! You met a man while I was gone, didn't you? That's what it is! You're in love. I should have seen it right off. But there's a sadness there, too, that doesn't quite fit with the glow." She tilted her head and lowered one brow. "I can see that it doesn't pay for me to turn my back on you for a minute. You can't be trusted to behave yourself when left alone."

Alisha handed Janine a glass and they wandered into the living room. "You have a point there," Alisha said, sinking into one of the stuffed chairs. "I have a question."

"Shoot."

"Before you left, did I mention anything about going away this summer?"

Janine's eyes narrowed. "Don't you remember? You wrote me a few days after I left. The letter arrived while we were still in Edinburgh."

Alisha leaned forward eagerly. "What did the letter say?"

Janine blinked. "You're asking me? You wrote the thing, don't you remember?"

"I'll explain in a minute. Can you remember what I said?"

"Hmm. It was something about you'd gotten a letter explaining a last-minute speaker cancellation for a teacher's conference in Paris. It was all unexpected, last-minute stuff. You were asked to fill in, your room and airfare were provided, and you'd decided to go."

"Who was sponsoring it?"

"You didn't mention that part."

"Where was it being held?"

"You mean, where in Paris? Gee, I don't know. I don't think you said. Now then, would you mind telling me what this is all about? When I didn't hear from you again I figured you were too busy to write, plus we were moving around so much I thought you might have sent something that never caught up with us."

Alisha stared at her friend in silence for several moments. Janine was her best friend and yet she was having trouble trying to decide how to tell her what had happened. The whole story was too bizarre for words. Finally she leaned back in her chair and said, "I have something to share with you that I don't intend to tell another soul. This will be our secret. It's nobody's business at school how I spent my summer vacation, but I have to tell someone."

She began with waking up in a hospital, not knowing who she was.

She ended with Raoul's phone call on the day she arrived back home.

Janine had not moved or spoken during the entire unfolding of events. She sat there staring at Alisha with her mouth slightly open. When Alisha finished with her story she got up and went into the kitchen, retrieved the iced-tea pitcher and returned to the living room. Janine still hadn't moved.

Once her glass was refilled, Janine picked it up and drank as though she had been the one talking nonstop, as though her throat had gone completely dry.

"That is the most— That is the strangest— Can't you see Catherine Deneuve playing a part like that? Of course, she'd play a dual role. It's really a beautiful... and sad story... and—"

"And I want your help."

"*My* help! What can I do?"

"I want you to help me find out if there's any connection between my birth and Sherye's."

"Do you really think there is?"

"Of course I do! Don't you?"

"But Sherye sounds awful! I mean, she treats her husband like dirt, ignores her kids, she's rude to her sister-in-law, not to mention the fact that she happens to have what sounds like a nasty drug habit—"

"That doesn't mean that we might not be related."

"You don't just mean related, and you know it. You're talking identical twins here, which would be pretty tough to prove considering two different women gave birth to you."

"That's what the birth certificates say, but Sherye's mother was a midwife."

"So?"

"I remember Mother telling me that she had wanted to have me at home and that they had it all planned to have a midwife, but once she was in labor there were complications. My dad called an ambulance and had her rushed to the hospital."

"So?"

"Don't you see? What if the complications included twins?"

"Oh, c'mon, Alisha. Isn't that a little farfetched? I mean, your mom and dad were there, for Pete's sake. Don't you think they would have known how many children she had?"

"Maybe. But they both talked about it later, about how scary it was. The pain was much worse than Mother had expected. My dad had panicked. Who knows what happened? But if I could find out the name of the midwife, and if it was Thelma Hopkins, I certainly think my theory would fly."

"You think there was a baby born at home without your mother's knowledge and the midwife took it?"

"I know it sounds crazy, but there's got to be some kind of explanation why people who knew Sherye well could mistake us."

"Did your parents leave anything in their personal papers that would shed any light on any of this?"

"No. After Dad died, Mom moved to Corpus Christi. I had to go down there after she died and pack everything. All the papers were standard stuff. My birth certificate has nothing unusual. If my mother did have twins, I don't think she ever knew about it."

"How awful."

"Yes."

"Then Sherye could be your sister."

"I think so."

"Which means you're in love with your sister's husband."

"You certainly cut to the heart of the matter, don't you, Janine?"

"Well? That's what we're really talking about here. While you didn't have a memory you lived in Sherye's house with Sherye's husband and children. You, in essence, lived your sister's life."

"My alleged sister."

"Nitpick all you want, old girl, but you're in a real pickle."

"Don't be silly. Everything's been straightened out. Whatever happens, I'm no longer a part of it."

"Don't you care what happens to Sherye?"

"I've been thinking about that. I don't have any particular feeling about her, other than seeing such a wasted life. She's made some pretty poor choices over the years and her life is really messed up. Unfortunately her husband and children are suffering right along with her."

"Don't you want to see her, talk with her, try to get to know her?"

"No. I hope for her sake that she recovers and that she'll be able to get her life straightened out, but I have no desire to have anything to do with her."

"You sound angry."

"I *am* angry. It's my belief that Sherye somehow found out about me. I don't know how or when, but I think she used the fact that she had a twin to put in her place so that she could pull her disappearing act and get away with it. If there was any way I could find out more about the so-called teachers' conference I was asked to attend—all expenses paid—I bet I could prove that Sherye was behind it."

"I hadn't thought of that."

"That's all I've had to think about since I found out that I wasn't Sherye DuBois. She used me, or at least she benefited by my being there. The doctors theorize that I was given some kind of drug that would cause amnesia, at least on a temporary basis. I can't fathom anyone being so wrapped up in their own needs and pleasures that they would manipulate and endanger another person's life."

"So you think she set you up?"

"Absolutely, even if I can't actually prove it."

Janine moved over to the sofa, sat next to Alisha and took her hand. "I'm sorry all of this had to happen to you. You've never done anything to deserve this kind of treatment."

Alisha gave her a weary smile. "Now you sound like Raoul. The worst of it is over for me. He still has to live with it every day, wondering if Sherye's ever going to regain consciousness or whether she'll remain in a coma indefinitely."

"You're very much in love with him, I can see that."

"I never said that."

"You don't have to. It shows every time you mention his name. From everything you've told me, he must feel the same way."

"It doesn't matter how either one of us feels. Nothing can ever come of it. I intend to put all of this behind me. Just to satisfy my own curiosity, I'm going to discover the truth about our respective births. Then I'm putting it all out of my mind. As far as anyone will ever know, I spent the summer here in Dallas. I know nothing about the former model, Sherye, her French husband or her fast life-style."

"Whatever you say. But some things aren't so easily forgotten."

As part of her teaching routine, Alisha regularly scheduled her annual physical the week before school started. She felt ready for her checkup this year. She'd been dragging around the house with no energy since she got home, blaming it on a combination of the heat, the humidity and the residual trauma from her head wound and amnesia. Either that or she had a permanent case of jet lag.

After dutifully turning her body over to the dubious delights of a medical examination, plus answering the doctor's questions and readily admitting to a lingering bout of lethargy, Alisha dressed and waited for the doctor to join her in his office. She hoped he'd offer some helpful suggestions on how she could boost her energy. Otherwise teaching a group of high-spirited girls was going to be a real challenge for her.

She'd been going to the same doctor for years and felt comfortable with him. When he walked into his office looking preoccupied she said, "I won't take up any more of your time, Troy. I know your waiting room's full and I—"

"Sit down, Alisha," he said, walking around his desk to his chair. He tossed her file down in front of him. "I'm never too busy for you, and you know it." He settled comfortably into his chair, tilted his head and looked at her over the top of his rimless glasses. "Besides, I think we need to have a little talk."

She'd made light of her head injury, admitting to occasional headaches that were becoming less frequent and less severe. There was no reason for him to look so worried. Determined to treat the whole thing as lightly as possible, she gave a little chuckle and said, "Uh-oh. I bet I'm anemic, aren't I? Actually, I'm not surprised. I seem to have lost my appetite lately and—"

"Alisha," he quietly interrupted her, "do you remember at the time you had your miscarriage that I told you there was no reason why you couldn't have a healthy, normal pregnancy?"

Pregnancy.

She froze when she heard the word. She'd ignored the possibility. No! She didn't want to think about it! She refused to consider that there was even a remote chance that she could be—

The doctor continued speaking as though what he was reporting was an everyday, run-of-the-mill occurrence. Of course, from his perspective, it was. "You've tested positive for pregnancy, Alisha. I would say you're close to six weeks along, making your due date around the last of March or first part of April."

Alisha stared at him in horror. No. He was mistaken. She couldn't be pregnant. She wasn't married. She was alone. She had a position of responsibility at a girls' school where she was expected to preserve, promote and maintain high moral standards.

Hadn't she had to deal with enough trauma in her life? Hadn't the events of the summer been difficult enough to overcome without long-term repercussions such as an unplanned, potentially explosive pregnancy to complicate matters?

The doctor watched her reactions with concern and compassion. After giving her a few moments to adjust to the obvious complications a pregnancy would create for her, he leaned forward in his chair and said, "As your doctor and as your friend, I guess the question I have to ask you now is—what do you intend to do about it?"

Chapter Fourteen

A strong gust of wind swept over the hillside, rattling the dry leaves that dotted the carefully groomed grounds of the cemetery.

Raoul stood beside the open grave while the priest's voice droned on, barely impinging on his thoughts. He held Jules with one arm while Yvette clutched his other hand with a fierce grip.

Danielle stood next to Yvette, while *Maman* stood beside Raoul. Few people had come to the graveside service. Raoul had kept the news of Sherye's death quiet, not wanting the media to sensationalize the family's troubles.

During the past four months he'd spent most of his time at Sherye's side. He had talked to her during the long hours as though she were aware of his presence. At times he asked questions. At other times he shared his pain and confusion with her.

He told her about Alisha, he asked how Sherye had found her, how she had known of her existence. He promised her help and understanding if she would awaken.

Sherye never gave an indication that she heard him, but over the months he found a certain peace and release in expressing his turmoil over her behavior.

The early-morning call two days ago from the hospital saying that Sherye had slipped away sometime during the night had caught him unprepared to have his bedside vigil over. He'd felt a sense of rage from the knowledge that once again Sherye had escaped the consequences of her actions without ever having to face them. Now as he watched the final scene of her life being played out, Raoul could acknowledge how dearly Sherye had paid for her actions. She'd forfeited her life.

He doubted that he would ever know what drove her to such extreme behavior. It no longer mattered. He recognized his own sense of inadequacy that he hadn't been able to make a difference.

A rumbling in the dark gray clouds overhead drew his attention and he glanced up, hoping that the rain would hold off until the service ended.

He studied the people standing opposite the family. Most of them lived and worked for the château and winery. None of Sherye's friends were there. He had made no effort to contact them, since he hadn't heard or seen anything of them since she was brought back to France.

He had wondered if the man known as Mario would appear. Had he managed to stay in touch with the hospital to monitor Sherye's condition? Did he care? Did he feel any responsibility for what had happened to her?

The priest was concluding his remarks and the casket was slowly being lowered into the ground when Raoul returned his thoughts to the service. Yvette buried her face against his leg. Raoul placed his hand on her head and gently stroked her hair.

Jules had fallen asleep, his head tucked into Raoul's shoulder.

Later the family rode back to the château in silence, each lost in his and her own thoughts. The rain that had been threatening arrived, beating against the limousine Raoul had hired to provide the family transportation. In some way the weather seemed fitting, as though the rain was Mother Nature's tears shed for one of her lost children.

As much as Raoul had attempted to protect the children from the strain of Sherye's death, he knew that Yvette had been deeply affected. The bubbly little girl who had danced across the lawns with her puppy had said very little since the news of her mother's death. Whatever she was feeling, she kept it locked inside.

He knew that she had suffered from the loss of Alisha in her life. She had cried for her, as had Jules. He understood their loss but was helpless to combat it.

You are free now, the tiny voice in his head whispered, repeating a refrain that had been running over and over in his head. He hated the voice, hated the grinding guilt that immediately followed in the wake of the tempting siren's call.

He knew that the medical profession had done everything they could to help Sherye. They had explained that her abused body hadn't been able to fight the long-term effects of her drug use.

He hadn't wanted her to die, even though he knew that he no longer loved her. Perhaps he could have dealt with honest grief better had he still been in love with her. Now his grief was strongly interwoven with guilt.

They arrived at the château and Raoul spent the rest of the afternoon with the children. It was after dinner that night, after *Maman* had gone upstairs, that Danielle asked, "Did you let Alisha know about Sherye?"

They were seated in front of the fire. Raoul had poured each of them a snifter of brandy.

He stared into his glass for a long moment before he answered. "No."

"I think she would want to know, don't you?"

He shrugged. "Perhaps. Then again, perhaps she has already placed all of the unfortunate events of last summer behind her."

"Have you been in contact with her since she returned to her home?"

"Once, on the day she arrived. After that there was no reason to stay in touch. She said that most of her memory had returned, that her home and the city all seemed familiar. Hopefully, she's fully recovered from what happened to her."

"Are you aware she still sends the children notes and small souvenirs from Texas?"

"I would have to be deaf and blind to miss them. The only time Yvette is animated at all is when she's heard from Alisha."

"I was amazed at how quickly she formed a bond with them. Perhaps we should have realized that such an abrupt change in personality could not take place."

"According to the doctors, such changes are not all that unusual for some severely injured people who recover. I thought that Sherye had at long last recognized how much her family meant to her."

"Does Alisha have any children?"

"No."

"That's too bad. She's so good with them."

"All right, Danielle! That's enough. You're about as subtle as a sledgehammer! I doubt very much that Alisha Conrad would appreciate being offered the opportunity to become a permanent stand-in as wife and mother in this household."

Pleased that she had managed to break through his reserve and get him to express what he was feeling, Danielle hid her smile by taking a sip from her glass. After a long silence that seemed to stretch into the shadowy corners of the room, Danielle once again set out to shake Raoul out of his brooding mood.

"How do you know unless you ask her?"

"You're being ridiculous," he muttered.

"And you've buried your head in the sand like a silly ostrich, which tends to put a person into a very awkward stance. You're just asking for someone to come along behind you and kick you in the derriere."

"I take it you're self-appointed for the task."

"If necessary."

"The idea is preposterous. Alisha has her own career, her own circle of friends. She may be involved with someone else by now... possibly married."

"At least you've given the matter some thought."

He leaned his head back against the chair and closed his eyes, realizing how much he'd betrayed himself. For months he had sat beside Sherye and looked for her resemblance to Alisha, finding tiny touches of comfort when he noted them. What a damnably awkward situation. Alisha would never be able to understand that he had felt nothing but contempt for his wife and had only fallen in love when Alisha had taken on the role. He found it a little difficult to understand himself. All he knew was that it had happened.

"I think you owe it to yourself to see her once more now that you are free to make a new life for yourself."

"My God, Danielle, we just buried Sherye a few hours ago!"

"And I watched you for months bury yourself every day at the hospital while you sat by Sherye's side without her ever being aware of your presence."

"We don't know that for certain."

"Are you feeling guilty because you couldn't die along with her?"

"Enough, Danielle. Enough."

She got up and came over to him, kneeling beside his chair. "Stop sacrificing yourself, Raoul. Stop denying your own needs. Anyone who knows you and loves you as I do could see the difference that Alisha made in your life. It was not your fault that you believed her to be Sherye. Sherye herself must have been responsible. Surely you're not blaming Alisha, are you? Do you think she and Sherye planned it together?"

"No! She'd been drugged and struck a severe blow to her head. She could have died. Of course she had nothing to do with it."

"Then the two of you are innocent of everything but the natural and very human act of getting to know each other and falling in love."

"It was nothing so clear-cut as that. Alisha thought she was married to me, so she assumed she loved me. When she found out the truth, I'm sure she was embarrassed, as was I, and would just as soon not be reminded of the awkwardness of our situation."

"That doesn't take into account your feelings, though, does it? Don't you feel that you deserve a chance at happiness after all this time?"

"What is your point, Danielle? God knows you've hammered at this subject long enough. What do you want me to say?"

"I want you to admit your feelings for Alisha, at least to yourself, and then I want you to go see her. Tell her how you feel, find out how she feels. Create an opportunity where you can discuss the matter." She touched his cheek. "You've always been one to fight other people's battles. Now you need to fight for your own happiness."

He shook his head. "I can't believe we're having this conversation today, of all days."

"We are having this conversation today because it's the first time I've had an opportunity to see you for more than five minutes at a time since you returned to France from Australia last summer."

"You're correct in one regard. I spent most of my time during these past few months either at the hospital or with the children and I have a business to run. I don't have time to go dashing about the world chasing fantasies."

Danielle shook her head and stood. "I give up, Raoul. You are a hopeless case."

He looked up at her, his eyes shadowed. "Thank you for caring about me. I appreciate your concern."

"Good night, Raoul. I'm going to bed."

Bright sunshine and temperate air greeted Raoul when he stepped out of the terminal at the Dallas-Fort Worth airport four days after Christmas. He hailed a taxi and gave the driver an address he'd memorized months ago.

Raoul had spent the past two days in New York on business. When he left France he hadn't intended to fly to Dallas. There had been a problem with a major shipment of wine to New York that had been ordered for a New Year's celebration. He had flown to the United States to deal with the matter personally.

The face-to-face meeting with his client had gone a long way toward soothing injured feelings and any misunderstandings that had occurred. He had left the man the evening before, well satisfied with the outcome. The crisis had been successfully averted.

He'd returned to his hotel room with a sense of relief. He'd done what he'd set out to do. Now he could return home, having accomplished his mission. However, instead of immediately arranging for a flight home, his thoughts turned to Alisha.

Here he was in New York, on her side of the Atlantic, after all. A few hours' flight would put him in Dallas. There was nothing to prevent him from dropping by to see how she was doing, was there?

He considered calling her to make certain she was home. Schools were presently closed for the holidays. She could be out of town, visiting friends. He would be foolish to fly to Dallas unless he knew for sure that she would be home.

In the end, however, he didn't call. He knew he was being a coward. He wasn't at all sure she would have invited him to visit if he contacted her. She might not want to see him.

He didn't want to give her a chance to say no.

If she wasn't there, then he would return to the airport, get a room nearby and book a flight out for the next morning. In the meantime he would see the city of Dallas for the first time. He would get to see where Alisha lived.

To be able to visit the area where she lived, worked and spent her days would help him better visualize her life. Besides, he had nothing better to do in the next few days. The family didn't expect to see him until after the first of the year. He would treat the time spent here as a vacation. Even if Alisha wasn't at home, he might rent a car and explore the area on his own.

By the time the taxi turned down the quiet street where she lived, Raoul had convinced himself that it was perfectly natural to casually mention that he had been in the neighborhood and thought he'd stop by to say hello.

He got out of the cab and glanced around. Neatly manicured lawns, lush and green despite the December date, graced the area. He saw several shades of golden flowers in bloom.

"Would you mind waiting until I see if anyone is there?" he asked. Since he gave the driver a large tip along with his fare he wasn't too surprised when the man readily agreed.

Raoul carried his small bag up the walk, carefully set the bag down in an unobtrusive place and rang the doorbell. He waited, but there was no sound of movement inside. There was no sound at all—no music, no voices, no radio or television.

She wasn't home.

Well, what had he expected, after all? he reminded himself. He punched the bell one more time, glanced at his watch, then out to the waiting cab.

He felt as though his body had suddenly gained two hundred additional pounds. He wasn't going to be able to see her, after all. He was leaning over to pick up his bag when he heard a slight noise on the other side of the door.

He spun around in time to hear the bolt of the lock being moved. The door eased open. He fought to control his unruly emotions, which had been bouncing around for the past several hours like a roomful of yo-yos.

It was Alisha. Since the light was behind him, he knew she couldn't see his features clearly. He had a moment to stare at her before she recognized him.

She looked wonderful to him. Absolutely wonderful. She was wearing an emerald green robe that fell from her shoulders like a voluminous tent. She'd cut her hair into a shorter, more casual style and lightened the color to a soft red. He'd forgotten how green her eyes were.

He saw the polite question in her face and heard it in her "Yes?" split seconds before she recognized him. She froze, her eyes widening in shock. "Raoul!"

"Yes. I know I should have called first. It was very impolite of me to show up with no warning, but I—" He stared at her hungrily. "I don't need to ask how you've been. You look won—um—quite well."

She blinked, almost as though she fully expected him to disappear as a result of the action. He grew more anxious. "If you have company or if you are busy I'll just—" He waved his hand halfheartedly at the cab parked out front.

"Oh! I'm sorry, no, it's fine. I mean, you've just surprised me, that's all. I had no idea— What I mean is, you were the last person I expected to see standing on my doorstep."

"Would you mind if I let my taxi go? I'll get another one when I leave, if that's all—"

"Of course. Please. Come in."

He signaled the cabdriver, who saluted and pulled away from the curb.

Alisha stepped back, leaving the door open for him while she led the way into the first room off her hallway. Her lounging robe swirled around her as she turned and faced him. "As you can see, I wasn't expecting company. There's no school this week so I've been rather lazy."

Following her into the room, Raoul walked over to her and took her hands in his. "Please don't apologize. It was inexcusably rude of me not to call."

"Are you here on business?"

"Yes, as a matter of fact. Well, actually, I had to fly to New York on short notice and decided as long as I was there, I'd come on to Dallas on the off chance I might be able to see you."

She blinked again, this time with something like astonishment that he would consider a flight halfway across the country a chance to "drop in."

"Would you like some coffee? Have you eaten? I could—"

"I'm fine. Really. Please, have a seat. I won't stay long. I just wanted to visit for a while, if that's all right."

She sank into a nearby chair as though obeying his command, but she knew it was because her shaking knees would no longer hold her weight.

Dear God, what was she going to do! Raoul DuBois was here. *Here!* Right in her living room. She had never expected to see him again. There had been no reason to ever see him again, certainly not now. Not here.

He sat across from her and she had a chance to study him. He was much thinner than she'd ever seen him, and he looked older. His thick black hair had silvery flecks that were particularly pronounced over his ears.

"How is Sherye?"

His gaze was steady when he said, "She died almost two months ago."

"Oh, no! Oh, I'm so sorry. I didn't know."

"How could you? We kept her passing private. I saw no reason to make a media circus out of the circumstances surrounding her death."

Leaning toward him, she folded her arms and rested them on her knees. "Did she ever regain consciousness?"

"No."

She felt a tearing somewhere deep inside of her, as though something had been ripped away. She'd meant what she'd said to Janine. She'd never known Sherye and had no desire to meet her. Still . . .

Her eyes filled and she fought to control her tears.

"I didn't mean to upset you," he said quietly.

"It isn't that. I mean, of course I'm sorry she never recovered. Who knows how different she might have been if she'd been given another chance. It's just that—" She stopped and cleared her throat. "I've done some amateur sleuthing on my own, with Janine's help. I was able to prove to my own satisfaction that Sherye and I were sisters."

He leaned forward. "You have proof?"

"Looking at us is enough proof, wouldn't you say? I don't believe in that kind of coincidence." She placed her elbows on her knees and propped her chin on her clasped hands, her knuckles white with tension. "I've been in contact with some of my parents' friends, as well as one of our neighbors at the time I was born. They remembered that my mother had insisted on having a home birth. Having a midwife and giving birth naturally was really being talked up back in those days."

His eyes narrowed. "I seem to recall that Sherye's mother was a midwife."

"Yes. Looking back it's clear that Mother wasn't aware she was carrying twins. Obviously Thelma Hopkins didn't tell her that she'd actually given birth to a child by the time the ambulance arrived and whisked her to the hospital, leaving the midwife to stay behind and clean up." Her gaze had gone inward as she recalled what she and Janine had discovered.

"A woman who knew Thelma told me that Thelma once told her that Sherye wasn't really hers. She'd said that Sherye's birth mother was a young unmarried girl who died during childbirth. Rather than turn the baby over to authorities Thelma decided to claim her as her own."

"You mean, no one ever questioned her about it?"

"The authorities had no reason to question a home birth and a single parent registering the birth."

"I wonder if Sherye ever learned the truth?"

"How else did she find me?"

"You mean she contacted you?"

"I don't know. All I know is that according to a letter I wrote to Janine I received an unexpected invitation to a teachers' conference in Paris, all expenses paid. I don't remember going, but it would explain my being in France at that particular time."

"Do you think Sherye had something to do with the invitation you received?"

"It seems likely to me. I don't like to speak ill of her. She's certainly paid for whatever she might have done, but whoever was behind it had carefully planned every detail, including dyeing and restyling my hair. No one but Sherye would have a reason to go to such lengths to duplicate her appearance."

"That's true."

"According to the people I spoke to who knew her, Thelma was always considered a little strange. Look what she did, after all. If she had any kind of conscience it must have eaten at her. From all accounts, she was obsessive about Sherye. I can't imagine what sort of childhood Sherye had under the circumstances."

"Sherye once told me that her mother was the one who was so eager for Sherye to model. That's how she got involved when she was so young."

"Thelma must have wanted to show her off to the world. If so, then she must have felt she successfully reached her goal, regardless of the long-term effects it had on Sherye."

"I can see that this episode didn't end for you once you returned home, did it?"

She shook her head. "I kept thinking about how it was for me growing up. I always wanted to have a brother or sister, but Mother never got pregnant again. If I'd had any idea that I had a sister, one who looked just like me, what a difference that would have made in my life."

"And in hers, as well."

"Yes."

Raoul couldn't keep his eyes off Alisha. There was a glow about her, despite her sad expression, that continued to draw his attention. When she caught him staring at her, he attempted to cover his lapse in good manners by hurrying into speech. "I wasn't at all certain you would want to see me again."

"Why?" She sounded honestly puzzled.

"Because I'm a reminder of what happened to you."

"That works both ways, you know. I'm even more of a reminder to you."

"Not anymore. Not really. You and Sherye have such different personalities that it is easy enough now to see how little you were alike. Physically, Sherye grew very frail during her last months, while you seem to be blooming with good health."

She flushed in embarrassment, which surprised him. He tried to figure out a cause for her uneasiness and kept the conversation simple. "I like your new hairstyle. The softer color is very attractive."

She touched her hair. "I've never worn my hair this short before. I decided to experiment, looking for an easy style to keep." Once again she inexplicably blushed.

There it was again. His presence must be making her uncomfortable, despite her polite acceptance of his unexpected appearance. Raoul glanced at his watch, then got up from the chair. "Well, I've kept you long enough, I'm sure. I just wanted to stop by to see you for a few minutes. The children have been delighted with your cards and letters. You've been very kind to remember them."

Alisha reluctantly came to her feet. "I've missed the children very much," she said softly.

He moved nearer. "And me? Have you missed me at all?"

She looked away, refusing to meet his gaze. "I've missed all of you, of course. I told you before that I enjoyed being a part of the life there at the château."

"Alisha, I know it's too soon to speak of this, and I—"

As soon as he began to speak she turned away from him and for the first time since he'd arrived Raoul saw her figure in full profile. The sight literally took his breath away.

She now had her back to him, walking behind the sofa so that the piece of furniture was between them, effectively shielding her from his view.

"Please don't say anything, Raoul," she said quickly. "I appreciate your stopping by and I..." She paused and lifted her chin slightly before calmly continuing. "We can't pretend that Sherye didn't exist, nor can we pretend that I don't bear an uncanny resemblance to her."

Raoul interrupted her, growling, "Why not? Aren't you busy pretending that you're not pregnant with my child?"

Chapter Fifteen

She hadn't really thought she'd be able to hide her condition from him. Actually, she'd been unable to think at all from the time she opened the door and saw Raoul DuBois standing on her front steps.

She'd hoped the casual robe she wore would be enough camouflage to give her time to adjust to his presence, as well as time to come up with the explanation he was sure to demand when he discovered her condition.

She'd just run out of time.

The unexpected news about Sherye had distracted her from the ominous realization that she'd made a serious error in judgment when she'd decided not to notify Raoul when she first found out that she was going to have his baby. Janine had warned her at the time that she would be sorry if she decided not to tell him. She'd pointed out that he sounded like the type of man who would insist on his rights as well as on taking care of his responsibilities. She'd also pointed out that he didn't sound like the type of man Alisha would want to antagonize if it could be avoided.

There was nothing more annoying than to have a friend who was invariably right.

Now that Raoul was here in her living room looking his most intimidating, Alisha discovered that she would have much preferred to discuss the subject with him with an ocean between them rather than a sofa.

Unfortunately her discovery was too late.

Raoul stalked around the sofa, so that she lost even that dubious protection from his thunderous gaze.

She took a deep breath, held it, then slowly released the air in her lungs, intent on finding and hanging on to some semblance of calm. "You surprised me," she admitted with a hint of a shrug. "I didn't know what to say."

"I surprised *you!*" He took her by the arm and guided her around the sofa, silently indicating that she should sit down. He sat beside her, facing her so that their knees touched. She could feel the heat radiating from his body. "Why didn't you *tell* me!"

How could she have imagined such a scene? She had never expected to see him again. She tried to pull her chaotic thoughts together to form some semblance of order.

"I seriously considered contacting you when I first learned about it, but so much had happened. You already had so much to deal with that I thought—"

"You're saying you didn't want to tell me because you wanted to protect *me?*"

"Well, yes, that was part of it. You aren't responsible—"

"If I'm not responsible, then who is? Oh, and if you're going to try to convince me of another immaculate conception, you're wasting your breath. I know exactly who's responsible."

"I didn't mean— What I was trying—"

Unable to sit still, Raoul left the sofa and strode across the room, running his hand through his hair. He spun around and faced her. "What an unthinking fool I've been. I never gave the possibility of pregnancy a thought. Not once! I let you walk out of my life without once considering the fact that you could be carrying my child."

"Well, you—"

"When is it due?"

"Will...you...please...stop...interrupting...me?" she shouted, jumping to her feet.

He froze and stared at her as though she had metamorphosed into an alien monster creature.

He was close.

She couldn't remember when she'd been so angry. He wouldn't give her a chance to explain, to defend her actions, or to offer her apologies. Raoul DuBois might be the unanointed ruler of his own private kingdom in France, but he was in her home at the moment and he was badgering her.

Enough was enough.

She seated herself once again and folded her hands in her lap. "Now then," she said in a quiet—a very quiet—voice. "I can understand that you're upset, but if you will attempt to calm down for a moment, I'm confident that we can discuss the matter like two rational adults."

He strode over to the window and glared at the unsuspecting view, grasping his hands at his back. "Don't count on it," he muttered between clenched teeth.

She took another deep breath and began to speak. "I found out I was pregnant when I went for my annual pre-school-year medical checkup in August—"

He spun on his heel, redirecting the glare to her side of the room. "August! You've known *for months and didn't find it necessary to—*"

She held up her hand much like a policeman stopping traffic. A muscle in his jaw jumped, but he said nothing more.

"I'd only been home a couple of weeks at that time. I knew that Sherye was in the hospital and that she was your first priority."

"Don't be ridiculous! I'm just as responsible for your condition as you are. Even though we thought we were married to each other at the time, I should have—"

Once again she held up her hand until he stopped talking. "I know what we thought at the time, but we were wrong. You were legally married to another woman. You are an honorable man. There was no reason to cause you any more problems than those with which you were already dealing. You see, there was nothing you could do at that point."

He looked at her in disgust. "So you were going to blithely carry on without any help."

She eyed him for a moment before making a sudden decision. "Very few people know this... and it isn't something I can talk about very easily... but I had a miscarriage not long after my husband was killed. Had I managed to carry that baby full term I was fully prepared to be both mother and father to it. I was devastated when I lost it. I knew that I wouldn't have any help, since both my parents and Dennis's parents were gone. But it didn't matter, then. I wanted very much to have my baby." She rested her hand on her softly rounded belly. "I still do," she said softly. "I don't deny that I was shocked to discover I was pregnant. I'd lost track of time and the possibility of a pregnancy had never entered my mind. But once I overcame the shock, I felt that God had given me another chance to have the family I've always wanted."

He studied her for a moment in silence, then sat in the chair across from her. She continued in a steady voice, praying he would understand why she'd made the choices she had.

"Because of the circumstances that occurred this summer, I knew there was very little you could do other than to help me financially. I don't need financial help. I'm perfectly able to care for myself. I teach because I enjoy teaching, not because I need to work." She gave him a rueful glance before saying, "I'll admit I told my classes that I had gotten married unexpectedly this summer—to a European who would not be moving to the States. I intimated that I would be spending my summers in France." She smiled, remembering that day. "I must say they found it all extremely romantic."

Raoul took his first deep breath since he'd discovered her secret. "Thank God for that. At least it will make things a little—"

She held up her hand and he stopped speaking as though she'd physically covered his mouth with her hand. In a very gentle voice she said, "I made up the story, Raoul. It is fiction...a fairy tale...something to protect the baby."

"Granted, but close enough to the truth."

"Close only counts in horseshoes and hand grenades, Raoul. As you know very well, we are not married. We were never married."

He gave her a heartwarming smile and said, "Which we can remedy immediately."

Sadly she shook her head. "I should have known that you'd feel honor bound to marry me if you could."

"True. I do feel honor bound. I can marry you...and I intend to marry you."

"No, you can't. Sherye's only been dead—"

"I can't concern myself about the conventions of the matter when there's a bigger issue here. You are carrying my child."

Of course she had known that he would feel possessive toward the child. She had gotten to know Raoul DuBois rather well last summer. In a conciliatory voice she replied, "Yes. I know that. Perhaps next summer if everything works out I can fly over to visit with you and the family."

Once again he gave her a look that conveyed quite convincingly that he thought she had lost her mind. "You're joking, right? This is your idea of a joke. You will come to visit us during summer vacations and bring my child with you? How very thoughtful of you. So kind."

"Please don't be sarcastic."

"Then please stop being so ridiculous."

"I'm not. There are many children who only live with one parent, but that doesn't mean they can't learn to love both parents."

"You're being unreasonable."

"Not at all."

"I disagree with your logic."

"A marriage would not work between us."

"How can you say that!" he shouted, then paused when he saw the look in her eye. In a deliberate whisper he leaned toward her and said, "How can you possibly *say* that when we had a perfectly acceptable, enjoyable marriage last summer?" He gestured toward her protruding stomach. "How else do you explain, even justify, how you got into this condition? We obviously enjoyed each other's company. My mother and sister admire you, my children adore you. Getting married is the absolute best solution."

She was beginning to realize that she wasn't in control of this conversation. With a hint of desperation she said, "But don't you see? Marriage is totally unnecessary. I know you're a proud man, Raoul, and you always face up to your responsibilities. Well, I intend to face up to mine, as well." Unable to sit still she rose and stepped behind the sofa once again. Placing her hands lightly on the back for support, she said, "I really think we've covered everything that needs to be said." She fought to keep the tremor from her voice.

"Thank you for stopping by. Please give the children a hug for me. Tell *Maman* and Danielle hello."

He stood and stared at her for a long, tension-filled silence. "You're right. You're not like Sherye. Even she would never have been so cruel as to deprive me of my child. I feel very sorry for you, Alisha. You are so determined to have your independence that you are refusing to see what you are doing to everyone else involved. You didn't become pregnant on your own. Our baby deserves a great deal more than you're willing to offer it. Our baby has a right to grow up with its brother and sister, to be a part of a loving family, but you in your wisdom—" he spit out the word "—feel justified in making godlike decisions for this innocent being."

She felt each word as a blow to her heart. Our baby. She had never thought of it that way. As soon as she'd learned of her pregnancy, it had become *her* baby, much as she'd felt about the baby she'd carried during those weeks after Dennis had died.

When she'd found out about this pregnancy Raoul had been dead to her, as well.

She loved him. Of course she did. But she hadn't considered the possibility of marrying him, even if he had ended up divorcing Sherye. The thought that Sherye wouldn't recover was one she'd refused to consider.

Now she had to face the unthinkable— Sherye was gone and Raoul was here, demanding in his usual arrogant manner to be allowed to do the "right thing." Was it fair to her baby, to their baby, for her to refuse him?

"Will you give me a little time to think about your offer?" she asked, her voice echoing in the tension-packed room.

His steadfast gaze touched her like a laser beam of light—probing, dissecting, judging. "If it will help you better understand my position in this matter, yes. If you intend to use the time to marshal more arguments against me, don't bother. I cannot force you to marry me. I can't think of anything that would be more inappropriate, given our peculiar circumstances. If you feel that being married to me will make you as unhappy as it obviously made Sherye, I'll leave now and promise to stay out of your life."

His bleak words and matter-of-fact tone wrenched her heart. Of course he was angry with her. She had handled today's unexpected meeting very badly. "I think we both need a little cooling-off time," she said carefully. "Our circumstances have changed dramatically. You've had two months to adjust to Sherye's death. I've only had a few hours."

Raoul became aware of how pale she was. He was still getting over the shock of learning she was pregnant and learning that she had lost a baby earlier. How could he have lost his temper with her in her condition? What if she lost this baby? What if he didn't have her pregnancy as leverage to coax her into marrying him?

He shook his head, disgusted with his behavior. Once again he approached her, this time stroking her cheek with his thumb. "I'm being an unmitigated ass, yelling at you...upsetting you." He brushed his lips across hers. "I'm sorry. I'm never quite in control of my behavior when I'm around you. You trigger my deepest emotional reactions."

His sudden and unexpected tenderness almost undid her. "I should have realized how you would feel being confronted by the news without warning," she said, finding his nearness extremely distracting.

"I will give you all the time in the world to decide what you wish to do and I promise to accept your decision, whatever it may be." Once again he gave her a light kiss. "For now, I will request the use of a phone to call a taxi and give you some space. Perhaps, if you don't mind, I will call you tomorrow to see what you have to say, hmm?"

Darn him. He knew very well how to charm her into agreeing to anything—to everything—he wanted.

"There's, uh, there's really no need for you to leave. What I mean is, I have plenty of room if you'd like to stay here."

"Are you sure that's what you want?"

"Well, it's rather silly to have you look for a place to stay, given our circumstances. Come. I'll show you the guest room and then I'll dress. You must be hungry by now. I can fix you something—"

"I would rather take you to dinner, if you don't mind. There's no reason for you to put yourself out, just because I dropped in unannounced."

"If that's what you want."

"Yes. Yes, it is."

She studied him for a moment, then nodded, walking toward the hall. He followed her and waited while she opened one of the doors for him. She gave him a brief, rather distracted smile, then turned and walked to the end of the hallway, where she opened the last door, closing it quietly behind her.

Raoul knew that the next few hours would be the most important ones he'd had to face. It was up to him to convince her to believe that they could make a relationship work, regardless of the irregularity of its beginning.

He retrieved his bag in the hallway and placed it in his room. The enormity of what he'd just learned hit him, causing his knees to buckle. Fortunately there was a chair nearby.

The most miraculous experience of his life had resulted in the beginning of another child. In the midst of tragedy and wasted lives, God had seen fit to offer him new hope and new dreams. He had to do everything in his power to win Alisha's trust and her love.

They had stayed out later than Alisha had expected, lingering over coffee and dessert while she shared some of her memories of growing up in Dallas, her schooling, a few things about her marriage and how she felt about teaching young daughters of prominent families.

Raoul had seemed engrossed in everything she had to say. How could she resist the captivating and flattering attention he'd given her all evening? He had driven them to and from a favorite restaurant of hers, following her directions without a sense of strain.

They pulled in to her garage and he helped her out of the car. "I'm sorry for keeping you up so late," he said when she fought to stifle a yawn.

She laughed. "I've enjoyed every minute of it. I'm just used to going to bed early because of my teaching schedule. I can sleep in tomorrow if I feel the need."

They stepped into her kitchen through the connecting door between the garage and her condo. "I enjoyed putting the frame of your background in context with the woman I know today. Thank you for sharing it with me."

She grinned. "I'll admit it's much more comfortable now that I have most of my memories, although talking about them reminds me of how ordinary my life has been." She glanced up at him, then quickly away. "Meeting you under such strange circumstances has been the most dramatic thing that has ever happened to me."

"If you'll excuse me," he said in a lazy tone, "there's something I've wanted to do all evening." Taking his time, he pulled her into his arms and kissed her. When she didn't resist, he held her closer, deepening the kiss.

This was what she'd been afraid of, Alisha told herself, in the back of her mind. This was also what she'd wanted very much. The rights and wrongs of their relationship were too much for her to deal with just then, and she gave herself to the moment.

When Raoul picked her up she didn't resist. Instead she clasped her arms around his neck and allowed him to carry her into her bedroom. There he carefully removed each item of clothing that she wore, placing kisses on each area of her body that was revealed, until he had her completely uncovered.

He pulled back the covers and placed her on the bed, then ran his fingers lightly over the contours of her body, coming to rest on her stomach. "You are so beautiful. I noticed the glow about you right away without understanding it. Perhaps it is wrong of me, but I am glad you are carrying my child. I am grateful that a part of me is now a part of you. I love you, Alisha, even before I understood who it was that I loved. I think I began to topple when you decided that if I was your husband that you had great taste in men."

She made no effort to cover her body, reveling in his enjoyment of her. When he reminded her of her embarrassing remark from her early days in the hospital, she couldn't control her blush. "I was hoping I hadn't really said that out loud," she admitted.

He grinned. "It was a startling comment totally out of character for my wife to make. Never wonder why I want to marry you, Alisha. I want you in my life because it is you that I love. The baby adds some urgency to the need, that's all."

"I've promised to work until the end of February."

"All right. I will return home and prepare the family, as well as take care of some business matters, then I'll come back here and stay with you until you are ready to go home with me."

"You'd do that for me?" she asked.

"There's no limit to what I'd do for you. You have become my heart. I do not want to be without you for any longer than absolutely necessary."

She leaned up on one elbow and reached for his tie. "One of us is wearing entirely too many clothes."

He smiled. "Does that mean you agree with my plans?"

Coming up on her knees, she pushed his jacket off his shoulders and began to unbutton his shirt. "I've always had a weakness for anything French. How can I possibly resist you?"

Chapter Sixteen

Once again she was returning to the French château with her husband, Raoul DuBois. However, there were several differences from the first time she had turned through the stone gateway and followed the paved driveway to its end.

Summer had dotted the landscape with lushness the first time she'd entered those gates. Now winter had its grip on the surroundings.

She'd come the first time with no memories of the place and with the name Sherye DuBois. Now she had a great many memories of the place—wonderfully fulfilling memories—and she knew that her name was Alisha Conrad DuBois. She wore the wedding ring that confirmed it.

The first time she'd come here she'd been confused and a little afraid. Her confusion was gone, her fear was gone, but there was a residue of anxiety that still clung to her.

Raoul had reassured her that the family was looking forward to her arrival. He had convinced her to discuss with her boss the possibility of having her replacement take over the first of February. Then Raoul had come back to Dallas in time to appear at the school to meet her students and to allow them to practice their French with him. Every single one of them had fallen madly in love with him.

Who could blame them?

After overseeing the packing and shipping of those items she wanted to keep, Raoul had helped her to list her condo with a real estate agent and found a buyer for her car.

His help had been a godsend and she had found herself falling more in love with him each day, even though she'd protested his high-handed suggestion soon after she agreed to marry him that they be married immediately. Nothing she said could sway him from his determination to have her his wife at the first opportunity.

She still felt their marriage was too soon, despite her increasing girth, but she had given in because he'd been so adamant.

When they'd arrived in Paris he'd surprised her by announcing that they would be staying in the city for at least a week because he wanted a honeymoon with her. He'd also arranged for her to order a new wardrobe, pieces that she could wear in comfort for the remainder of her pregnancy as well as other things for immediately afterward.

He wanted her to fill her closet with items that she personally had chosen, and she had been whisked around the city for measurements, fittings and some sight-seeing. However, he'd made certain that she spent a considerable part of that time in bed.

Resting was only part of his carefully planned agenda while she was there.

By the time they reached the château Alisha felt pampered and well loved by the man who sat beside her in the car. She glanced at him, delighted to see how much better he looked now than he had little more than a month ago.

Besides looking more rested, he had gained back some of his weight, although he still appeared too thin to her. He smiled more now, which softened the rather harsh lines that had appeared on his face.

"Why are you looking at me?" he asked without taking his eyes off the road.

"I enjoy looking at you," she promptly replied. "Don't tell me it makes you nervous?"

"And if it did?"

She laughed. "I'll never believe that anything ever makes you nervous."

"You'd be surprised."

The truth was that she was the one who was a little nervous about the upcoming reunion with his family. "You did tell them that I was pregnant, didn't you?" she asked, more for reassurance than real concern.

He snapped his fingers. "I *knew* there was something I was supposed to do."

When he didn't look at her, she leaned forward to see his eyes. As soon as she did, she made a fist and hit him on the shoulder. "Oh, you!"

"I'm certain I'm wasting my breath, but I would like to point out that it really doesn't matter what anyone else thinks, you know."

Alisha nibbled on her bottom lip. "In theory, that's true. Practically speaking, it makes a big difference to me."

They pulled up and stopped at the front door. He immediately got out of the car and came around to help her out. She was rapidly becoming a size where she actually needed the help, particularly in a small car.

They were still in the foyer when Danielle came out of the salon. "I thought I heard you!" she said, dancing toward them. She hugged Alisha. "Oh, it's so good to have you back here." She drew back and looked at Alisha. "You're positively glowing with good health."

"I told you," Raoul pointed out, as though he was personally responsible for her condition, Alisha decided. Actually, he probably was, for the most part.

"You're looking rather glowing yourself," she said to Danielle.

Danielle laughed and held out her hand for Alisha to inspect the sparkling ring she wore. "For good reason. You've arrived just in time to help me plan a wedding!"

"That's marvelous! Oh, Danielle, I'm so happy for you." Alisha gave her another hug.

"It would never have happened without you," Danielle said, her eyes sparkling.

"Me! I haven't even been here."

"But you were here last summer and you befriended me, made me feel like I'm attractive, even if I'm not beautiful like you."

"Oh, Danielle. I can't believe you ever thought you weren't beautiful." Alisha looked up at Raoul. "Would you listen to her?"

Raoul hugged his sister, dutifully admired her ring and said, "I'm ready for something to eat and a chance to relax in front of a warm fire." He took each woman's arm and escorted them into the salon. "Ah, there you are, *Maman.*"

The older woman stood and faced them, her eyes on Alisha's protruding stomach. Slowly she raised her gaze until it locked with Alisha's.

Alisha didn't know what to say. She didn't know how to handle the blatant once-over. Then her jaw dropped when Felicity gave her a welcoming smile and held out her hands. "You must be very tired after your trip. Come, sit here by the fire and tell me how you've been doing. I want to hear all about Dallas and your students. Yvette has shared every card and letter with us."

Alisha walked over to the older woman and put her arms around her. "Thank you, *Maman.* It's wonderful to be home again."

The same thought continued to run through her head several days later when she lay in Raoul's massive bed, waking up after a restful night of sleeping with his arms around her, holding her close.

All of her nightmares had been fought and dealt with. The children were so happy to see her. She couldn't get over the changes in them. Yvette was now going to school. Jules was no longer a baby. Instead he was a sturdy little boy with a very stubborn mind-set. He knew exactly what he wanted at all times and fought to get it, a trait he'd obviously inherited from his strong-willed father.

She stretched, missing Raoul. He'd left early, promising to be home early this evening. He'd insisted there was no reason for her to get up so early and she had obligingly gone back to sleep.

Everyone treated her with loving attention. No one referred to Sherye, or how Alisha had come to be at the château in her stead last summer.

Yesterday she had driven to the cemetery to visit Sherye's grave. She'd stood there a long time, and when she had left she'd determined to leave the past there in that peaceful spot.

The baby decided to shift at that moment and Alisha smiled, rubbing the spot and feeling a wealth of love and contentment sweep over her.

Driven by hunger more than a great desire for activity, Alisha forced herself to get up and face the day. When she reached the dining room, her setting was the only one left. Obviously everyone else in the household had been and gone.

She filled her plate with brioches and croissants and sat down, noticing for the first time there was a letter beside her place. Janine must have written almost as soon as Alisha had left Dallas.

She picked up the letter, smiling, before she really looked at it. Only then did she note that it had been posted in

France and that the handwriting was unfamiliar. The letter was addressed to Madame Raoul DuBois. Puzzled, she opened the envelope, and several sheets of paper fell out.

As soon as she unfolded them she froze, staring at the top line with a sense of dread. Reluctantly she scanned the expensive paper containing the slashing scrawl.

Dear Sherye,

So you think you're too good to acknowledge an old friend, do you? Saw you earlier this week in Paris. You sailed past me like you'd never laid eyes on me. Sorry, babe, but it won't work.

I was glad to see you up and about these days. I don't mind admitting you had me a little worried with that fainting act you pulled last summer. From the looks of things you've decided to cozy up to the unsuspecting hubby. Nice try, but then you've always been a ballsy woman.

You owe me big time, babe. You missed the last two quarterly payments and it's getting hungry around these parts. I'll expect to see you at the usual place on Friday.

You wouldn't want me to tell the unsuspecting hubby just whose baby you're carrying, now would you?

Ciao,
M

Alisha had trouble reading the last few lines because the paper was moving. Only then did she realize she was shaking.

Somebody thought that she was Sherye. From the tone of this letter it must be the man known as Mario. She had seen him in Paris! She'd actually walked past him, unaware of his identity. Had Raoul been with her? She thought back over the week in Paris. He must have been. She'd never gone anywhere alone.

That's why he hadn't approached her.

He wanted money, and he didn't know that Sherye was dead.

She stared at the letter for a long time, trying to decide what to do about it. Her first thought was to ignore it completely. He couldn't hurt her. Raoul would quickly see that the man was arrested.

Wasn't any of this going to end? The nightmarish quality kept creeping back, despite all she could do to keep the past in proper perspective.

"Ah, there you are," Danielle said, coming into the dining room. "Mind if I join you? I'm ready for a cup of coffee and some advice."

Alisha tucked the letter into a pocket. "I don't know how helpful my advice will be, but I'm certainly willing."

Danielle filled a cup from a carafe and sat across from her. "Are you sorry that Raoul pushed you into a quick wedding?"

"Not sorry, exactly, but I felt it was somewhat rushed."

"No, I mean, didn't you want a big wedding with a long invitation list and bridesmaids?"

"That would have been totally inappropriate under the circumstances, but even without that, I preferred a small ceremony. My first wedding was headache enough with the friends and the few family members we had attending."

Danielle leaned over the table and said, "You know that very few people realize that you aren't Sherye. Because we kept her illness and death so quiet, people assumed she was away. Now that you're here, they think everything's back to normal."

"I'm beginning to realize that. I'm not sure how to handle it."

"Do you have to? I mean, it's really no one's business. I realize we're protecting Sherye's reputation as well as our own, but it seems so needless to put the children through any more heartache."

Alisha forced herself to eat a few bites before she said, "What about Sherye's friends?"

"It's obvious they weren't friends in any real sense of the word. No one ever tried to contact her. Whoever she was traveling with obviously didn't want to be involved in what happened to her. That one fellow was the only person who gave us any information and he refused to name any of the others on board the yacht."

"Danielle, did Sherye ever mention Mario to you?"

"Sherye never spoke to me about anything, why?"

"I just wondered."

"Oh, I meant to see if you'd like to go shopping with me tomorrow. I want to have my hair trimmed and I thought we could have lunch, then browse. I need your idea on the type of gowns we could have for the bridesmaids. Plus, we want something special for Yvette and Jules to wear."

Alisha smiled. "I'm not getting around very fast these days, but I'd enjoy going with you."

"Good. Now, then. Here's some ideas I have about the wedding invitations."

Alisha forced herself to listen to her sister-in-law and to forget about the letter that seemed to be singeing her pocket.

Alisha was thankful for the mild weather the next afternoon. She and Danielle had been in several stores before time for Danielle's hair appointment. They agreed to meet at the restaurant at an appropriate time and Alisha wandered through the shops, admiring the lace and looking at baby clothes.

Because she was tired of being on her feet, Alisha arrived at the restaurant early, thankfully finding a booth and ordering coffee. What a relief to sit down. She knew her ankles were swelling, even though she rarely caught a glimpse of her feet these days. Absently she rubbed her stomach and closed her eyes.

"Did you get my letter?"

Alisha opened her eyes and stared across the small tabl at the man who seemed to have materialized out of thin ai

"Where did you come from?"

"I saw you on the street and decided to follow you. Whe you came in here, I figured it was a good chance to say hell and make sure you got my letter."

Alisha looked at the man, trying to remember if she ha ever seen him before. His skin was swarthy and he ha glossy black hair and equally black eyes. He wore an obvi ously expensive suit and from his smile it was also obviou that he knew how good he looked. There was no denyin that he was a very attractive man, if you cared for the type To Alisha, there was no contest between this man an Raoul.

She didn't like the familiar way he was looking at her. Sh felt that he had stripped her with his eyes in one glance an obviously liked what he saw.

"Look, you've made a mistake—"

"No, Sherye, you're the one making the mistake if yo think you can just brush me off like that. You and me g back a long way, babe, a long way. Don't you forget i Haven't I always been there for you? Haven't I always riske everything for you? Hell, I even found that teacher dam that was your spittin' image, didn't I? Well, don't forget doll face, that we both pulled that one off, and we could'v gotten into some big trouble if the truth had ever come out." He laughed. "But it never did, huh? Damn, but you've go a devious mind. What a stunt to pull. I checked with m friends in Dallas last fall, you know the ones. Their daugh ter goes to that fancy school where the gal teaches. They sai she was still there teaching school. So what did you tell her Did you explain that it was a gag, that we didn't mean an harm?" He leaned back in his chair, crossed his arms an grinned at her. "From the looks of things ol' Raoul neve suspected a thing. You're really something else."

"Ah, there you are. I'm sorry I was late, but there was this—" Danielle realized that Alisha wasn't alone and stopped talking. During the pause Alisha jumped to her feet and grabbed Danielle's arm.

"Don't worry. I think we'll still make our next appointment." She nodded at the man who was slowly pushing back his chair. "Don't bother getting up. I hope you enjoy your lunch." She practically dragged Danielle through the front door, out on the street and was almost running to the car.

"Alisha, what in the world is wrong with you? Have you lost your mind? If you don't slow down, you're going to trip and fall. What is the matter?"

"Please, just get in the car. I'll explain as soon as we're gone. Please!"

Danielle took one look at Alisha's face and said nothing more until they were in the car and moving. "All right, tell me."

"Would you mind driving me to the winery? I've got to see Raoul right away. I'd hoped we could just ignore it, but I can't handle this on my own. I've got to talk with him."

"Yes, of course. Who was that man back there? Did you know him?"

"No, no, I didn't. I'll answer all your questions once we get to Raoul's office, okay?"

Alisha could feel her heart pounding and she concentrated on slowing her breathing before she began to hyperventilate.

What a bizarre situation. Once again she was being mistaken for Sherye, by the very man who had helped to arrange the first switch. She didn't know what to do. All she knew was that she had to reach Raoul. He would know how to handle this.

Thank God she had Raoul.

Chapter Seventeen

Raoul was talking on the telephone when Alisha and Danielle arrived. He waved them into his office with a smile, finished his conversation, then came around the desk and put his arms around Alisha. As though he couldn't resist the opportunity, he kissed her rather thoroughly before looking over at his sister with a grin.

"This is quite an honor, having you drop by to visit. Have you eaten?"

Before Alisha could gather her wits after that blatantly sensual kiss, Danielle spoke up. "No, we haven't. If there's anything around here to nibble on, I'd appreciate it, because I for one am starved."

Raoul looked back at Alisha with a puzzled frown. "I thought the two of you planned to have lunch out today."

"We did, but—" She tried to think of a way to begin the story she had to tell him.

"We had unexpected company at our lunch meeting," Danielle said. "Alisha was upset, so..."

He looked down at her. He must have seen something in her expression because he immediately led her to a chair. "What happened?"

"Mario is here."

"Mario?"

"The man with Sherye."

Raoul stiffened. He nodded at Danielle to sit down, then leaned against his desk and folded his arms. "How do you know?"

Alisha felt so awkward. "I—actually, Sherye—received a letter from him yesterday."

Raoul lifted his brow. "Oh?" he asked in a neutral tone.

"The letter was addressed to Madame Raoul DuBois, so I opened it. The salutation was to Sherye and it was signed with an *M*. He said he saw me on the street in Paris and that I ignored him. He reminded me that I hadn't paid him the past two quarters and told me to meet him at our usual place. Otherwise he would tell you who fathered my baby."

Danielle gave a small gasp but said nothing. Raoul eyed her thoughtfully. "Why didn't you show me the letter?"

She had known he would ask that question. Impatiently she replied, "Because I chose to ignore it and saw no point in bringing it to your attention. There was no return address on the letter—no way to report his whereabouts. Since I had no idea where the usual meeting place was, I hoped that if I didn't show up he would leave me alone, assuming I was no longer interested in him."

"You mean that Sherye was no longer interested."

"Yes."

"So he isn't aware that Sherye died," he mused.

"Obviously not."

"What happened today?"

"He said he saw me on the street and followed me to the restaurant where I was to meet Danielle for lunch. He brought up all the things he'd done for me—for Sherye—

including finding the schoolteacher. He wanted to know if you'd ever discovered the switch."

"Did you tell him who you were?"

"No. I couldn't think, I was so unnerved. As soon as Danielle arrived I made an excuse about having to go. We left immediately and drove straight here to tell you what had happened."

"I appreciate your including me." His bland tone didn't fool either woman.

Danielle said, "Raoul—" but stopped abruptly when he turned his gaze on her. When she said no more, he returned his attention to Alisha.

"I'll notify the authorities that Mario's in the area. Perhaps you could give me a description of him."

His voice remained smooth but Alisha could see he was exerting a great deal of control over his temper. All right, so she should have told him about the letter. She'd made a wrong choice. Now wasn't the time to apologize or explain any further. She'd done what she thought was best, after all.

Alisha gave Raoul a description of the man who'd sat down across from her. When she finished he repeated one of her words.

"Attractive?"

"Yes."

He glanced at Danielle as though to confirm Alisha's assessment and Danielle nodded.

"Is there anything else either of you can think of to help the authorities find him?"

After a long pause Alisha shook her head.

Raoul straightened. "Then I suggest the two of you go home and I'll discuss the matter with you when I get there. In the meantime, I'll give the information to the police."

He made no attempt to kiss Alisha goodbye.

The women wasted no time leaving his office.

"Whew! He was furious," Alisha said once they were in the car and Danielle was driving them home.

"He was worried about you and it showed."

"He's got such a temper!"

"Which he controlled admirably," Danielle pointed out dryly. "Under the circumstances."

"I know," Alisha admitted. "I should have told him about the letter."

"You didn't know that at the time. I happen to agree with you. What point was there in reminding him that his wife was seeing another man?"

"Exactly my reaction." She glanced at Danielle. "I've been trying to put the past behind us and build a new life with Raoul. I know it must be difficult for him to have me in his life as a daily reminder of his first marriage."

"I think you're more self-conscious about the situation than anyone," Danielle said, watching traffic. "Yes, you look like Sherye. There isn't much you can do about that. However, you need to remember that the family had several weeks to get to know you, Alisha. You helped us to overcome our reactions to Sherye. When we look at you now, we see Alisha. I know it's difficult for you to believe that, but it's true."

Alisha touched her sister-in-law's arm. "Thank you for saying that. At the moment I'm feeling anything but secure. Raoul married me because of my pregnancy and I—" She stopped speaking because Danielle laughed. "What's the matter?"

"I'm sorry, I didn't mean to be rude," Danielle replied, still chuckling. "I was just amused that you think Raoul married you because of the baby."

"He's an honorable man."

"And he loves you, Alisha. You. It's so obvious to the rest of us. You would have had to know what Raoul was like before to see the tremendous changes you've brought about in him. You've been very good for him."

"I have?"

"Most definitely. I had no idea you were feeling so insecure. Obviously my brother needs to be a little more forthcoming about his feelings. I'm surprised he— What's this?"

A truck carrying crates of winter vegetables had broken down near the stone gates of the château. Three cars were pulled up in a line behind the truck and the drivers were shouting for the driver to get the thing out of the way.

Alisha chuckled. "Sometimes these narrow roads can be a real hazard, can't they?"

Danielle stopped the car. "We'll have to wait, since there's no other way to get to the château. By the time I finally get something to eat, I'll be near fainting."

"I know what you mean. I—"

The door to the passenger's side flew open. Alisha's seat belt was jerked loose and she was hauled from the car before she knew what was happening. She heard Danielle's scream and fought to get her balance, only to find herself lifted into a pair of strong arms.

"What is—" She couldn't get enough breath to finish the sentence.

Mario loped along the shoulder of the road until he reached a side road, more of a trail than a road. He opened the passenger door of a car parked there, shoved her inside, locked the door and ran to the other side.

"What are you doing?" she stammered as he threw the car into reverse and backed out onto the roadway, then headed away from the château.

"I don't know what kind of game you're playing, Sherye, but I'm getting a little tired of it. It's a little late to be worrying about whether your sister-in-law sees us together or not, wouldn't you say? Forget about your need for financial security. You're carrying my baby now. That's more important to me than all the money in the world. We'll work all of this out together, somehow. You'll see."

"But you've got it all wrong. I'm not Sherye. I'm—"

He glared at her before switching his gaze back to the road. "Don't play games with me anymore. Okay? I can't take much more of this. After I left you at the hospital in Perth I was afraid to go back right away, for fear the police would hold me for questioning. When I finally managed to sneak in you were already gone. I've been trying to contact you for months. I didn't know where you were or how to contact you. Then when I finally do run into you, you ignore me, like I was dirt under your feet. Well, it's a little late for you to decide to forget about me. There's too much between us. You know that as well as I do."

He was driving too fast and his agitated speech scared her. She didn't know what to do but she knew he had to calm down before he wrecked the car.

"Where are you going?"

"To a place I found. You've never been there but I know you'll enjoy it. I suppose we can expect Raoul to spend some time looking for you. Once he gives up, we'll be able to leave France, maybe go back to the States or wherever you want to go." He gave her a quick glance. "When is the baby due?"

"In about three weeks," she replied absently. "But, Mario, I can't go off with you like this." She had to think, had to stay calm. Getting upset would not help the situation and could harm the baby. Alisha didn't know how to tell him that she wasn't Sherye. If he discovered who she was, would he harm her in some way? *Think!* she told herself. What can you say to him in order to convince him to let you go? He was talking once again and she forced herself to listen to his rambling speech.

"I know you think you've got to stay with him for the money and the prestige, but we mean too much to each other to keep on with this farce."

Stay calm, Alisha, she kept repeating to herself. *Don't do anything that will cause distress to the baby. You're too large to try to run away. Danielle will get in touch with Raoul and he'll find you. If Mario's telling the truth, he won't do anything to harm you, at least not intentionally.*

"Please slow down, you're scaring me," she finally said, gripping the armrest.

Mario laughed. "Who are you kidding? Nothing scares you. You've always been a speed demon. The faster the better."

She fought to sound calm. "I don't want to take any chances at the moment. I wouldn't want to do anything that might harm the baby."

"Yeah, I guess you're right." He raised his foot off the accelerator and Alisha let go of her pent-up breath. "Man, oh, man, I'm still having trouble believing it. Me, a daddy." He laughed exultantly. "I was shocked out of my head when I saw you last week, let me tell you! All that time you insisted you wouldn't get pregnant because you were on the pill." He glanced over at her with a smug grin. "Guess I showed you what a real man can accomplish, huh?" He looked back at the road, still smiling. "I always did have trouble keeping my hands off you. If we hadn't had that big blowup you never would have ended up married to that stiff Frenchman."

"We've known each other for a long time," she said in a tentative voice.

"Yeah, we go back a long way. You got high for the first time with me. Remember that, babe? After that you were insatiable." He laughed again, sounding pleased with himself.

During their conversation Alisha watched for landmarks. If she could keep him talking, if, somehow, she could continue to allow him to think she was Sherye, he would have no reason to suspect that she wasn't happy to stay with him. She'd have a much better chance of making a phone call if she didn't give him any reason to become suspicious of her.

For the next hour she asked him questions that he seemed pleased to answer about what he'd been doing since last summer. She coaxed him into reminiscing about their past together, responding vaguely when he brought up places and happenings for her to remember.

She kept reminding herself that he wouldn't harm her as long as he thought she was Sherye. It was obvious that he loved Sherye very much. She knew he was going to be devastated when he learned the truth.

By the time they arrived at the small cottage tucked away in the hills, Alisha wasn't certain she could make it into the house unaided. The past few hours had taken their toll on her. The nagging ache in her back that had started in Raoul's office hadn't gone away. If anything, it had become more persistent. Her body wasn't used to carrying so much extra weight and she was in the habit of resting every few hours.

Now she had no trouble convincing Mario that she needed to lie down. He solicitously helped her into the bedroom, one of three rooms in the house, and encouraged her to rest.

Her heart sank when she saw no sign of a telephone anywhere on the premises. How was she going to contact Raoul? She was shaking as though she were having a chill. She was scared and the pain in her back wouldn't go away. She knew it was nerves and reminded herself to calm down. She had to think about the baby.

From every indication, she could see that she wasn't in any immediate danger from Mario, particularly as long as he thought she was Sherye. She'd played that role enough to have some understanding of what he expected Sherye to be. What she had to do was to keep Mario distracted until she could think of a way to get help.

Alisha knew she was too on edge to sleep, but at least she could stretch out and ease the strain on her back. She slipped off her shoes and lay down, pulling the folded quilt on the bed over her.

The soft mattress felt wonderful after the long hours she'd spent moving around today. She rolled to her side and pulled up her knees in an attempt to get comfortable. At this stage in her pregnancy, true comfort was only a memory. She placed her hand on the baby protectively and closed her eyes, willing herself to rest.

A kiss awakened Alisha sometime later and she smiled as she stirred, knowing Raoul would—

She opened her eyes and stared into Mario's smiling face. "Hey, sleepyhead, are you going to sleep the evening away?" He straightened. "I made us something to eat. We've got to keep up your strength, you know."

She was back in the nightmare once again. She was with Mario, and Raoul had no idea where she was. More important to her immediate well-being, she was physically uncomfortable.

Alisha pushed herself up until she sat on the side of the bed. "I, uh, need to—" She looked around the room, embarrassed by her situation. She was alone with a man she didn't know, the man who was responsible for her being in France in the first place. How could she hide her negative reaction to him?

"Yeah, sure," he said, nodding. "The bathroom's right in here. That's one of the things that sold me on this place. It's been modernized and updated but still manages to keep its rustic charm."

Thankfully Alisha found herself alone for a few very necessary minutes. She had to gather her courage. She'd been gone for several hours now. Surely Danielle would have immediately contacted Raoul to tell him what had happened. She knew him well enough to know that he would waste no time looking for her. All she had to do was to keep Mario from discovering her real identity. She would let him think she was ready to leave Raoul in order to be with him. She must do whatever she had to do to save herself and the baby.

When she could find no other excuse to linger, Alisha joined Mario in the kitchen. He'd set the table with colorful pottery and had a simple meal prepared.

"You know, babe, you're really looking good, nice and healthy compared to the last time I saw you. I guess maybe we kind of overdid our partying last summer." He shook his head, remembering. "I know you scared the hell out of me. I tried to convince myself you were just kidding around, but I couldn't take the chance. That's why I told the others. They insisted we get you to a hospital. I knew you'd be furious when you woke up and found me gone." He reached across and took her hand. "I'm sorry for running out on you like that, babe. Real sorry. I'll make you a promise. I'll never leave you again." He patted her hand and smiled, his eyes glowing. "I figure with us having a kid and all we need to back off from the heavy-duty stuff, kinda take it easy. Who knows? We might make damn good parents. Wouldn't that be a laugh?"

Alisha didn't know what to say. She didn't want to think about the results of their drug-using spree last summer.

Here she was, once again playing the role of Sherye DuBois. How could her life continue to be so bizarre? She felt as though she was in a nightmare. Instead of waking up, she kept finding herself in a new and different nightmare.

Alisha fought her panic. What if she couldn't make contact with reality again? What if she was doomed to play out various roles of another woman's life? What if—

"What's wrong? Are you feeling all right?"

She stared at the stranger sitting across from her and registered the worried expression on his face. "Not really," she murmured. "My back is bothering me. I can't seem to get comfortable and I—"

"Here. These chairs aren't the most comfortable things I've sat in. We'll go into the other room and sit in front of the fire. How does that sound?"

She nodded. He slipped his arm around her waist and helped her into the other room. "Your face is flushed," he said, lowering her to the small sofa. "Is it too warm in here?"

She leaned her head back and closed her eyes. "No. I'm just not feeling very well."

"I'm sorry, babe. I guess all of this has been hard on you, hasn't it? Me deserting you like that, leaving you to face your husband on your own. I've been a real heel, but I promise you things are going to be different for us. Wait and see. I'll be everything you need. I'll help you with the baby, I'll—"

"Mario, I—"

"Tell me what happened last summer after I left. I've got so many questions...like, how long you were unconscious, how you got back to France, what you said to the schoolteacher, did that stuff we gave her really work on her memory the way it was supposed to, did Raoul ever catch on to the switch? You know all the stuff we planned. Did it work out okay?"

She had to concentrate on what he was saying, not how she was feeling. She didn't dare think about the increasing frequency of her back pain, or the way her abdomen seemed to clench and draw, then release. It was too soon for the baby. She had to relax, that was all. She had to force herself to remember what he was saying. "The, uh, the schoolteacher went home," she panted, forcing herself to fill her lungs with air before releasing her breath in a sigh.

"Yeah, yeah, I knew that. Did she remember me meeting her at the airport as soon as she landed?"

That was easy enough to answer. "I don't think she remembered anything."

"Great, then the psychotropic drug worked the way it was supposed to. I kept telling you the guy who sold it to me insisted there was nothing to worry about."

He stroked her hair and Alisha fought not to react to his touch. If only—

"What a touching scene," came a voice from the doorway, a voice that had never sounded so wonderful to Alisha before. She almost cried out with relief when Raoul walked into the room and paused beside the sofa. "That happens to be my wife you're mauling, Pirini." He didn't look at Alisha. Instead he kept his attention on Mario.

Mario had risen at the first indication that someone was in the room. He stared at Raoul in shock. "How the hell did you find us?"

"I alerted the police that you were somewhere in the area as soon as my wife mentioned seeing you."

Mario spun around and glared at Alisha. "You told him? You actually told him that I was here?" he repeated incredulously.

Raoul went on. "Fortunately my sister had enough presence of mind when you showed up again to follow you on foot until you drove away. She memorized the license and described the make, model and color of your car to the police."

Only then did Raoul sit beside her and take her hand. "I've been worried about you." He searched her face, frowning. "Are you all right?"

She was so relieved to see him that it was all she could do not to throw her arms around him and burst into tears. She'd been so frightened that he wouldn't find her. At the moment all she could do was bite her bottom lip and nod her head.

"Of course she's all right. She's been with me, where she belongs," Mario said, striding back to the sofa. "I guess it's time for you to hear some unpleasant truths, DuBois. Sherye always insisted that you would divorce her if you found out about us. Well, that's exactly what I want." He gestured toward Alisha. "Surely you aren't so stupid as to think that's your baby. Sherye would never have had another one of your brats. She could barely tolerate living in the same place as you."

Raoul didn't move from Alisha's side. He looked up at Mario, standing belligerently in front of them, and quietly said, "She could have left at any time. I never forced her to stay."

"Maybe *you* didn't," Mario sneered, "but your money did, and your prestige did. Sherye always wanted a home and family, that was her dream . . . until she got it and realized what a boring life that was. She needs me to help make life more exciting for her. Now that we're finally together again, I don't intend to give her up, to you or anybody. We belong together. We're going to become parents together. We're going to build our lives together. I'm the man she truly loves."

Raoul's eyes met Alisha's and she saw compassion and understanding for the other man in his eyes. He was aware that whatever this man had done had always been for Sherye. Whether Sherye had deserved such devotion was irrelevant.

Alisha knew that the relationship she and Raoul had established had gone a long way toward his accepting the truth about Sherye and his marriage to her. Somewhere along the way he must have come to terms with and accepted Mario's presence in Sherye's life.

Raoul looked over at Mario and nodded his head to one of the chairs. "Sit down, Pirini. I've got some bad news for you."

Warily the man sat down across from them, glaring at Raoul when he slipped his arm around Alisha. "Yeah? What sort of bad news?"

"Whose idea was it to have someone take Sherye's place last summer?"

Mario looked at Alisha, frowning, before glancing back at Raoul. "You found out about that?" He clearly wondered why Alisha hadn't warned him.

"Just answer the question."

Mario looked at Alisha again, shrugged and admitted, "We both thought it up, didn't we, babe?"

"How did you find Alisha Conrad?"

"Who? Oh! You mean the schoolmarm." Once again he shrugged. "Hey, we got lucky. I guess that's what first gave us the idea, right, Sherye?" Alisha kept her eyes focused on her hands, refusing to meet his eyes. When she didn't answer him, Mario continued. "I was visiting some friends in Dallas last spring and their daughter was showing us a bunch of pictures she'd taken and I got a glimpse of the teacher. Except for her hair color, she was a dead ringer for Sherye. I asked if I could keep one of the pictures to show a friend, and I got the lady's name." He scratched his ear and said, "Of course, she isn't as beautiful as you, babe. No one could be, but she came close by the time we colored her hair and put her in some of your clothes."

"That's kidnapping, Pirini," Raoul said in a low voice.

Mario straightened in his chair. "So who's gonna complain? Don't forget that Sherye's in this up to her neck. You gonna tell the police on me? You think I won't explain how she was just as much a part of it as me? And for what! Nobody was hurt. The teacher's back home, happily teaching her little classes, me and Sherye are getting that divorce you're so willing to give her, so everything's working out fine without the police having to know anything about what we did. After all, there was no harm done."

Raoul stood, placing his hands in his pockets as though to prevent himself from reaching for the other man. "I'm afraid it's not quite that easy, Pirini. You see, you and Sherye did too good a job. I identified Alisha as Sherye just as I was obviously meant to do. While you and Sherye took off on your cruise I spent those weeks with Alisha. I fell in love with her."

Mario got a pained look on his face. "So why are you bothering to tell me all this stuff? Who cares? No wonder you're so willing to let Sherye go. I can't believe you'r standing here telling me all of this right in front of her. S what have you been waiting for, her to have my baby so yo can kick her out and chase after the other gal?"

"There's no easy way to tell you, Pirini. Sherye never re covered from that drug overdose last summer. She died i November of last year."

Mario stared at him, looked over at Alisha blankly, the returned his gaze to Raoul. "What is this, some kind of sic joke?"

"There's no joke."

Mario looked back at Alisha. "C'mon, Sherye, explai to the man. He's suffering all kinds of delusions or some thing. Tell him the truth."

For the first time since Raoul had entered the room A isha spoke. "He's telling you the truth, Mr. Pirini," she sai quietly. "I'm not Sherye. I'm Alisha and I taught school i Dallas. When I regained consciousness in the hospital didn't remember who I was. Raoul convinced me and th doctors that I was his wife, so I went home with him an spent several weeks there." She touched her stomach "That's when I became pregnant."

Mario jumped up from the chair. "But that's imposs ble! You—Sherye—whoever—doesn't sleep with him. Yo haven't slept with him in years."

She looked him in the eye and said, "I did. He came to se me in Dallas several weeks after Sherye died. When he di covered that I was pregnant he insisted on marrying me That's why you saw us together in Paris."

Mario's skin turned a pasty gray. "Sherye's really dead? he whispered. "She died? No. That isn't possible. Sh couldn't have died. I would have known somehow. Sh wouldn't have done that. She wouldn't have left me...." H sank back into the chair as though his legs would no long hold him.

Alisha caught a movement out of the corner of her eye and turned. Two men stood in the doorway, one wearing a police uniform.

Raoul looked at Alisha and said, "Are you ready to go home?"

She nodded and he helped her from the sofa and past the two men. When she glanced around at Mario, she saw that he was sitting hunched over, his hands covering his face. She wasn't certain whether or not he'd seen the other men, or if he was aware that she and Raoul were leaving.

Once they were in the car Raoul said, "Are you sure you're all right? I've been out of my mind with worry."

"He wouldn't have hurt me. He thought I was Sherye. That's why I decided not to try to explain. He was too convinced and I was afraid of what he might do if he knew the truth."

"Danielle thought he was rough when he grabbed you out of the car. I was afraid he might accidentally injure you."

"I can't deny that he frightened me, showing up that way, but he was really very gentle with me." She sighed. "I'm glad it's over...I mean, completely over. All the questions have been answered. I can't help but feel sorry for Sherye. She never understood how blessed she was, how much she had."

"Each of us has a different idea of what it takes to be happy. Hers was different from yours."

"That's really obvious. Even without my memories, my life seemed so perfect to me last summer. I was living the life I had always wanted...only to discover it wasn't my life, after all."

He reached over and took her hand in his. "It is now."

"I do have one rather minor problem."

"What's that, love?"

"I'm afraid this child has decided not to wait any longer to become a part of the family."

Raoul jerked his head around and peered at her in th shadowy car. "Alisha! Are you having labor pains? Whe did they start? How far apart? Do you need to get to th hospital now?"

She closed her eyes and counted for a brief moment be fore she sighed and said, "I know that first babies usuall take their time, but this one seems to be in something of hurry. Since I'm not nearly brave enough to have it at hom I think we need to go to the hospital."

"A simple yes would have done it," he muttered, step ping on the gas and shaking his head. "I can't believe yo never said anything. How long have you been—"

"I'm really all right, Raoul. Stop worrying. We've go plenty of time."

He brushed his palm against her cheek for a brief mo ment before returning it to the wheel. "That's true, love We've got the rest of our lives."

Epilogue

She fought her way to the surface, knowing there was omething she needed to do. She hated to leave the soothng, restful place where she had found peace, but it was ime—time to surface and face whatever it was that awaited er.

She opened her eyes. The room seemed to be filled with olden sunshine, pouring through a large window. She linked from the brightness and waited for her eyes to adust. Once she could see, she discovered that she was not lone in the room.

Raoul stood next to her bed, holding her hand between oth of his. He looked tired, but extremely pleased with imself and with her. Sleepily she peered around the room, ecognizing the faces of Danielle, *Maman* and Janine.

"Janine," she whispered. "What are you doing here?"

"Making the acquaintance of your family and gazing with great deal of awe and admiration at that handsome young on of yours."

Alisha smiled. "He *is* beautiful, isn't he? Just like h papa." She squeezed Raoul's hand. "We did it, didn't we?

"I was very proud of you," he said gruffly.

"Thank you for staying by my side."

"I wouldn't have missed it for anything."

She smiled at the others. "I'm sorry I'm so groggy. I f nally asked for something to take the edge off toward th end."

Raoul grinned. "Yes. Now the delivery room staff and have a very good idea what sort of drunk you make...ver very jolly."

Her eyes widened in horror. "Oh, no!"

He nodded, his eyes filled with amusement. "Oh, ye You serenaded us for a while, in both French and English.

"How embarrassing! I'll never be able to face any c them again."

"Nonsense. They were amused but not particularly su prised. People react differently to medication. Fortunatel what they gave you was quite mild. I had an opportunity t talk with your doctor about your susceptibility to drug We're really very fortunate that you recovered as well as yc did from the drugs you received last summer."

Danielle leaned over and said, "The authorities called th morning to say that Mario gave a full statement about wh occurred and is cooperating with them, so they won't nee to bother you or Raoul anymore with the matter."

Alisha caught Raoul's eye, and he returned her gaze whi he kept a firm grip on her hand.

Maman spoke up. "Yvette and Jules are delighted know that their new brother has arrived. They have a manner of things to show him when he gets home."

She smiled, thinking about the children. "I'm eager to g home to see them. I already miss them."

"Right now you need your rest," Raoul said. "You' had a rather exciting last few days."

Each of the women kissed her on the cheek and lef leaving her alone with Raoul. He pushed a wisp of hair b hind one of her ears. "I was thinking as I stood here watching you sleep about the time when I was actually seeing you for the first time. You were lying in a hospital, much like this. You were very pale and wearing a head bandage. I thought I knew you. Then you opened your eyes and my life was never the same again. You turned my thinking upside down . . . you kept me confused and on edge. You woke me up to my own prejudices and set opinions. You made me reassess everything about my life and myself."

"I didn't mean to. I was just trying to find out who I was."

"Well, you helped me to find out who I was, as well. Thank you. I thank God every day that He sent you to me."

He leaned down and gave her a tender kiss. When he would have stepped away she tightened her grip on his hand. She met his gaze as she said, "I thought of a name for the baby."

"Ah. We never talked about names, did we, thinking we had some more time. So? What have you thought of?"

"Michael René. I wanted him to have your name—the René. Your mother mentioned once that was your middle name. Michael was my father's name. I always hoped if I had a boy that he could carry part of my father's name, since he never had a son."

Once again Raoul kissed her. "Whatever you want, love, is fine with me."

She looked up at him. "Are you going to always be such a mellow, accommodating husband?"

"If I'm not, I'm sure you can whip me into shape in no time."

She yawned, then laughed at her sleepy state. "I think you're perfect just the way you are. You see? I have wonderful taste in husbands."

* * * * *

A Note from the Author

I hope that you enjoyed Alisha's story. Her story has ci cled in my head for several years. It was one that I knew had to tell at some point in my writing career.

Have you ever wondered what would happen if you lo your memory? Would the person you are still be there, hi den away from your conscious mind? Just think about ho unnerving it would be to have the people around you tell y all sorts of things about you that were painful to hear, thin that made no sense to your idea of the kind of individu you feel you are.

It would take a very strong personality to withstand su an onslaught of confusing information. The most herc thing a person could do, in my opinion, would be to hang to a belief in yourself when no one else believed in you.

Raoul is a man of honor and integrity faced with son very tough choices. His quiet strength and stubborn tena ity intrigued me. I knew that he would have to be a ve special man, because Alisha is a very special woman.

INDULGE A LITTLE 6947 SWEEPSTAKES
NO PURCHASE NECESSARY

HERE'S HOW THE SWEEPSTAKES WORKS:
The Harlequin Reader Service shipments for January, February and March 1994 will contain, respectively, coupons for entry into three prize drawings: a trip for two to San Francisco, an Alaskan cruise for two and a trip for two to Hawaii. To be eligible for any drawing using an Entry Coupon, simply complete and mail according to directions.

There is no obligation to continue as a Reader Service subscriber to enter and be eligible for any prize drawing. You may also enter any drawing by hand printing your name and address on a 3" x 5" card and the destination of the prize you wish that entry to be considered for (i.e., San Francisco trip, Alaskan cruise or Hawaiian trip). Send your 3" x 5" entries to: Indulge a Little 6947 Sweepstakes, c/o Prize Destination you wish that entry to be considered for, P.O. Box 1315, Buffalo, NY 14269-1315, U.S.A. or Indulge a Little 6947 Sweepstakes, P.O. Box 610, Fort Erie, Ontario L2A 5X3, Canada.

To be eligible for the San Francisco trip, entries must be received by 4/30/94; for the Alaskan cruise, 5/31/94; and the Hawaiian trip, 6/30/94. No responsibility is assumed for lost, late or misdirected mail. Sweepstakes open to residents of the U.S. (except Puerto Rico) and Canada, 18 years of age or older. All applicable laws and regulations apply. Sweepstakes void wherever prohibited.

For a copy of the Official Rules, send a self-addressed, stamped envelope (WA residents need not affix return postage) to: Indulge a Little 6947 Rules, P.O. Box 4631, Blair, NE 68009, U.S.A.

INDR93

INDULGE A LITTLE 6947 SWEEPSTAKES
NO PURCHASE NECESSARY

HERE'S HOW THE SWEEPSTAKES WORKS:
The Harlequin Reader Service shipments for January, February and March 1994 will contain, respectively, coupons for entry into three prize drawings: a trip for two to San Francisco, an Alaskan cruise for two and a trip for two to Hawaii. To be eligible for any drawing using an Entry Coupon, simply complete and mail according to directions.

There is no obligation to continue as a Reader Service subscriber to enter and be eligible for any prize drawing. You may also enter any drawing by hand printing your name and address on a 3" x 5" card and the destination of the prize you wish that entry to be considered for (i.e., San Francisco trip, Alaskan cruise or Hawaiian trip). Send your 3" x 5" entries to: Indulge a Little 6947 Sweepstakes, c/o Prize Destination you wish that entry to be considered for, P.O. Box 1315, Buffalo, NY 14269-1315, U.S.A. or Indulge a Little 6947 Sweepstakes, P.O. Box 610, Fort Erie, Ontario L2A 5X3, Canada.

To be eligible for the San Francisco trip, entries must be received by 4/30/94; for the Alaskan cruise, 5/31/94; and the Hawaiian trip, 6/30/94. No responsibility is assumed for lost, late or misdirected mail. Sweepstakes open to residents of the U.S. (except Puerto Rico) and Canada, 18 years of age or older. All applicable laws and regulations apply. Sweepstakes void wherever prohibited.

For a copy of the Official Rules, send a self-addressed, stamped envelope (WA residents need not affix return postage) to: Indulge a Little 6947 Rules, P.O. Box 4631, Blair, NE 68009, U.S.A.

INDR93

INDULGE A LITTLE
SWEEPSTAKES

OFFICIAL ENTRY COUPON

This entry must be received by: APRIL 30, 1994
This month's winner will be notified by: MAY 15, 1994
Trip must be taken between: JUNE 30, 1994-JUNE 30, 1995

YES, I want to win the San Francisco vacation for two. I understand that the prize includes round-trip airfare, first-class hotel, rental car and pocket money as revealed on the "wallet" scratch-off card.

Name ______________________

Address ______________________ Apt. __________

City ______________________

State/Prov. ______________ Zip/Postal Code __________

Daytime phone number ______________________
(Area Code)

Account # ______________________

Return entries with invoice in envelope provided. Each book in this shipment has two entry coupons—and the more coupons you enter, the better your chances of winning!

 MONTH1

INDULGE A LITTLE
SWEEPSTAKES

OFFICIAL ENTRY COUPON

This entry must be received by: APRIL 30, 1994
This month's winner will be notified by: MAY 15, 1994
Trip must be taken between: JUNE 30, 1994-JUNE 30, 1995

YES, I want to win the San Francisco vacation for two. I understand that the prize includes round-trip airfare, first-class hotel, rental car and pocket money as revealed on the "wallet" scratch-off card.

Name ______________________

Address ______________________ Apt. __________

City ______________________

State/Prov. ______________ Zip/Postal Code __________

Daytime phone number ______________________
(Area Code)

Account # ______________________

Return entries with invoice in envelope provided. Each book in this shipment has two entry coupons—and the more coupons you enter, the better your chances of winning!

© 1993 HARLEQUIN ENTERPRISES LTD. MONTH1